WHO SERVED WELL

WHO
SERVED
WELL

Lawrie Johnston

Matador
Unit E2 Airfield Business Park,
Harrison Road, Market Harborough,
Leicestershire. LE16 7UL
Tel: 0116 2792299
Email: books@troubador.co.uk
Web: www.troubador.co.uk/matador
Twitter: @matadorbooks

ISBN 978 1803133 119

British Library Cataloguing in Publication Data.
A catalogue record for this book is available from the British Library.

Printed and bound in Great Britain by 4edge Limited
Typeset in 11pt Minion Pro by Troubador Publishing Ltd, Leicester, UK

Matador is an imprint of Troubador Publishing Ltd

For Lily and Lilly.

ACKNOWLEDGEMENTS

I first had the idea for this book while researching war memorials in southwest Scotland, specifically those in the village of Creetown and the parish church at Bargrennan. The characters in *Who Served Well* are entirely fictious, but inspired by the real lives of local men and women. I would like to thank the volunteer staff at Creetown Museum for access to primary source material, and the staff of Newton Stewart Library for access to the microfiche copies of the *Galloway Gazette*.

Thanks are also due to Jayne Baldwin, who was Literary Advocate for Wigtown Festival Company. Jayne gave me the confidence to proceed with this, my first novel.

I am indebted to Phillipa Thomson for her patience in reading and correcting my first draft. Also, for setting me deadlines, which I mainly stuck to.

A million thanks to Gwen Gordon, who kept me right in all matters medical, for tolerating my incessant bletherings about the progress of the book over the last couple of years and for her suggestions, which have made this a better read than it might otherwise have been.

And to my editor, Leona Skene, for her expertise in editing and general encouragement, and whose advice has been invaluable.

Lawrie Johnston

VIII

ONE
EXECUTION

The first bullet penetrated the forehead, just above the left eye socket, singed the top of the blindfold as it entered, and shattered the back of the skull. It sent fragments of brain and bone in all directions. Almost simultaneously the second, third, and fourth bullets hit the large square of blue-coloured cotton pinned to the khaki jacket at chest height. The soldier's body slumped forward from the waist, then jerked back slightly as the rope tied round the wrists held fast to the wooden stake. A trickle of urine ran down the kilted leg and formed a puddle on the dusty ground. It was quickly joined by two streams of blood, one from the head and the other from the chest wounds. Thankfully, there had been no missed shots or ricochets, but the noise in the chalk cave was deafening as it echoed around the walls. The sound of two of the firing party retching was barely audible.

As the noise died down, Captain Denis Wilson of the 6th Battalion King's Own Scottish Borderers stepped towards the body. He undid the stud on his leather holster and removed the Webley Mk IV revolver, the lanyard forming a bow between the gun and Sam Browne belt. As he strode forward, it took him a moment to realise that the revolver would not be necessary. Probably the first errant bullet would have been lethal. He should have been angry at the soldier who missed the chest target, but instead he was relieved that he had no need to finish the job. The soldier was already dead. Personally, he found the whole affair distasteful. Wilson had offered to defend him at his court martial, but the soldier had refused, so determined was he to prepare his own defence. It was an arbitrary choice, as the result was inevitable. Very few junior officers had any real legal training or expertise, and the rank and file even less so. But Wilson had felt duty bound to offer his services, given both the soldier's previous exemplary record and his popularity within the company. The outcome of the court martial was as certain and predictable as the verdict: guilty of desertion and sentenced to execution. The hasty appeal to HQ for clemency had just as hastily been denied. There were rumours of unrest and mutinous sentiment in the French battalion further down the line, so British High Command could not be seen to go soft on deserters.

Wilson was relieved he did not have to recruit the firing squad from the ranks of his own company, but from a neighbouring battalion of infantry. His unit had been through so much recently he could not expect them to dispatch one of their own. The 'neighbours' had rightly earned a reputation as hard bastards, and a squad of eleven soldiers and a sergeant had been formed quickly, given a double ration of rum, and informed of their dire orders.

The site of the execution was also out of the ordinary. The chalk caves and tunnels in and around Arras were a combined feat of medieval and modern engineering. For centuries French workers had formed the caves as they hewed the chalk for buildings. More recently, New Zealand and bantam sappers were given the task of linking them by tunnels so that 25,000 troops of the Third Army could be sent deep into no man's land and close to the German front line trenches. Wilson had noted the graffiti left by the medieval French miners, mainly names and dates, including that of 1314. As a keen student of military history, he wondered if the artist may have heard of the Battle of Bannockburn, Robert Bruce of Scotland, or Edward II of England; it was highly doubtful. He also noted the cruder graffiti left by his own soldiers. Mary must have been a popular girl. The caves were now mainly devoid of troops. They were currently used to transport the wounded back to field hospitals, and to store supplies for the front. Few noticed the small party making its way underground to perform its grim task.

With the help of a medical orderly, Wilson untied the soldier from the stake, laid his body prostrate on the ground, and covered it with an army blanket. He called forward some of the firing squad and ordered them to form a stretcher party to take the corpse for burial. Strictly speaking, he should have organised a separate unit for stretcher-bearer duties, but he had simply run out of time. They duly lifted the remains and unsteadily made their way along the maze of tunnels until they emerged at the entrance of what had once been the Hotel de Ville, now a shattered remnant of its former Gothic glory. They loaded the body on to a waiting cart. It was 6.30 a.m. on a cold April morning. Only the odd remaining patch of snow glistened white in the morning sunshine, but the wind was still bitter cold, and the men shivered as the effects of the rum wore off. The noise of artillery exchanges had been a constant clamour in this section of the line since the beginning of the attack. One side would open up and the other would retaliate. Heavy artillery would boom exchanges, medium guns likewise, only an octave or two higher, it seemed, and field mortars would lob missiles to and fro. Each piece of armament had its own distinctive sound, known only too well to the experienced troops. This morning it sounded like the 18-pounders were letting fly.

The horse and cart plodded back from the front against this familiar cacophony. It made its way down the sunken road set against a now-featureless landscape to the point known as Dead Dump. The driver stopped, and the four executioners each grabbed an entrenching spade and found a place to begin digging the grave. They were grateful for the physical work, which began to warm their muscles as the last of the rum's glow diminished. The shelling sounded uncomfortably close as they worked hurriedly to finish the digging. They returned to the cart and carried the covered corpse to its fresh grave, carefully laid it to its shallow rest, and began to cover it with the wet earth. Captain Wilson had handed to the sergeant the soldier's identity tag, so he could scratch the details on the wooden cross which would serve as a temporary headstone. With cold fingers the sergeant fumbled in his pocket to find the reddish-brown asbestos disc with its trailing cotton cord. He lifted it close to his face to read the army standard information: number, name, regiment, and religious denomination. He paused for a second and then read it again in complete disbelief. Over the last week he had very little sleep and was extremely fatigued. He knew how delusional one could become in this state, as it was not uncommon for soldiers to shoot at apparitions or see fields of lush green grass and pretty hedgerows set against bright blue skies, where in reality there was only grey mud, shattered tree stumps, and tangles of barbed wire. So, he took a deep breath and read the tag for a third time. He barely noticed that the thunder of the artillery bombardment had stopped, only to be replaced by something even more sinister and alarming. The soft plop, plop, plop of mustard gas shells landed around the burial party. He watched as his men frantically fumbled to pull gas masks from their satchels and rammed them over their faces. It was the last thing he remembered.

TWO
SPRING 1914

I t wasn't the right type of weather for a funeral, Andrew McDowall thought to himself, as he greeted and shook hands with the mourners at the door of Kirkmabreck parish church. Dark clouds and rain would have been a better match for his sombre mood. The church, with its impressive Regency-style tower, dominated the landscape of the eastern end of the town. He looked across to the blooming white hawthorn trees, over to the sloping pale green fields by the shore, and beyond to the Cree estuary, dappled by the bright spring sunshine. At one time a small ferry had operated from here across the river to Wigtown, saving travellers some time from the long road journey around Wigtown Bay. But with the arrival of the railway, the ferry was long since gone. He still preferred the old name for his village: Ferry Toun of Cree. It sounded far more poetic than boring old Creetown.

Andrew greeted the last few mourners, then made his way inside the church and took his place at the front pew, stopping briefly to touch the top of his mother's small coffin. He sat down on the hard wooden seat, sighed quietly to himself, and unconsciously stroked his thick black moustache with his right hand as he waited for the minister to appear. The shuffling of feet and sporadic coughing subsided as the Reverend McWhirter addressed the congregation.

The minister had nothing but praise for Andrew's mother. She had been known and respected in the parish as a good Presbyterian woman. She had been deeply proud of her family's Covenanting traditions: 'Let no man, be he laird or ferm laddie, come betwixt you and the guid Lord,' she had been fond of telling her son. The Reverend McWhirter reminded the mourners that not only had she attended service every Sabbath, but every Saturday evening; while others in the parish may have been indulging in more pleasurable pursuits, Mrs McDowall was on her hands and knees cleaning every pew in the church. She believed that 'in Scotland it is the poor that look after the poor', saving a few pence every week for those less fortunate than herself and depositing them in the alms box. Andrew remembered that in his younger days he would spend Sunday afternoons delivering her fresh baked bread and scones to the houses of the less fortunate. Sitting in the musty church, he could recall the sweet yeasty smell of her baking, stimulating his salivary glands. In the autumn he might also deliver a pot of bramble and apple jelly, and would be delighted when one of the neighbours invited him in to share a mug of tea and the baking. On the way home of a sunny evening he would stop and collect brambles for her next batch of jam making, his hands stained a deep red from the berry juices. Despite being a strict Sabbatarian, Mrs McDowall had allowed her son to deliver baked alms to the neighbours, so long as he was home in time for Bible reading before bedtime. Andrew always was, greeting her at the door of their small cottage as she prepared the Bible text for their evening prayer together.

As well as a distaste for frippery or anything faintly Popish, Mrs McDowall also had a deep abhorrence for the demon drink. She had been a leading light in the local Temperance movement. Many a publican, of which there were a few in the town, would cross the road rather than feel the sting of her moralising tongue. Woe betide any innkeeper who had served her husband, Willie, drink until he was fit to drop. Fortunately, Willie was a very benign drunk without an aggressive bone in his body, but she had resented the way he would squander their meagre earnings by buying drinks for all and sundry in the local hostelries.

As the minister recalled her further charitable deeds, it was with a slight sense of guilt that Andrew remembered how he had readied her breakfast in the last few months of her life. Ever since she had become ill Andrew would prepare her a bowl of milky porridge and a mug of strong tea, laced with a teaspoon of Challenge Scotch whisky. If only she had been aware of this 'medicinal' addition, the wrath of God would have descended on her son's head, along with a few choice words. She possessed an impressive skill in delivering alternatives to oaths, blasphemies, or obscenities, which still hit home whenever she was angered. He had consoled himself with the thought that the medicinal tea had at least perked her up and brightened her for a time each morning, and he had enjoyed their short conversations before he left for work. Her increasing frailty had pained him a great deal as he waited for the inevitable.

She had been unwell for a long time, but Andrew could not fail to notice how quickly she had gone downhill after the death of his father. She had always said that drink would be the death of her husband, and so it had proved. What had really surprised him was the effect of his father's death on her. For years it had appeared to Andrew that his mother could barely tolerate Willie, her husband. She would harangue him about his drinking and become exhausted and desperate when her lectures had no effect on his behaviour. Yet after his father's death it had become obvious to Andrew that she had loved Willie very deeply, and was far more dependent on him than he had ever realised. It seemed to him she had decided to conceal the depth of her love for her errant husband from the rest of the world, and had simply died of a broken heart after his demise.

'Is your faither no home yet? Ah wonder what's keeping him?' became as familiar a question to Andrew as her incessant repeating of Psalm 23 in the days after his father's funeral, It had not surprised him, then, that she had only lasted a few months without him. Andrew's thoughts returned to the present as the minister completed his elegy.

Two pews behind Andrew sat his younger friend, Tam Murdoch. He cut an awkward figure compared to Andrew. Whereas Andrew was of average height and build, Tam was several inches taller, and his ill-fitting, borrowed suit accentuated his lankiness. His unkempt mop of sandy hair made him stand out further from the rest of the mourners. He too found the pews uncomfortable, and fidgeted back and forward throughout the service. Unlike Andrew, Tam was not a regular churchgoer. Rather than follow the solemn order of service, his mind wandered to thinking about why every Church of Scotland minister he had heard seemed to speak in the same way. They had a knack of accentuating and amplifying words of doom and gloom. They must have been trained to do it, he thought. Tam remembered how he would entertain his younger brothers by mimicking and exaggerating the minister's voice and actions:

'Alexander and William Murdoch, the wrath, and I mean the wrath of God will descend on both yer heids if you do not go and buy ten Woodbine from the shop for your good brother Thomas. Do you want to risk hellfire and damnation for the price of a packet of fags? Oh, remember, in hell there will be much gnashing, yes, gnashing, of teeth!' His mock commentary would be accompanied by wild hand gestures. He would contort his face by protruding his lower jaw to expose a front row of irregular, yellowish teeth, just as he pronounced 'gnashing'. His brothers had roared and laughed with delight, feigning terror as they headed to the store for Tam's tobacco.

Tam grinned to himself at the memory, then, realising where he was, tried to look serious again. He surveyed the congregation to see if anyone had caught sight of his small indiscretion. His gaze stopped at a row of young women towards the back of the church. The Reverend McWhirter was quite forward-thinking in allowing women to attend funerals in his church. Tam was glad he did, as he thought women always looked so elegant in their long black dresses and bonnets. Really, it was just one young woman he was gazing at: Kathleen Marr. He could only see the side of Kathleen's pale face, as most of her red curling hair was hidden under her black hat, but he still thought she cut a fine figure of a woman. Tam had always admired Kathleen from afar, but took his interest no further, as Kathleen and Andrew were courting and no doubt would announce their marriage after the mourning period ended.

When the minister completed his blessing, the pall-bearers lifted the coffin out into the warm sunshine of the church graveyard and set it down carefully next to the freshly dug grave. The minister said another few comforting words and invited Andrew to throw a few grains of earth on top of the lowered coffin. Andrew duly did so, but also unclasped his mother's Temperance medal from his hand and threw it into the grave. It made a metallic whirring sound as it spun through its descent, before abruptly coming to rest on the coffin lid. He whispered, 'Goodbye, Mother' to himself and turned away from the grave. It was one of those clear, bright, crisp spring mornings where the light was focused and sharp, giving excellent views across Wigtown Bay. He paused for a moment and then signalled to the funeral party to make their way down through the town to the Ellangowan Hotel for the funeral purvey. As he walked from the churchyard he thought to himself: *the old lady is well and truly gone now*. He felt sad and relieved at the same time.

The meal of cold ham with boiled potatoes and carrots was to everyone's satisfaction. Andrew spent an hour or so after the meal conversing with relatives and neighbours, who offered him their commiserations and support. Slowly, the crowd of mourners thinned out, a few of them the worse for drink. *Not the best way to remember my mother.* Andrew smiled to himself. Finally, Tam and Andrew had a chance to talk alone. They each drew up a chair and sat at a round oak table near to the fireplace. It was that time of year when it could feel colder inside a building, shaded from the sun, than outside. The roaring fire had at least warmed up their corner of the room. Tam had removed his black tie and loosened his collar. He draped the jacket of his borrowed suit over the back of his chair and headed towards the bar, then stopped halfway and returned to the table. He slid the black armband from the empty sleeve of the jacket and slipped it onto his left arm. 'Sorry, Andrew', he muttered, before making his way to the bar once more, returning with two pints of pale ale and two nips of whisky. Both men took a generous draught of the beer. Tam offered his condolences again.

'Two funerals in such a brief time must have been an awful shock to you, Andrew', were the only consoling words he could come up with. Andrew licked the froth from his moustache and replied, 'Thanks, Tam. The old man I was expecting, as the drink had ruined him, but I was surprised at how quickly Mother went down. She was such a hardy type too. I hope this is my last funeral for a long time.'

Tam nodded, offering a cigarette, and as the two friends lit up he questioned Andrew about his future. 'I suppose you will wait a month or two, Andrew, before you announce your engagement to Kathleen? There is nothing to stop you now, is there?'

Tam, like most of the local community, expected them to marry soon, as it was well known that his mother had not considered Kathleen, or any of the local girls for that matter, good enough for her son. With the old lady laid to rest, surely he would ask Kathleen to be his betrothed? They were well-matched, the locals thought. Both were from good families, and members of the same church. They were seen together frequently at social occasions. When Kathleen played the piano and sang, beautifully, Andrew would accompany her on the fiddle.

Andrew smiled to himself and said, 'Tam Murdoch, if there is one thing I admire about you, it is your directness. But lad, you are ower hasty. I really haven't had a chance to discuss things with Kathleen yet, but I promise you will be the first to know.'

Tam blushed slightly and replied, 'Didn't mean to pry, just thought you might like to think about something cheerier today, after all you have been through. I suppose you have a lot to think about now. Have you decided what you'll do with the land?'

Andrew thought to himself that only Tam could apologise for asking a personal question and then follow it up with another one. 'No, not yet, Tam. I may rent it out, perhaps.'

'I could be very interested in renting it myself, Andrew. What a chance to get away from the old Major. Would you give me it at a low rate, seeing as we are friends and all?'

'We are friends, Tam, but you know business is business,' replied Andrew. He could tell from the slightly bemused look on Tam's face that his inquisitive young friend would not be following this line of questioning any further. Andrew was aware that when he pulled his strict schoolmaster's face and tone it was more than enough to kill a conversation.

Renting the land to Tam would have been a worthy way forward, but Andrew had, in fact, other plans for the land. He was on the verge of making a huge decision about his future, but was not ready to share it with anyone just yet. As an only son and now a twenty-two-year-old orphan, the only local ties that remained for Andrew were his parents' house and the smallholding which his grandfather had owned. Andrew had never had any interest in farming, and his mother had encouraged him to be a man of books rather than of the fields. She had high hopes that he might become a minister, but after three years at Glasgow University he had had enough, and took up teaching instead. So, for the last three years he had taught the pupils at the local school. He liked to teach, and he cared for his pupils a great deal, but he had now decided that there had to be more to life than thirty or forty years of the three Rs and Bible reading. Kathleen had hinted that she would accept such a local domestic life with him, but try as he might, he could not feel enthusiastic at all about that prospect.

'You're right about one thing, Tam. I do need to think about my future.' The two men raised their measures of whisky and toasted the future.

'Warms you much better than any fire,' Tam responded. Davy Kennedy, the barman and a mutual friend, passed to load more coal on the glowing embers in the grate. Andrew caught his attention and ordered another round of drinks. The wet coals sizzled on the fire as Davy returned with two more ales and whiskies.

'These are on the house, Andrew,' he said. Davy locked the front door, added the cash from the till, and took the money through to the main house. He returned shortly, poured himself a pint and joined his friends. The three sat talking and drinking in the smoky corner, well into the wee small hours of the night. They all agreed they had given Andrew's mother a fine send-off, although Andrew doubted she would have approved.

Within a month of the funerals, not only had Andrew sold the land and house for a fair price, but he had also used some of the money raised to buy his passage to Canada for the beginning of a new and, he hoped, exciting life. Now he anticipated the most difficult part of his decision: namely, informing Kathleen of his intentions. He had spent hours going over in his head how he would approach the subject. He rehearsed his carefully chosen sentences and anticipated how she would react to him.

Above all else he dreaded a tearful scene. These thoughts ran through his mind as he approached the Marrs' house one evening in May. It was one of the finer and larger houses in the town, built, as most were, from the local grey granite, but with windowsills and cornerstones in contrasting red sandstone. It stood detached, in its own fine gardens. Andrew was dressed in his black mourning suit and tie. His face looked pale against the darkness of his clothes, hair and moustache. He approached the front door, scraped his shoes on the cast iron boot grid, and rang the doorbell. The housemaid showed him into the small parlour, where he was presently joined by Mr Marr, the local bank manager, a tall, thin man, with greying hair and piercing blue eyes. They exchanged pleasantries and Andrew listened as the older man recited the usual formalities to one still in mourning. He also remarked about the sale of Andrew's house and land, which his bank had been involved in.

'I suppose you will be looking for something more substantial in the village?' he asked. 'Drop into my office and I can discuss properties and finances whenever the time is right, young man.'

To his slight alarm, Andrew suddenly realised Kathleen's father was thinking of a marriage home, and probably thought the purpose of Andrew's visit was to ask him for Kathleen's hand in marriage. As the stream of small talk dried up, an awkward silence filled the room. Mr Marr fidgeted in his pocket, produced his watch and checked the time against the grandfather clock in the corner. Its bass, rhythmic ticking was the only sound in the room. After what seemed like an eternity to Andrew, the housemaid returned with a silver tray laden with tea and scones. He tried to hide the relief from his face, but couldn't fail to notice the crestfallen look on Mr Marr's.

'I will see what is keeping Kathleen,' he managed, and then as an afterthought: 'I will be in the drawing room should you need to see me before you leave, Andrew.'

Kathleen heard her father mutter, 'Odd, most odd' to himself as he passed her and entered the drawing room She apologised to Andrew for being late and poured tea for them both from the patterned china pot. It was obvious Kathleen had spent some considerable time making herself presentable. Her red hair was tied back in three ringlets, she wore a pale blue, full-length dress with a white embroidered collar, and the scent of her perfume filled the room like a lily in full bloom. As their conversation inevitably moved to the point which Andrew dreaded, he was taken by surprise by her forthright manner.

'Andrew McDowall, I know you well enough to tell that you have spent the last half hour beating about the bush and changing the subject to avoid telling me what you came here to say.' Before he could recover or respond she continued, 'I also know that the purpose of your visit was not, as my silly old father supposed, to ask for my hand in marriage. Was it, Andrew?'

He blurted a reply along the lines of that she was correct, but he did not wish to hurt her feelings. He apologised, far too many times.

'Father let slip you had sold the cottage and land, and from that moment I knew you planned to leave. I could tell from the time of your father's death that your mind was elsewhere, and now I know for certain. So where are you going to, Andrew? Edinburgh, or London perhaps?'

His reply was the only time in their conversation when he detected a hint of surprise and maybe even regret on her face.

'Rather further than that, Kathleen. I am afraid I have booked a passage to Quebec.'

She recovered her composure quickly, and reassured him that she would be fine and that he was doing the right thing. Canada was a land of opportunity, she said, and with his talents and qualifications he should make a bright future for himself. She pledged to write to him regularly and he promised the same. As he left the house and walked to his lodgings, he was overcome by a sense of regret and relief. He truly enjoyed Kathleen's company and would miss her as a friend, but no more than that. Unbeknown to him, Kathleen felt much the same, and was very composed as they parted for the last time. Her serenity was shattered, however, when later her father chose to make an ill-timed remark about Suffragettes and how any self-respecting young man would be quite correct to stay well clear of a girl associated with such nonsense. She stormed upstairs to her bedroom, completely and utterly exasperated.

A week later Andrew stood on the deck of the Donaldson Line steamer *Asthenia*, looking back in the direction of Liverpool docks. The grey granite harbour walls and the tall warehouses had a familiar look to them. Not surprising, really, as they were built with the same Galloway granite as his house and school back in

Creetown. Andrew's grandfather on his mother's side had been a quarryman who hewed the stone, which was then shipped south to England.

The coastline of the north west of England was fading into the horizon as he gave a wry smile, remembering how friends and neighbours had reacted with great surprise to his decision. In their eyes he was a devoted son, a hardworking, dependable teacher and a pillar of the local community at a relatively early age. They had expected him to marry Kathleen soon enough. The only person who seemed pleased with his decision was Tam Murdoch. Tam had shown unbridled enthusiasm for Andrew's decision to go. He had also vowed to join Andrew on his great Canadian adventure, at the very latest before the summer was out. That thought greatly cheered Andrew but, knowing Tam, it was very unlikely that he would ever save enough money to make the journey. Still, he might surprise him.

THREE

SUMMER 1914

The plan was so simple that Tam wondered why he had not considered it sooner. He would run in as many local sports and gala day events as he could over the summer. Although not a sprinter, this being where the big prize money was found, if he placed in the half mile or mile races he should be able to raise the £6. 10s. for his passage to Ontario. Of course, he would have to deduct the entry fee and his railway tickets from his winnings first. Most important of all, he must steer clear of the beer tent. His pals would say Tam was 'fond of a wee drink', and it was true that after a few pints and drams his generosity would know no bounds. Having stood several rounds, all he would have to show for it was a sore head and an empty wallet. Despite a few lapses earlier in the summer, he had still managed to put away £4. 7s. in winnings. Now he had entered two local races: the Castle Douglas Athletics Games on Bank Holiday Monday, quickly followed by the Garlieston Regatta and Sports the following Saturday. A couple of strong performances and he should have enough for his Canadian passage. He imagined himself walking into the steamship agent's office on Victoria Street, Newton Stewart, with a huge smile on his face, demanding to know when the next Allan Line steamer was departing.

On the Monday morning Tam was out early, tending to the sheep on the lower slopes of Cairnsmore of Fleet, one of the highest Galloway hills, which dominated the local landscape. The granite massif rose sharply through mixed woodland, then levelled off to a moorland top. In the summer months the sheep grazed on the high ground, which offered fine views to the south of Wigtown and Luce bays, as far as the Mull of Galloway. Tam regularly spotted golden plovers, black grouse, and the occasional golden eagle on his trips to the hill. There was to be no bank holiday break for Tam, although that did not deter him from attending the games. He had assured his employer, Major Black, owner of Kirroughtree Estate, that he would be roaming the hills with Sammie, his collie cross sheepdog, to round up stray sheep. So the Major should not expect him back at the farmhouse until late. Tam figured that the old man would be none the wiser, and even if the miserable old bastard read about his exploits in the Galloway Gazette's sports page, Tam no longer cared. He would take great pleasure in telling the Major that he was bound for Canada. That was Canada, where he would be paid at least three times his measly estate wages.

After a cursory check on the sheep, Tam tethered Sammie to a gatepost next to a burn where the dog could drink, picked up his bicycle, which he had stashed the

evening before, and headed off. He could not chance being
seen at Creetown railway station, so he cycled up the moor
road to the more remote Gatehouse of Fleet station. It was
a stiff climb, as the station was several miles above the
village, but he was spurred on by the sight of puffs of smoke
from the steam locomotive in the distance as he neared his
destination. He bought his ticket and left his cycle in the
waiting room. As the train steamed east, Tam had a little
time to catch his breath and eat a cheese sandwich. One
of the few advantages of working on the Major's estate
was that the workers' food was excellent. Mrs McKnight,
the cook, was renowned in the area and had a soft spot
for Tam, which he used fully to his advantage. Even his
simple sandwich was delicious: fresh, homemade, slightly
sweet brown bread combined with the tangy saltiness
of the cheese was the perfect pre-race meal, he thought.
The train slowed as it approached Loch Ken Viaduct. He
stared at the loch, watching the large raindrops disturb the
surface, as the carriage tentatively crossed the bowstring-
girdered bridge. Tapping his hands on the seat and feet
on the floor, he could hardly wait to be at the start line.
Fortunately, Castle Douglas station was right next to the
park used to hold the games. Several large marquees had
been erected and Union Jack bunting trailed from one
tent to the next. A good crowd of all ages was gathering,
mostly around the bandstand, where the local silver band
was playing. Leaping from the train, already changed into
his running gear, who couldn't notice what a fine figure
he cut in his cotton vest, thigh-length shorts, and rubber-
soled canvas shoes? His work clothes were in an old duffel

bag, left in the corner of the pavilion. It escaped Tam that some would see him as an ungainly lad who had not quite left the awkwardness of youth behind him.

He lined up at the start line opposite the pavilion, his height and mop of sandy brown hair making him stand out from the other runners. He gave a quick glance left and right to size up the opposition. A few younger lads, enjoying their day off school, would set off like hares and then fade badly. There were two or three more seasoned runners whom he would need to keep an eye on, although one of them looked the worst for drink already. Tam knew he would be less than popular if he beat the local champion, Jim McRoberts. Not so much a case of civic pride, more the fact that there was a lot of money bet on McRoberts. The beer tent crowd would turn ugly in the event of Tam winning, so he might have to hold something back after the race for a sprint to the train station. He and McRoberts exchanged a less-than-friendly nod to each other, the older man with a contemptuous grin on his angular face.

The gun went off, startling Tam, as the runners headed off around the perimeter of the park. Just as he had predicted, the younger runners bolted to the front, keen to impress the gathered crowd they passed on their way out of the park and down the Crossmichael road. Tam ignored the cheers and waving handkerchiefs to concentrate on his stride. Breathing heavily, but bearably, he would be about ten or twelve from the front, he reckoned. As he turned at the halfway mark, all the front runners were in sight. In his previous races he liked to hit the front at this stage if he could, as it was the fear of being caught which spurred him on. He so dreaded the thought of anyone catching him that the sound of approaching feet would trigger the last ounces of effort and energy out of him. It was not unusual for him to finish races in complete red-faced exhaustion, retching up whatever he had eaten and collapsing on the ground. But it was more than worth it to him, knowing that he had won by giving his all. There were now only three runners in front, but McRoberts did not appear to be one of them, he realised. No sooner had that thought occurred than the champion caught and passed him, giving Tam a hefty dunt in the ribs with his sharp elbow as he did so. Tam let out a grimaced gasp – 'Bastard!'– and pulled up from the pain. 'Is that the only way you can beat me, McRoberts?' he yelled.

'See you at the finish line, son,' came the reply. He slowed almost to a stop for a second or two, gave his aching ribs a quick rub and then tried to get back into his stride. Every time he exhaled, though, he felt a sharp pain in his side. Undeterred, he ran on. By the time he re-entered the park for the last lap there were only two competitors in front of him, including McRoberts. He was quickly onto the heels of second place, closing ground with every stride. The sun was out now and Tam was sweating heavily. Steam was rising from the wet grass as he came towards the finishing straight. The crowd had gathered around, cheering loudly. His lungs ached, and his heart pumped ten to the dozen as he pushed the last effort from his tiring legs. He closed the gap on McRoberts to within a yard as they crossed the line. His first instinct was to grab for McRoberts and plant a left hook on his grinning face.

Just in time, he came to his senses and thought about the ten-shilling prize for second place. It was simply too much to risk. He needed the cash for his Canada fund, which was building up nicely. Besides, a fair crowd of well-wishers had gathered around McRoberts. They offered him their congratulations or gave an encouraging slap on the back. If Tam had swung a punch, he would have taken a sorry beating from the locals and spent the night in the cells. It might just be a bit tricky explaining that to the old Major.

So instead he shook McRoberts by the hand fiercely. 'Next time I'll have you, fair and square, you big cheat!'

'I'll look forward to that, son. Any time you fancy.'

Ignoring the older man's taunts he endured, half-heartedly, the prize-giving ceremony back at the pavilion. He barely applauded McRoberts, before more enthusiastically collecting his prize money for second place. He picked up his duffel bag, bypassed the now-heaving beer tent, and headed for the train home. He could wait to get his revenge another day, and get it he would, that was for certain. His level-headedness had pleasantly surprised him.

Thank the Lord, the cycle back was mostly downhill. His leg muscles ached and complained on each small rise. It had turned into a beautiful summer's evening, with the sun setting over the Cree estuary. He could hear the plaintive *cour-leee* of whaups in the distance. He untethered Sammie and was relieved to see that the late evening warmth had not affected the old dog too badly. Tam produced the remains of a slightly stale cheese sandwich he had kept in his pocket, which the dog gulped thankfully. No one noticed or remarked on his return to the farmhouse. Mrs McKnight had retired for the evening, but had left Tam a pot of new tatties simmering on the range and some gutted and filleted herring in the larder. He fried the fish with a knob of butter in a large black pan, and helped himself to the potatoes. After the meal he savoured one, then a second, mug of tea, to his great satisfaction. He loved this type of tiredness brought on by cycling and running, and the slight sting of sunburn on his face, arms, and legs. He felt the ten-shilling note in his pocket – he would add it to his Canada fund. As he started to nod off in the old armchair to the rhythmic ticking of the kitchen clock, he thought to himself: *I would have really loved to beat McRoberts.* But all in all, Monday August the third had just about been as perfect a day as possible. He would sleep well tonight.

To the outside world it may have appeared astonishing that Tam had not foreseen what occurred the following day. Only the week before, he had been at the Territorial Army training camp on the south Ayrshire coast. As soon as he left school Tam had joined the 2nd Company of the 5th Battalion King's Own Scottish Borderers as a Territorial. He knew he looked good in the uniform, and hoped to catch the eye of the local girls. The combination of the smart uniform and his very good looks would prove irresistible, so he thought. Besides, he loved to get away to the training camps, and laughed at the fact the old Major had to let him off work to go, given the old man's own military background. Not only that, but the army paid them too. Most of the local lads had joined with him, and

Tam enjoyed their company. After a hard day's drilling and training, the part-time soldiers would take over the local pub. He would always be in the thick of things, and loved to be the centre of attention when he told his jokes and stories. It was in marked contrast to his usual job, where he only had Sammie and the stupid sheep for company. At the most recent camp, as well as the usual banter and rivalry with the other companies, one or two of the more serious-minded had mentioned the problems in Europe and that they might have to help stop the German Kaiser in his tracks. The conversation had then moved to the attractions and attributes of the French *mademoiselles*, which was the only part of the conversation Tam had paid much attention to. It had therefore come as a bit of a shock that, on the day after his race, he was given the news that Great Britain and the Empire were at war with Germany. Very soon his company would be called up. At least the news had preoccupied the old Major to such an extent that he did not ask any awkward questions about Tam's previous day's 'work'.

The following day Tam sat impatiently in the Mission Hall in Creetown, as the usual local dignitaries took to the stage to express their support for this new war and exhort the young lads to do their duty for king and country. There was the Reverend McWhirter, Mayor Huxtable, and the old Major, of course. They all lamented that they were sadly too old for this conflict, but that they would do their bit at home. The Major was keen to stress that any young man who came forward would never regret doing his bit for the Empire. Tam found himself agreeing with the

Major for the first time in years. If only they would shut up soon, he could get off the uncomfortable wooden bench, find Colour Sergeant Irving and get on with enlisting. As the last patriotic speech was drowned in enthusiastic applause, Tam noticed that Kathleen Marr, along with two of her older brothers, was also in the audience. As far as Tam was concerned Kathleen was the most beautiful girl he had ever seen. Bright red curling hair, striking blue eyes and high cheekbones, and oh, when she sang! Tam thought it was as close to hearing an angel as you could get on this earth. The fact that in Tam's own opinion, Kathleen was unattainable for the likes of him, only made her even more desirable. True, he, like most others in the village, had expected her to marry his friend Andrew, but he had recently left for Canada. At the very least Tam hoped Kathleen would be big-hearted enough to grant him the honour of a dance at the soldiers' leaving ceilidh. He might even be bold enough to steal a kiss, and then it would be off to France, where the girls would greet him as a hero. He could hardly contain his excitement.

He briefly realised that Andrew would be far from all the troubles in Europe, and wondered how he was reacting to the news over in Canada. His own plans for Canada would be put on hold, but like most others he believed the war would be short-lived and that he would pick up on his plans the following year at the latest. The war was giving Tam a different chance for adventure, and he could not let that pass him by.

The formalities of signing up were dealt with efficiently in the neighbouring town of Newton Stewart, where the 5th Battalion had orders to muster. Tam was more preoccupied with the coming event that evening. Whoever thought of the idea of a farewell ceilidh for the departing soldiers should get the first medal of the war, according to Tam. The Territorials heading for France would be there from all over the local area. That also meant there would be lots of girls who had not yet had the pleasure of meeting Tam. He vowed that he would dance with every single one of them, and when the chance came, he would even ask Kathleen. As the night progressed a steady stream of uniformed soldiers began to fill one side of Newton Stewart's McMillan Hall. Facing them on the other side were more pretty girls than Tam had ever seen gathered in one place, all dressed in their Sunday best. Everyone looked much better-presented, more confident, and happier than they did on a usual work day. This war seemed to be bringing out the best in everyone, and Tam was determined to enjoy each new experience to the full. It was time for him to join the rest of the lads for a refreshment. Or two.

Around the back of the hall a group of the Creetown boys had gathered. David Kennedy, a friend since schooldays, hailed him over and held out a half bottle of Brig o' Turk whisky for Tam to take a swig. Not needing to be asked twice, Tam held the bottle to his mouth, savouring the aroma as he took a hefty gulp. He loved the sensation of the first drop: the rich smell, the strong bittersweet taste, followed by the warming effect, which seemed to spread from his throat to his lungs and heart and then up to his cheeks and head. It was like someone had placed a warm blanket between his skull and brain. Was there a better feeling in the world? He licked his lips and passed the bottle on. He was feeling just grand.

'Right lads, let's say farewell to all these girls in fine style.'

The whisky also did his confidence the world of good.

'Lead the way, General Murdoch, lead the way.'

An hour or more later, having danced every strip the willow, eightsome reel and dashing white sergeant, Tam was half-exhausted and happier than he could ever remember. He had taken a shine to a girl from Wigtown called Anne, who was a fine dancer. He had danced with her at least three times. At six feet tall, Tam towered over most girls, but she was a bit taller than most and they made good partners. She even complimented him on the lightness of his feet.

'If ye can move that fast in France, ye will dodge they German bullets nae bother.'

As he sat drinking tea and eating sandwiches at the interval, his attention was swiftly diverted to the stage. As soon as the band had asked for singers the cry had gone up: 'Go on Kathleen, give the boys a song.'

Kathleen Marr was renowned for her beautiful singing voice. What most people did not realise was how very nervous she was when she took to the stage and became the centre of attention. She could be very good at hiding her emotions. The evening was very bittersweet for her. Of her four brothers, two were already serving in the armed forces: Edward was an officer in India and Walter an able seaman in the Royal Navy. Her two remaining brothers, Robert and Alexander, had volunteered and were in the audience tonight. She herself had attended a meeting of the Red Cross Voluntary Aid Detachment and was determined to serve as a nurse, in France if need be. Over and above that, she sorely missed Andrew's calming presence on the stage and his wonderful fiddle playing. As all these thoughts flashed through her mind, she considered it more than appropriate to start with 'The Braes of Galloway'. The hall hushed as she began singing.

The lines, 'Come on, bonnie lassie, will ye gang wi' me, and share yer life in a far country,' were sung laced with emotion. She barely made it to the chorus when thankfully the crowd belted out an enthusiastic, if not always tuneful:

'Oh, the Gallowa' hills are covered wi' broom

Wi heather bells in bonnie bloom'

Tam was one of the more enthusiastic singers as he stood transfixed watching Kathleen, resplendent in her soft green silk dress, singing on the stage. Again, the hall hushed as Kathleen cleared her throat and this time unaccompanied sang the Burns ballad 'Ae Fond Kiss'. It was almost as if Burns had written the song with the intention of having Kathleen sing it. Every heart-wrenching word and phrase was caressed by her voice, lifting and soaring. There was a silent pause when she finished and then, as if the crowd were drawing breath again, a burst of warm, emotional applause. Tam's face was flushed with the heat in the hall, his hands were red with clapping, and a tear ran down his cheek. He told himself it was a whisky tear, of course.

He did not remember much of the second half of the ceilidh. Yes, he had continued to dance but without really paying much attention to his partners. He was overwhelmed with the feeling that he must see and speak to Kathleen before the end of the night. He even passed on the next few rounds of illicit whisky-drinking for fear that he would miss her. Finally, his chance came. As he approached her in the corridor he felt his heart beat faster than during any race. Not only did she look and sound beautiful, but the floral scent of her expensive perfume made her smell beautiful too.

The scent gave Tam his opening line: 'Would you like me to bring you back a bottle of that scent from Paris, Kathleen? It smells so good it must have come from there.'

She turned and smiled at Tam. 'I would like that a lot, Tam, but will you be able to carry so many bottles for all the girls you have promised?'

'Only for you, Kathleen, only you.' He grinned back.

'I am not too sure about that, Tam, from what I have heard.'

'Ah, you know this place, Kathleen, full of gossips. Don't believe a word o' it.' Tam liked to think of himself as a bit of a ladies' man, even if in truth most of the local girls did not share his opinion.

The conversation continued in this light-hearted manner for a time. Kathleen enjoyed his company and his attempts to impress her, as it took her mind off more serious matters. He had an impish look on his face which Kathleen found attractive. Tam thought he was doing very well and noticed the envious looks from some of the other young soldiers. He plucked up the courage to ask, 'Will you be at the train station tomorrow, Kathleen, for the big send-off?'

When she replied honestly that she was not sure she could bear to see her two remaining brothers depart, he began fumbling in his jacket pocket.

'Will you keep this for me then, Kathleen, just until I come home?'

He produced a mother-of-pearl brooch with the silver insignia of the King's Own Scottish Borderers in the middle. As she took it from his open palm he reached out with his other hand and held hers gently. Her perfume was intoxicating as he leaned forward to embrace her. Kathleen demurely turned her head a little and allowed him to plant a brief but tender kiss on her cheek.

'It will bring you luck,' he said.

'I am sure it will,' she replied, adding, 'I will keep it safely for you, Tam. You will be home again sooner than you think.'

She wrapped the brooch in a silk handkerchief and placed it in her purse. She vowed to look after Tam's sweetheart badge – even though he was not her sweetheart.

Tam did not sleep well that night. It was partly because he was back at his parents' house for his last evening at home. Ever since he had started working for the Major at the age of fourteen he had only been back at the family home on the occasional day off over the last six years. He wondered how his mother and father would take his leaving in the morning, He had found it hard enough to say his farewell to his sheepdog, Sammie. The dog could sense there was something amiss. Tam took comfort from the fact that his two younger brothers were still too young to be called up, so they would be of good support to his parents, he hoped.

As he flitted in and out of sleep, over and over in his mind he replayed his conversation with Kathleen. Sometimes he smiled and sometimes he sighed about what might have been. He tried to imagine what the next few days and weeks would be like.

How long before his battalion sailed for France? Would his company see action? What did a German look like? Could he kill someone? Were French girls as pretty and as free as they said they were? Would the Major keep his job open until he came back? Why had he not tried harder to kiss Kathleen properly?

The following morning the small company of Creetown soldiers formed up in front of the Ellangowan Hotel. Tam stood next to Davy Kennedy, and immediately behind him were the brothers John and Kenneth Glendenning. Behind them again, Craig Wallace. All old school friends. Led off by Colour Sergeant Irving and accompanied by the local pipe band, the ten volunteers proudly marched through the small cheering crowd, then up over the bridge towards Newton Stewart. As the strains of the regimental anthem 'Blue Bonnets O'er the Border" faded behind them, Tam looked around at his fellow soldiers and friends. He felt a pride and a comfort in their company. He didn't mind the five miles or so march to Newton Stewart railway station, but he did wonder why his company could not have simply embarked at Creetown, where the train would pass through anyway. That was army life, he supposed, and best not to question orders. They were joined at Newton Stewart by other companies, and they endured more worthy speeches from local dignitaries. Friends, family and neighbours gave them a rousing send-off, crowding on to the narrow platform as the troops boarded the carriages. Shouts, sobs, and laughter could just be heard over the hissing of the steam engine and the slamming shut of carriage doors. Anne's presence on the platform almost compensated Tam for the lack of Kathleen's. Anne blew him a kiss and waved a linen handkerchief at him, as she implored him to write to her as soon as he arrived in France.

The two-hour journey to Dumfries passed quickly enough, as the lads chain-smoked cigarettes given as farewell presents and speculated about when and where they were likely to arrive in France. Some predicted they would be thrown straight into action, whilst others reckoned they would be held in reserve and only used if the regulars were in serious bother. Tam had never been so excited in his life and already felt he was a bit of a hero, even if he had done nothing of note yet. As he glanced around his local company, crammed into the small compartment, he wondered what Andrew was doing right then.

FOUR

CANADA

ndrew's mental image of Canada was largely based on a large blackboard map of the British Empire, which he had used for geography lessons with his pupils. He had keenly pointed out the enormous difference in size between small Scotland and the vastness of the Canadian territories. Sitting high on his tall teacher's desk, he had considered what a journey across such a large land would be like: the excitement, adventure, and characters he might meet. He eagerly gathered books, leaflets, and newspaper clippings about all things Canadian. Almost all the information Andrew read about emigration to Canada was enthusiastically positive. New opportunities, better wages, and cheap fertile land were all there for the taking, apparently. Having made his bold decision to go, he then pondered which occupation would suit him best. If land was so cheap he would be able to buy a decent amount from the money raised by the sale of his grandfather's smallholding in Galloway. Yet that idea did not really enthuse him, given his antipathy to all things agricultural. Or he could go back to teaching; but that would be much like back home, too. Eventually he had decided that an office job with a railroad or logging company would suit him fine to start with. He had the educational qualifications, which were much in demand. Furthermore, if he invested his remaining capital well, he could make quite a small fortune. Railway, logging, and fur companies were all enjoying a boom. He might eventually start up his own business.

Stories about conditions aboard emigrant ships had been less positive. He had heard too many tales of the awful, cramped accommodation on the steerage passages, so had willingly paid extra for second-class cabin accommodation. He had enjoyed the comparative luxury of a single bed, lavatory, and bath, and the freedom to wander between smoking and music rooms. There had even been a barber's shop on the *Asthenia*. As Andrew strolled the decks in the daytime he would see steerage passengers, mostly young families with many children, huddled together and eating meagre meals of mainly dried food that they had brought with them for the journey.

Ten days later the TSS *Asthenia* steamed into the St Lawrence River and docked at Quebec. It was early May and the port was once again ice free. Andrew was completely overwhelmed by the size, beauty, and bustle of the city, or *la cité*, as the French-speaking inhabitants called it. His grasp of the French language was enough to get him by in terms of finding accommodation in the Lower Town area of the Cape Diamond promontory. Quebec was a confident city, founded on the fur, timber, and wheat trades. It was now establishing itself as a centre for the burgeoning tourist industry. Andrew could see why. He used his brief stay to marvel at the sites: the grandeur of the Old Citadel was only outdone by the more recently constructed Chateau Frontenac, which completely dominated the city skyline. He thought the Ellangowan Hotel back in Creetown looked like a byre in comparison. This grand chateau hotel was built for the Canadian Pacific Railway, so Andrew thought it might be just the place to begin his enquiries regarding his job prospects. The following day, Andrew was met at the entrance by a sharply dressed bellboy, who escorted him through some of the grander public rooms to the office of Callum McGregor, depute manager of the hotel, who had responsibility for recruitment. Andrew had thought it wise to dress in his Sunday best, but still felt slightly intimidated by the surroundings. He was led through the main dining room, with its carefully-set-out round oak tables covered with crisp, starched white table linen. Six huge glistening crystal chandeliers hung impressively from the ceiling. Andrew was conscious that his good leather shoes were squeaking on the highly polished floor. He drew a deep breath as the bellboy knocked on the office door and a loud voice bellowed, 'Enter.' Any apprehension Andrew was feeling was dispelled immediately when Callum McGregor introduced himself. He was a large, jovial man, with a full beard and ruddy face. His waistcoat barely managed to fit round the girth of his stomach. After a very hearty handshake, he motioned for Andrew to sit down, and then spent the next ten minutes enquiring about the old country.

McGregor was second-generation Scots and loved to hear stories from the land his parents had left behind. Andrew enjoyed his company and was pleased and encouraged by his advice. He suggested that Andrew should head west, where a lot of the territory was opening to the railways and other industries. There would be ample opportunities for him out there.

'It's a great country, Andrew boy, and they have a high regard for us Scots. You will do well, but let me give you a bit of advice, son. Assuming you still have some funds available, see a bit of the country first before you settle anywhere. The scenery is breath-taking, and you strike me as a lad who likes a bit of adventure. You have arrived at just the right time of year to take full advantage of the improving weather.'

McGregor scribbled the names of a few useful contacts in Montreal and suggested to Andrew he head there next, at his leisure, of course.

Andrew felt satisfied with his day as he walked back to his lodgings. He couldn't help but notice the number of black-robed priests who happened to pass by. Andrew thought of his mother and laughed at how she would have shuddered at the sight. He had also decided to take McGregor's advice. He would indeed award himself the luxury of some leisure time. He reflected that his life to date had been one of duty and doing exactly what was expected of him. Out here, he was developing a sense of freedom, and the prospects thrilled him.

His next stop was Montreal, where he stayed a week in a lodging house in Saint Catherine Street, trying to get the lay of the land. He strolled along the busy tree-lined streets, taking in the sights and sounds. Everything and everyone appeared bright, exciting, and vibrant. People were moving in all directions: office workers in suits heading to their places of business, mothers with children in hand walking towards the elementary school, paperboys on street corners belting out the morning headlines, and horse-drawn carts making deliveries to grocery stores, their wheels clicking as they crossed the tramlines. He would walk from one end of the town to the other to take in the sights and sounds, and then enjoy the simple pleasure of taking a trip on the new electric tram back to his lodging house. The tram had a slightly sideways to-and-fro movement as it travelled forward, and gave a little bump as it crossed junction points. The local people were friendly and polite, but above all Andrew enjoyed his anonymity, which had been impossible back home. He introduced himself at various logging company and railway offices in the city. They told him that if he was prepared to head out west, a man with his education and experience would have the pick of the best jobs. *Well, I have come this far*, he thought. *Why not a bit further?* His next destination would be Calgary, an important staging post on the western end of the railway line. He would travel across country using the Canadian Pacific Railway. A great deal about this latest decision appealed to him. He had pored over maps of Canada before his departure. and he could not help but notice the plethora of Scottish place names: Elgin, Hamilton, Paisley, to name a few. There was even a North and South Dumfries.

They were, of course, testament to the pioneering Scots who had first settled there. He did, however, wonder if they shared the same small-town mentality as their namesakes back in Scotland. Full of moralising ministers and endless gossips, he wouldn't wonder. Those places would not be for him. Calgary, on the other hand, sounded new, exciting, and perhaps a little dangerous, with people arriving from all parts of the globe. It might just be the place where he could finally find himself.

The very next day he found himself heading west along the railway line that stretched from Montreal to the Pacific ocean. The following days passed very quickly for Andrew. He was still completely overwhelmed by the size of this new country, realising that he had travelled further in the last fortnight than he had in all his previous life combined. He marvelled at the changing landscape of aqua blue lakes, dense green forests, and grassy plains that stretched forever. Elk, mouse, coyote, and brown bears were regularly spotted by excited passengers. The distances between towns and settlements astounded him, and he thought that whoever described them as 'beads on a string' had aptly summed up their distribution.

His enjoyment of the journey intensified after an overnight stop in Winnipeg, where he was joined by the most affable and interesting of travellers. Two young Swiss alpine guides joined the passengers in Andrews's second-class carriage. Hans Stager and Nils Ansler were on their way to take up jobs as mountain guides for wealthy American and European tourists in the Rocky Mountains. Ever since the accidental death of a tourist on a mountain trekking holiday a few years earlier, the Canadian authorities had become much more safety-conscious. Bringing in experienced and knowledgeable climbers and mountaineers from Switzerland had helped greatly in that respect. Both guides spoke excellent English and retold stories of hikes, climbs, avalanches, and near-death experiences in the Alps. They were returning for their second season in the Rocky Mountains. Andrew was impressed by their expertise, but also their carefree spirit and sense of adventure. He felt almost embarrassed and ashamed to recount his own comparatively dull life. Nils, with his tall, athletic build, short blond hair, and piercing blue eyes could have been quite an intimidating character, were it not for his affable nature and sense of humour. The three became good friends in the space of a couple of days and Andrew could at least tell of his hiking exploits in the relatively tame Galloway hills.

'It does not matter the height of a hill, Andrew. Even your small Scottish hill can be as dangerous as the Matterhorn if the weather turns bad and you lose your way,' said Nils, in a slightly condescending manner. They clearly all shared a love of nature, a sense of adventure and the ability to tell a tall tale. As the train approached Calgary, Nils spoke again:

'Do you know what, Andrew my friend? Why do you not join Hans and I for a time in the Rockies? I am sure we will find some job for you.'

Andrew could scarcely believe he heard himself agree to join them for a time in the mountains, icefields, and glaciers of Canada's Rocky Mountains. Permanent employment could wait a little while longer, he recklessly decided. Callum McGregor would surely approve, although God alone knew what his mother would have thought of his hasty decision.

Each new day on his journey brought fresh experiences and excitement. They were met in Calgary by a black Model T Ford, which would be their transport as far as Lake Louise. Andrew had never been in an automobile before, but kept that fact from his more experienced colleagues. Although it was late May, the wind was still very chilled as the motor headed north into the snow-capped mountains. The three friends huddled together in the back seats of the car for warmth, singing in turn Swiss, German, and Scottish songs. Andrew could not remember a time in his life when he had ever felt happier.

'I can't remember the last time I had so much fun!' he exclaimed to them both.

'Oh, this is only the start of it, Andrew,' Hans promised.

On occasions their transport struggled up steep climbs, the engine roaring loudly as if in pain. Following Nils' lead, the three would jerk their bodies back and forth in mock encouragement and sympathy for the driver and car as it struggled to the summit. Hair-raising descents prompted nervous jokes about the last time the driver had checked the brakes. It was the most thrilling journey of Andrew's life, and he was almost sad when it ended.

Their destination was the Chateau Lake Louise. Andrew had to admit it was the most wonderful scene he had ever set eyes on. The chateau was situated on the eastern shore of the lake. Its emerald-green waters were surrounded by spectacular high Rocky peaks, their tops still thick with snow, sparkling in the spring sunshine. Cornelius Van Home, general manager of the Canadian Pacific Railway, had chosen the ideal location to build a hotel for outdoor enthusiasts and Alpinists. The hotel, originally a log cabin which had burnt out several years earlier, was now replaced with a splendid stone building befitting its surroundings. Wealthy tourists were transported from various railway stations to this new centre of outdoor adventure. The two Swiss lads were about to start their second season at the hotel as mountain guides. Having convinced Andrew to come along, they persuaded the hotel manager that Andrew would be a very capable porter of the pack horses which were required to take the tourists and their equipment into the lower slopes of the Rockies. In return, Andrew was given his board and lodgings in the staff quarters of the hotel.

He thoroughly enjoyed the weekly treks into the mountains and was well used to handling horses, from his time helping on his grandfather's small farm. He marvelled at how Hans and Nils could pick a route up a very challenging peak, but one which could nevertheless be climbed by even the most apparently unfit tourist. Andrew would wait behind to attend and feed the horses, and prepare the tents and food if the hike involved an overnight stop. He had become a competent cook in the last few months of his mother's life. Evenings at camp would start with whatever meat stew Andrew had put together – elk, for example, tasted very much like venison – accompanied by bottles of wine and beer carefully transported from the hotel. As the campfire embers dimmed and the last song was sung, the guests retired to their tents and the guides to their own. Furs, pelts, and body heat were the only protection against the night's bitter cold. On their occasional day off, and if the weather was fine, the three guides would take a canoe and paddle along Lake Louise. Nils explained that silt-like rock flour carried by the glacial melt water gave the lake its distinctive blue-green azure, and that even in high summer the lake temperature was barely above freezing.

'Did you know,' said Nils, 'that the local Stoney Nakota Indians called it "the lake of the little fishes"?'

'But,' Andrew protested, 'I have been gazing into the lake and can't see any sign of aquatic life.'

'Ah – that's because all the little fish must have died of cold,' said Hans, joking.

The highlight of his stay at Lake Louise was a long trek into the Rockies with a group of wealthy and energetic American tourists. The week-long expedition included an ascent of Mount Snow Dome. Although it was not the highest peak in the area, it was none the less a challenging and interesting climb. Guides and tourists wearing snowshoes traversed their way across an icefield to begin the trek. Due to the biting cold and strong piercing wind they did not stay long at the dome-shaped summit, so Nils kept his tales about the mountain until camp that evening. As this had been the final climb of the week, Andrew had prepared a fine spread for the returning climbers: all the remaining vegetables and tail-ends of meat had been concocted into a thick hearty broth that his mother would have been proud of. One large American tourist named Bill joked that he could smell the broth from the top of the mountain and it had given him encouragement to make it back to camp. They devoured the thick, tasty soup gratefully. Andrew had baked several huge sockeye salmon in the campfire and these fishy treats completed the meal. A bottle or two of Canadian whiskey was passed around the group, and Nils sensed the moment was right to entertain them. To an enthralled audience, he began his tale about the fate of a snowflake on Snow Dome:

'This mountain, this very mountain where we sit right now, gentlemen, is the only place on earth,' he claimed, 'where a snowflake might melt into one of three different rivers and subsequently has the choice of three oceans. If it dissolves into Bryce Creek it will head west to the warmth of the Pacific.' He pointed in the general direction and his audience turned their head to look.

'Or, if it melts into the Athabasca river, it will head north to the frozen Arctic Ocean. And finally, if it lands on the North Saskatchewan River, it will flow east to Hudson Bay and the Atlantic ocean. One snowflake, three possible fates,' Nils summarised. 'The frosty Arctic, the balmy Pacific, or the stormy Atlantic. A harder choice than picking a lover.' Then, looking back towards Andrew, he asked playfully:

'So, dear Andrew, if you were the snowflake, which would you choose?'

Andrew deliberated dramatically, to add to the fun before answering. His choice was quite easy really, he declared:

'I would head west to the charms of the Pacific.'

'Why so?' Nils enquired, trying to draw him out.

'Well, if I headed east I would be retracing the steps that brought me to here, and I have no intention of ever returning to Scotland. I have had enough wind and rain for one lifetime.'

'So why not north, then?' Hans asked.

'Because north means it would be even more bloody cold than here and I simply could not bear that.' He shivered, mockingly.

'An excellent choice, then,' Nils responded approvingly.

The others proceeded to ponder and debate the merits of each direction. The comparisons with women became bawdier as the night progressed, alongside the quantity of alcohol consumed.

Andrew realised that his own adventure had reached a crossroads. Another reason for his answer he had kept to himself. He was having more fun and enjoyment with his two Swiss friends than he had ever had in his entire life. He felt completely at ease in their company; their views and attitudes were so refreshingly different from the narrow-mindedness back in Scotland, and as a result their conversations were far more interesting. Yet his strict Presbyterian upbringing was nagging at him that no good would come of such a light-hearted approach to life. He was also concerned about how close a friendship was developing between himself and Nils. He admired him, he enjoyed his company, and yet only a month earlier had never met him. Painfully aware of the deteriorating situation in Europe, he foresaw the time when they could be on opposite sides of a serious armed conflict. He convinced himself this was a good reason to end his association with the German Swiss guides and move on again, to Vancouver probably, before things became too strained and awkward. Besides, it was about time he made a proper living for himself.

So, when the group returned to Lake Louise tired and exhausted, Andrew made his announcement to a surprised Nils and Hans and was on his way the following day.

*

'Best get yourself below deck, Corporal,' shouted a deckhand.

The Liverpool accent was familiar to him from his outward voyage, but Andrew was still getting used to his new title.

'It is going to get real choppy, and you army boys don't have sea legs.'

Andrew would have happily gone below if his present ship was anything like the vessel he had first sailed on across the Atlantic about a year ago. And the ever-present fear of a German U-boat attack made him think he would have a better chance of survival above, rather than below deck. Now, here, he was on board the overcrowded SS *Missanabie*, heading in the opposite direction. There had been more twists and turns to his life this last year than all the previous put together. At least he had plenty of company for this voyage. A thousand-plus other souls of the 6th Brigade of the 2nd Canadian division were crammed on board alongside Corporal Andrew McDowall of the 29th Vancouver Infantry Battalion.

His mind backtracked again. His journey west to British Columbia had been amazing. He knew that Canada was vast, but still he had been unprepared for the sheer scale of the landscape or the array of wild animals spotted on the long train journey west to Vancouver. He had found acceptable lodgings near Stanley Park and then employment with the Vancouver School Board, teaching basic English at a night school to the Chinese and Japanese workers who had flocked to work in the canneries along the Fraser river. After a class, he enjoyed taking a late evening 'owl car' home and would hope that the conductor might be the famous *spieler*, Teddy Lyons. His stories and jokes were legendary in Vancouver. Andrew smiled to himself as he remembered his favourite: 'Ladies and gentlemen, observe the seagull flying above the car just now. You are viewing the richest bird in all of Vancouver!'

'How so?' a gullible passenger would ask.

'Why, earlier today it made a large deposit on a brand-new Cadillac.'

His other favourite pastime was to take afternoon tea at the Clachan tearoom in West Vancouver, run by two Scottish sisters, Jessie and Helen Stevenson. The home baking and familiar accents reminded him of home. He was enjoying some of the sisters' fare one afternoon in early August when a sweaty and breathless newspaper boy burst into the genteel surroundings with news of war in Europe. He was taken aback by the reaction of the normally polite clientele, who clapped and banged on the lace-covered tabletops, sending bone china teacups and saucers dancing across the tables and causing some to fall and smash on the floor. His own reaction was more subdued and considered. He wondered how the colonial government would react to the news; he considered the predicament of his new Swiss German friends, Hans and Nils, and how old friends in Scotland, particularly Kathleen and Tam, would respond.

The first batch of regular Canadian soldiers left Vancouver before the end of August. As in other cities in the Empire, Vancouver had become immersed in a wave of patriotism and enthusiasm for the European war. Andrew was not immune to its effects. One sunny afternoon as he lay on the grass in Hastings Park, enjoying the late autumn sunshine on his face, he watched the newly formed 29th Vancouver Battalion's ungainly attempts at marching and drilling. A rather attractive young lady introduced herself very politely and handed him a leaflet which exhorted him to do his bit for King, Country and Empire. This encounter was enough to trigger his Presbyterian sense of duty, which had been gnawing away at him for months anyway. He joined his local regiment, the 29th Vancouver, soon to be given the nickname 'The Knights of the Roller Coaster' in reference to the huge roller coaster in Hastings Park which formed the backdrop to parade photographs. Surprisingly, he excelled in the winter months of training and was promoted to corporal in charge of a section of twelve fine young men, most from farming backgrounds and some with a Scottish connection. One tall lad, Anders, of Norwegian parents, reminded him of Nils, the Swiss mountain guide. Finally, after further months of training, his regiment were transported on the long journey to the port of Halifax in May 1915. So here he was, on board a troop ship, a corporal in Col. Henry Seymour Tobin's battalion, heading for England to do his bit. The snowflake had melted back westwards after all.

FIVE
GALLIPOLI

As his company changed trains in Dumfries, Tam impatiently asked Sergeant Irving:

'How long will it take us to reach France frae here, Sarge?'

'What's the hurry, son? Are you another that thinks this war will be over afore it starts?'

'Just want to do ma bit, Sarge. What a disappointment it would be if they French lassies didnae get to see me.'

'Ah don't know how they'll have coped until now, Murdoch. Any roads, we are going tae France via the scenic route.'

'What do you mean, Sarge?'

'Did they no teach you any geography at the school? France is south from here, and what platform are you standing on?'

Tam had a quick look round, a wee bit befuddled by the sergeant's last few remarks. He noticed the word 'Dumfries' painted in the livery of the Glasgow and South

West Railway Company, and then below that, a smaller sign with smaller writing: *Platform 2 Northbound Trains.*

'Am no' a gambling man, Sarge, but am guessing north?'

'You're a fucking genius, Murdoch! While the regulars are bound for Gay Paree and visits to Mademoiselle Fifi's bordello, we Terries are off to relieve them of their duties.'

'And they duties would be what, Sarge? Marching up and doon outside Edinburgh Castle?'

'Naw, lad – East coast defence duties. Just in case the Prussians fancy a wee hop across the North Sea, me and you wi' bayonets fixed will send them back tae Berlin.'

Turning to the rest of the company, he bellowed: 'Right, 2nd Company! Get your arses on that train in double time.'

The following months would mostly drag by for Tam. He was bitterly disappointed not to be going to France immediately. The most exotic place name he came across at that time was Tillicoultry, a small village nestled at the bottom of the Hillfoots, on the road between Stirling and St Andrews, where his battalion was billeted. Most days consisted of fatigues and drills. At least he enjoyed and looked forward to the forced marches. As others in his platoon, such as Davy Kennedy and the Glendinning brothers, moaned and groaned and attempted to find ways out of the marches, Tam would lace his boots, whistling and singing to himself. He was first in line every time. He particularly liked a Sunday, when after the church hall service at ten, the men had free time until two in the afternoon. The local pubs like the Woolpack and the Volunteer were closed on the Sabbath, so Tam would set off on his own and climb the Ochil hills via the glens at places like Menstrie, Alva, and Dollar. At the top of Ben Cleuch, he would rest for a while and, from habit, reach out to give Sammie, his absent collie, a pat. He enjoyed the views along the snaking river Devon during the descent back to his billets. There was a waterfall along the way where he liked to stop to listen to the roaring water and feel the spray on his face. Those few hours alone every week were enough to relieve him of the tedium of army life. He thought it funny that before the war his lonely occupation meant he craved company. Now that he had plenty of company, he liked nothing better than to go off on his own. His mother did call him contrary.

These early, dull months of the war contained a few brief highlights for Tam. The first was Christmas dinner. He was sorely disappointed not to be given home leave. Not only had he wanted to see his own family and Sammie again, but he was also hopeful that Kathleen might still be there too. They did not celebrate Christmas much at home, as Ne'er Day was deemed far more important. However, an army Christmas dinner of turkey, roast sausages, and spicy plum pudding had more than cheered him up. There was plenty of beer, too, and a lot of fun with the NCOs who served the ranks their meal, as was the regimental tradition at Christmas. Sergeant Irving in particular was in fine form, overstating the servility of his task with a large dollop of heavy sarcasm. The locals had done them proud too, and even gave each soldier a packet of cigarettes. These nicely supplemented the parcels, cards, and letters from back home in Galloway. He kept the card from Kathleen in his breast pocket. It had simply said: 'Thinking of you, Thomas, at this festive time. Kindest regards, Kathleen.' It was strange to read his 'Sunday' name as, apart from his mother, very few addressed him this way. He must reply to Kathleen soon, but letter-writing was a real struggle for Tam. He didn't let that thought trouble him too much as he loosened his belt and drew heavily on one of his cigarettes. The warm fuggy atmosphere of the hall made him feel contented and sleepy. He reckoned his company must have eaten much better than the poor sods in the trenches in France, although he was still no less keen to join them. The evening ended with the singing of Christmas carols, and Tam joined in with great gusto, although he could not help yearning for the sweet sound of Kathleen's melodic voice.

Early in the new year the company was sent to South Queensferry, to guard and transfer a group of sorry-looking German sailors to Edinburgh. They had been picked up after their ship, the *Blucher*, was sunk out in the North Sea. The sailors arrived as a right bedraggled bunch. Some still wore the uniform of the Imperial German Navy, but most had an assortment of clothes and blankets given to them by the sailors on HMS *Lion* and *Tiger*, who had fished them out of the freezing North Sea. Tam considered it his first absurdity of war. The sailors had tried to knock the living blazes out of each other, then as soon as the *Blucher* went down, all their energies went to rescue the sailors whose ship they had just sunk. He supposed the Germans may have done the same. The other thing that occurred to Tam was that the Germans, although clearly not looking their best, did appear pretty much like any other lad you might pass in the street; more blond heads, right enough.

A few had some English and would mutter comments of thanks, or ask: 'Where are you taking us?' or, 'Can you post this letter to my mother in Frankfurt? She will be worried about me.'

While they sat on the train Tam shared a couple of cigarettes with his prisoners, fogging up the third-class compartment. Their arrival at Waverley station had resulted in the gathering of a curious crowd. On the road up to Edinburgh Castle the escort was met with a combination of cheers for themselves and boos directed at their prisoners. One old biddy had made her way through the crowd and spat forcefully in the face of a young German sailor.

'That's for the wives and bairns o' Scarborough, ken, ye German bastard!' she had yelped at him. A couple of the company had had to push her back into the crowd.

So Tam had now seen a German, in fact over a hundred of them, but he still yearned for some real action. Rumours spread among the battalion that they were shortly for the off. A football match was arranged between the officers and men. Tam had been delighted to be selected to play, although he failed to score in the one-each draw. In the pub after the match some of the junior officers let it slip that they would all be allowed on home leave the following day. That certainly meant they were on their way to the front very shortly. Tam was beside himself with excitement. He hoped Kathleen would be at home.

He would see his parents and brothers and Sammie soon, and then finally, finally, it would be off to France and the real action.

The train journey back to Galloway seemed to take an age. Tam was in a compartment with Sergeant Irving, Davy Kennedy, and some other local lads. There was the usual banter and jokes, with admiring glances and comments to any young ladies who joined the train, but Tam's mind was elsewhere. He should have replied to Kathleen's card, but had never got around to it. What would she be doing in the war? No doubt organising parcels for the boys and fundraising of all sorts.

He was relieved and happy to find his parents and brothers in good form. If his mother was becoming anxious about him heading to the front, she made a good fist of hiding it. In fact, she seemed to be preoccupied with the adverse effect on his health of a certain type of French woman rather than the more obvious danger of the Kaiser's armies.

'Thomas, don't you be going with any of those filthy women, now! They will give you the pox and you will go blind; your thing will fall off and ye will die. Tell me you won't, Thomas.'

'Of course no, Ma.' Tam had never really entertained the notion of doing so, but his mother's warnings had completely dampened his ardour. He shivered at the prospect.

He was able to spend his last afternoon at home back on the estate, where he took Sammie for a walk on the lower slopes of the hills. Once again, the local community had done the lads in uniform proud. A special tea was laid on for the departing King's Own Scottish Borderers, followed by a dance that lasted well into the early hours. His enthusiasm for the send-off was dampened when he learned that Kathleen was no longer at home. She had volunteered for the Red Cross Voluntary Aid Detachment and was in Aberdeen at a training camp. As the night went on and Tam drank more and more whisky, he felt a bit consoled by the presence and company of Anne, whom he had met at the previous send-off in 1914.

Her opening remark had been: 'So the Huns havnae killed ye yet, Tam Murdoch? Jist as well, because they would have me tae answer tae.' It had made him laugh. They continued to laugh and danced most of the night. Tam held her close, enjoying the warmth of her body as they waltzed late into the night.

It was a bleary-eyed company of soldiers who entrained from Newton Stewart railway station the following morning. Even with a thumping headache, Tam resolved that he would spend the journey writing a letter to Kathleen in case he did not get a chance in France. He might write a short one to Anne, as well. It couldn't do any harm.

Tam had never spent so much time on trains until he joined the army. Now they were finally on the journey south. As he gazed out of the window the lights of each passing town and village illuminated the dark. He thought about the houses close to the line where he could see into a lit kitchen or parlour. Had the mothers in those homes seen off sons like him? Had they uttered the same dire warnings about French *mademoiselles*? They must have passed hundreds of towns and villages during the night.

The port of Dover was as close as Tam was to get to France in the meantime. When his company embarked again, they were to learn that their sea voyage would be a little longer than the hop across the channel. Instead of Flanders fields, they were bound for the sandy shores of Alexandria in Egypt, to join the Mediterranean Expeditionary Force. There was much talk as to why they were being dispatched there and what the purpose of their visit would be. Even the usually well-informed Sergeant Irving was in the dark . As each day passed, Tam noticed an increase in the temperature. By the time they reached Alexandria the heat was stifling. There were moans and groans when the lads found out that they would have to remain on board for two days before clearance to land. Tam had never seen so many ships and such a level of activity before. Freshly arrived troop ships like his own lay at anchor. The brightly coloured red and green hospital ships sailed back and forth in and out of dock. Hundreds of little lighters conveyed men and supplies out to the larger ships. The dockside was groaning with supplies of all kinds, from ammunition boxes to carts and wagons. Egyptian civilians seemed to be everywhere, hawking all sorts of wares, but mainly tobacco, the strong aroma drifting with the breeze onto the anchored troop ships. The cries of *baksheesh, baksheesh* were incessant, as the local porters tried the generosity of the soldiers they helped to disembark, singling out the better-paid officers.

After a chaotic day in the mayhem of Alexandria, Tam's company moved out to the huge Mustapha barracks. Here the routine was familiar, even if the temperature and scenery were not. Training consisted of days and days of long, gruelling marches into the hot desert to build up stamina.

'It's just like marching at home with the added joys of heat and sand. I remember when you buggers complained about the wind and rain in Bonnie Scotland,' Sergeant Irving would joke at the start of every day. Sometimes he would amuse himself by adding, 'Come on, ma wee sand dancers, on your way.'

Tam struggled in the heat, but was determined to tough it out, and was always at the front of the column. The most exhilarating part of the day was after the company stopped for food and water. The signal was given for open-order skirmishing. Tam and his unit would dash forward in full kit for about seventy to one hundred yards. They stopped, took aim, and fired off many blank cartridges from their Lee Enfield rifles towards an imaginary enemy on the heat-shimmered horizon. A short sharp bugle call, and glistening bayonets were fixed to the rifles for a frantic charge at the enemy. Every known expletive and a few more were shouted and screamed with delight during this crescendo of action.

'I wish to fuck these bastards would stop running awa' and face us wan day,' Davy Kennedy joked.

'I will no' have a clue what to do when they do.'

High command disagreed, and after six weeks, Tam's unit was deemed fit to enter the battle fray at Gallipoli. A major, on inspecting the troops at drill one day, had singled him out, impressed by his speed and enthusiasm. He told him:

'You will make a damn fine runner, soldier.'

Sergeant Irving made a mental note to use him for that when the time came.

Tam was relieved when at last they left Alexandria on board the HMS *Aquitania*. Their vessel was luxurious compared to the ships which had transported the first assault troops back in April. It was also a huge vessel, holding 6000 troops of the 52nd Division. He chummed around with his fellow KOSBs and lads from the 5th Royal Scots. The sailors also reassuringly informed the infantry that this vessel was far too swift for the slow Turkish U-boats, which apparently had no chance of pranging her. He hoped they were right. It only took a week for such a speedy ship to approach the shores of the Gallipoli peninsula. For the final part of the journey the men slipped down rope ladders on to lighters: small ships, no bigger than a fishing trawler, which took them to the beaches of Helles.

The war had finally come to meet Tam now, and after all his impatience he was not sure how to react. Like many inexperienced soldiers, he felt a mixture of fear, bewilderment, and excitement. It was the noise that struck him first. There was the distant dull thud of Turkish artillery, and as they neared the shore a rhythmic rattle of machine gunfire interspersed with the crackle of rifle shots. He could see puffs of black smoke on the hills overlooking the beach. 'Someone must have told the Turks we were on our way,' joked one of the lads. In fact, the fire on this part of the peninsula had been incessant since the first landings. Experienced soldiers had counted the seconds of silence between Turkish shells, and fifteen was the record to date. The run-aground HMS *River Clyde*, used in the first assault, now acted as a jetty for the men to clamber over and on to the beach. From there they were semi-organised and marched past the cemetery where the Scots, English Irish, Ghurkha, and Sikh soldiers of the first attack in April lay buried. It was an unnerving experience.

'Welcome to Fuckin Helles,' boomed a friendly soldier from the 29th division. *Too true*, thought Tam, *too bloody true*. This is what he'd been waiting for, to finally take part in real action. All he could think was *make the best of it lad, do your best*, as he tried to stop shaking.

His company gathered in the reserve trenches and attempted to get some sleep before morning. It was an all but impossible task. The unfamiliar noises and smells, coupled with the cramped conditions in the trenches, meant any rest was temporary. The next few days were spent ferrying equipment, weapons, and precious water supplies from the shore up to their reserve position. Tam could not believe the searing heat of the midday sun, which made him sweat and his skin prickle. The tasks were much the same as had been performed in drills back in Alexandria except for the noise. On one journey a Turkish shell found its mark about thirty yards from Tam. It sent a neighbouring party of four KOSBs sky high. Obliterated body parts, fragmented shards of rock, and a cloud of sand were sprayed in every direction, covering Tam with a grotesque blanket. He screamed out and began wiping the debris furiously from his uniform, unable to decide if what he'd just witnessed was real or some heat- and thirst-induced delusion. Sergeant Irving snapped at them, 'Get the fuck out of here. There is sod all you can do for those lads.' He was right, of course, but it would take some time for Tam to become casually nonchalant, and then callous, about death. Over the next few days he would get plenty of experience.

Everything about Gallipoli was chaotic. Tam was regaled by stories from the troops they were relieving: tales about the horrors of the initial landings to the ferocity of the Turkish counter-attacks and the monotonous, awful food. Everyone was permanently thirsty.

'The only way we'll beat the Turks is like this: lob over cans of McConachie's bully beef to the Turk trenches and then wait for the bastards to die of thirst,' an old regular had suggested to Tam. He didn't get the joke at first.

If Tam's division had been fortunate to miss the murderous mayhem of the first stage of the ill-fated campaign, they were joining it at an equally tough time. The grand strategy of the campaign had been to open a new front against the weak underbelly of the Alliance powers –Turkey, the so-called sick man of Europe. From the Gallipoli peninsula, British Empire and French soldiers would take Constantinople, opening a fresh sea route to supply Russia, defeat Turkey, and heap pressure on the Germans. Instead the campaign had ground to a halt and the attritional trench fighting of the Western Front was transferred to the sand and rock of Gallipoli. As well as the traditional horrors of trench warfare, Gallipoli was to add heat, thirst, and a brave and very determined enemy, fighting to repel the infidel invaders. Add to that a complete lack of sanitation, resulting in dysentery and typhoid which compounded the misery.

Tam was largely unaware of the grand scheme of things, except that he knew his company and division would take part in another fresh assault to try and dislodge the Turks. Could they succeed where others had bravely gone, but failed, before?

The bombardment began at 4.30 a.m. on 12 July. It was already becoming light. Tam and his company huddled into the side of their sandy trench, hoping and praying that the artillery was doing its work on the Turkish positions. The ground around them was shaking and the noise deafening. At 7 a.m. a corporal came around with a billy can full of rum and proceeded to dish it out via a large copper soup spoon. Tam gulped it down and momentarily enjoyed the warm glow.

' Have ye a pint to go wi' that, Corporal?' Private Kennedy half-joked. Their mouths were sand-dry, half with thirst and half from fear.

AT 7.30 a.m. Sergeant Irving whispered, 'Fix bayonets,' and there followed a mad scramble to do just that. It was not at all like the slick well-rehearsed drills of the parade ground. Instead, men fumbled to find space, so cramped were they in the makeshift trenches.

'Keep the rifles pointing up, you daft bastards,' he told them. 'Save the stabbing for the Turks. Whistle's about to go, lads. When you go over, run like your arse is on fire. See you in the first Turks' trench.'

At 7.35 a.m., over they went. It was fifty yards to the first line of Turkish trenches. Every man was weighed down by two bandoliers of ammunition, a backpack, water bottle, plus the weight of their rifles. Tam was one of the first over and instinctively kept his head down and to the side, as if sheltering from a hailstorm rather than the bullets and shrapnel which were whizzing and exploding all around him. Somehow, he made it breathlessly into the first trench. He was joined by Irving, Kennedy, and some of the other lads They looked to their left and right for Turks, but none were in sight. They had fallen back to the next line.

'Two minutes, boys, and we're off again,' instructed Sergeant Irving. They went back over the top: another barrage of fire from the Turks and into the second line. This time there were Turks in the trench and ferocious hand-to-hand fighting occurred. Tam came face to face with a Turkish soldier of around his own age. They both froze for a split second, and as the Turk raised his rifle to fire, Tam lunged ferociously at him with his bayonet, which pierced through his chest and pinned him to the sandbags on the far side of the trench. Trying to ignore the anguished look on the young Turk's face, Tam twisted and turned his bayonet in a vain effort to retrieve it from the dying soldier. Frantically he lifted his left foot high, pressing it against his foe's chest while pulling with both hands to free his rifle. There was no time to stop and think about what he had just done. A call from Sergeant Irving down the line had him scrambling to meet up. There were fewer of them this time, but Irving and Kennedy were still there.

'I think I got one,' Tam spluttered, in so much as a dry mouth can splutter.

'Good lad, Tam. Bagged a couple myself. Right: five minutes and it's third line for us.'

A private raised a periscope from the trench to survey the next objective.

'Beg pardon, Sarge, but where is the third line?'

Irving looked for himself and could see what the soldier meant. The scene didn't look like a summer's day: the thick clouds of smoke, sand, and dust blackened the sky. There was no obvious trench line forward of their position. 'Right. We wait here for other platoons to join us,' he decided.

Within an hour the old Turkish second line was bristling with advancing British troops. A captain gave the order to advance and over they went for the third time that morning. The third line was also empty of Turkish troops, but it wasn't really a proper line at all. The 'trenches' were at best two feet deep. Orders went out to widen and deepen them, but this proved almost impossible. Entrenching tools hit flinty ground and no noticeable improvement could be made. Tam and his company were alive, elated to be so, and overjoyed to have reached their first objective mainly unscathed. The exhilaration would soon wear off, to be replaced by exhaustion. Water bottles were guzzled in the lull. No one considered that it might be some time before fresh supplies could be sent up to their advanced position. Tiredness and extreme thirst, as they baked in the glaring summer sun, were their main problems for the next few hours. They were soon to forget about tiredness, thirst and heat, as the Turks launched one of their infamous counter-attacks.

First there was a retaliatory artillery bombardment from a 7.5-inch gun, which found their range after a few attempts. Tam buried his head in the ground and hoped for the best. As quickly as the shells stopped, the Turkish infantry were on to them. To stay in the flimsy trenches against such an onslaught was suicidal. The general order was given to retreat back to the second line they had captured earlier in the morning. Even in this relatively safer position, the Turkish attack, if anything, intensified. Tam and the others had to admire the courage of their enemy, as on they came against rifle and machine gun fire. Tam thought he downed at least two. And still they kept coming.

'Right, Murdoch: get your sorry arse over to the captain and be fucking quick about it,' barked Sergeant Irving. And then, more softly: 'And keep your head down, boy.'

Tam didn't need to be told twice. A few hundred metres back from the front line meant he might be just that little bit safer. He jack-knifed along the sandy trench towards Captain Taylor. Turkish shells were sending showers of shrapnel either side of him. Amidst the din of the artillery he could hear the ping-pinging of sniper fire. This was getting serious. The closer he got to the captain, the more intense the bombardment became.

'Right, Private, get this message back down the line pronto. I've no time to write, and the lads to your right need to get out of here sharpish. Tell the Major: "2nd company under severe pressure. Very heavy losses. Seek withdrawal to start point." Got that?'

'Yes, sir.'

'Then go.'

Tam took off like he was in a race back home. The adrenaline was already pumping. Only fifty yards on, a machine gun began to trace across his path. He instinctively started to zig-zag as he heard the bullets whiz around him A lung-bursting sprint took him further down the beach and out of the range of the gun. He'd never been so terrified in his life, yet he also experienced exhilaration beyond words. His euphoric state was soon burst when he relayed his message to the major.

'Are you quite sure that is what the captain said?' the major asked, disbelievingly. 'Could you not have misheard him, what with all the noise?'

The major found it hard to comprehend that a fresh company could suffer so badly after the artillery support he had organised from land and sea.

'No. That is exactly what Captain Taylor said, sir, I could see the bodies piled up just beyond our trenches myself, sir.'

As the major stood there contemplating and processing the information from the runner, Tam was becoming more and more irritated by his prevarication. He was just about to ask, 'Sir, what I shall tell the captain?' when a second runner from a different company arrived to convey a similar message to Tam's.

'Very well,' the major finally decided. 'All clear to fall back.'

'Thank Christ for that,' muttered Tam, as he made his way back towards the captain's precarious position. He decided to take a different route, just in case the machine gunners were still trigger-happy. As he approached the position, he noticed that both the artillery and the machine guns had stopped. That could only mean one thing: Johnny Turk was storming over the short gap between the trenches for some hand-to-hand scrapping. Some of the lads had not waited for the official orders, and were already streaming past Tam as he made his way to the captain.

'Major says withdraw, Sir.'

'About time, but I don't think anyone told the Turks.'

The captain ordered the remaining troops to stand fast. If they turned tail now and the Turks caught them, it would become an even bigger massacre.

'Take your positions, choose your man, and bring him down,' he yelled. A salvo of Lee Enfield bullets stopped the first wave of Turks hard. Most collapsed and were trampled on as the second brave wave advanced. Again, they recoiled against the withering fire of the KOSBs. Some Turks had sheltered behind bodies or in shallow sandpits, and were returning fire. Soldiers next to Tam were being hit. One straight through the head; another had most of his left arm blown off. In the brief lull before the next Turkish assault, the captain bellowed: 'Fall back, fall back now. 2nd platoon covering fire.' Tam took to his heels for the third time that day.

He was soon leading the retreat, as his superior fitness saw him pass the others. That feeling of exhilaration hit him again. He did not know whether to laugh or cry, so he just kept on running, beads of sweat dripping from his forehead. He could hear friendly troops to his immediate front yelling and yelling at him and his slightly slower comrades. Tam assumed they were cheering them to safety. Not quite. To their left a group of Turks had broken out and were heading across their path. Tam thought he would have more of a chance if he kept running, rather than turn to face them as others did. He could have been no more than twenty yards from the reserve line when he felt a searing hot pain in his left buttock.

'Oh for fuck's sake! I've been shot in the arse...of all places, my bloody arse,' he moaned.

And it was bloody, too. He limped the last few steps to safety where a medical orderly tore off fabric around the bullet hole and applied a field dressing.

'It's off to the hospital ship for you, lad. Don't look too serious: you will be back in a few days to get your revenge.'

And he probably would have been if he hadn't had to lie – face down – on a stretcher for two days on the beach. Why was it that no one showed you any sympathy if you got shot in the arse? A 'Blighty one' in any other part of the body would draw envious remarks and well wishes for your return home. A more serious wound would get you an offer of a fag, or maybe a word or two from the padre. But an arse wound? You only got laughed at, with comments like 'I see Johnny Turk got you up the arse then, Tam?' or 'Never mind, lad. Wait until Nursey has to kiss it better for you.'

The wound, however, stopped being a laughing matter after two days in the glaring heat and sun. Tam had never seen so many flies in his life, not even when he had disturbed a maggot-ridden dead sheep and swarms had burst everywhere. Here, they targeted the food and the wounded in equal measure. Open a can of bully beef and a thousand guests appeared for lunch. In between mouthfuls a soldier had to clear them with his sleeve from his face and mouth. When they crawled on to his eyelids or up his nostrils it could drive a man insane. They were also experts at spreading infection and disease. Dysentery and typhoid were endemic among the troops. The few medical orderlies on the beach were doing their best, but they were overwhelmed by the sheer number of casualties. They scurried here and there, applying field dressings and trying to prioritise cases for the hospital ships. They were supposed to divide the men into wounded and sick. No one had seemed to realise that many casualties would be both. The padres were also working full pelt, offering comforting words and prayers to the wounded. More importantly, they helped to distribute the water rations to the distressed soldiers. 'A mouthful of water over here please, Padre,' was a common cry.

The two days baking in the heat with a wounded and now infected backside were agony for Tam. But worse was to follow. He was finally heaved painfully aboard the black ship and taken below deck. Nothing in this world could have prepared Tam for what he was about to experience.

SIX

COMING AND GOING

The previous night, as he lay on the beach, Tam had been convinced he would die, as many around him had. Now in the hold of a 'black ship', he thought: *not only have I died, but I am consigned to hell.* The stench was insufferable, causing him to dry-retch involuntarily. The wounded and sick had been hastily hauled on board in the darkness and crammed into every available space. There had been no chance on the beach to grade the sick and wounded, so men with severe dysentery lay next to those with fractures and next to those with infected bayonet, bullet, and shrapnel wounds. The 'lucky' ones were accommodated in cot beds, but most had to make do with soiled mattresses or, like Tam, seawater-soaked stretchers. Latrine facilities were next to non-existent. The few chamber pots overflowed with dark urine caused by dehydration. It had the most intense sickly-sweet smell, not unlike pear drops. Worse was the fact that the dysentery cases had so little control of their bowels that their watery and bloody defecations trickled around the deck floor, seeping into mattresses, stretchers, and hammocks. Some orderlies on the beach had even tied string round the ankles of these poor creatures' trousers in a vain attempt to help. The putrid stench was made worse by the searing heat in the hold. Each new breath was a struggle for Tam's lungs and an assault on his nostrils. The stifled air felt solid. The sounds of crying, moaning men demanding attention were amplified in the overcrowded hold. The only people who were quiet were the few overworked nurses and their untrained assistants. With methodical calm and quiet energy, they made their way to each patient, sometimes having to clamber over their neighbour, so limited was the space in which they had to work.

It took over two hours for an Australian nurse to reach Tam. She removed the old field dressing and washed his wound with a bucket of seawater. His wound was now infected and leaking pus, but it was far from the worst she had seen. Tam winced as the salt from the water stung the wound, but was relieved to know it was freshly dressed. He even summoned the energy to ask the nurse her name, and when she responded, 'Connie,' he asked: 'Connie, you wouldn't have an old fag for a wounded soldier, would you?' To his delight, she produced a packet of Greek cigarettes and lit one for him. He propped himself up on his left elbow and took the cigarette with his right hand. The first drag was joyously magnificent. The tobacco temporarily blocked out the other smells and anaesthetised his senses. Each draw was longingly savoured right down to the butt. He fell flat on his stomach again and drifted into a disturbed sleep.

Parts of the previous day's actions replayed in his dream. He relived his stabbing of the young Turkish soldier, but this time Tam could see his horrified face, feel the Turk's gasping breath on his own face, and hear his last desperate cries, as the life drained from his eyes. Then he was confronted by a small Turkish woman, dressed completely in black, who wanted to know why he had killed her son. He was a good boy and a shepherd who tended his flock carefully. *Why have you come from a strange land to kill my son? Why, why, why?* she sobbed. Her dream cries startled Tam from his sleep. The cries continued until an exhausted and confused Tam realised they were coming from his companions in the hold. When he drifted off again the old woman would reappear, then morph into his own mother, who asked him: *Why did you kill that poor boy, Tam? Whit had he ever done to you? I never brought you into this world to be a murderer. Whit was ye thinking of?*

Tam cried himself awake, shouting, 'Sorry, I'm sorry. Sorry, Ma.' When this nightmarish sequence repeated itself several times, he woke in a cold sweat. Nurse Connie decided to give him a shot of morphia to let him, and those around him, sleep a bit longer. With over a hundred patients to deal with by herself, this was a much-practiced procedure.

Over the next few days a semblance of order came to the transport ship *Ionian* as it steamed toward the Greek island of Mudros. As the few nurses became familiar with their patients, the most serious cases were prioritised for operations. Unlike the official white and green hospital ships, medical facilities were basic aboard the so-called 'black ships' such as the *Ionian*. However, the few doctors and nurses performed admirably and saved many lives, even if it did not seem like that to them at the time. Tam had noticed two stretcher cases near to him being lifted out to a storeroom, not realising it served as a temporary morgue. After a soldier was operated on, he was moved to one of the scarce cot beds, freeing up a little more space for Tam and his comrades on the hold floor, still waiting their turn for treatment. Tam at least had the chance to converse with different patients as this grim game of 'medical chairs' progressed.

Amongst the frantic comings and goings, Tam began chatting with a familiar-looking soldier. Jim Melrose was in the 7th Royal Scots, a regiment mainly recruited from Leith. The two had met briefly while they were on North Sea duty in eastern Scotland. They were delighted to see each other again, and talked for hours about life back home and their own war experiences to date. Tam moaned to him about his own short war record.

'Aye Jim, I dinnae think they will be giving me any war medals. More than a year dossing around back home, and when I finally make it to the action I last a whole two days until a Turk blows half ma arse aff.' (Ironically Tam's commanding officer had given him a mention in dispatches for his gallantry during the attack and subsequent withdrawal.)

'Don't make me laugh, or ma stitches will come out,' replied Jim. And then, more seriously:

'At least you made it here, Tam. Did you no hear whit happen to the 7th on their way to Gallipoli? A fucking great train crash at Gretna; more than 200 men and nearly all the officers killed. Most of them burnt tae a crisp after their train was hit head on by the London express. Poor bastards didn't even get to fire a shot at the Huns or the Turks. Aw ma neighbours back in Leith had somebody killed. Glad ah didn't have to go home – don't think I could have faced that.'

Tam commiserated with Jim and thought maybe he was quite lucky after all. Later that day Tam was taken into the makeshift operating theatre on board ship. Originally the ship was to stop at the island of Mudros and send the wounded to hospital there. However, all the hospitals on the island were overflowing with wounded and even the proper hospital ships, which lay at anchor in the harbour, could not take any more casualties. They were now headed for Alexandria, and in the meantime, the overworked medical staff were performing more and more operations on board the black ship.

It was a different nurse, not Connie, who attended to Tam, along with a young English surgeon. Tam lay face down as she cut away at his stained trousers with an enormous pair of scissors. The surgeon administered the chloroform drip meticulously. Tam did not have a particularly clear view of the dimly lit theatre but, just as the anaesthetic took effect, he could have sworn he saw a bucket in the corner which contained two bloodied legs and an arm. His dressing was removed, revealing a badly suppurating wound, seeping with a huge volume of disgusting-smelling pus. The nurse quickly cleaned it as best she could, and the surgeon applied stitches to begin closing the gaping hole.

'Nurse, make sure a Carrel-Dakin dressing is applied every four hours to the wound. Also, make sure he stays lying on his stomach, and try to get him on deck when you can,' ordered the surgeon as he turned to make a brief entry in his medical log:

Thomas Murdoch, private KOSBs. A single through and through rifle bullet wound. Entered posterior to right lesser trochanter through gluteal muscle exiting anterior to left greater trochanter. Discharged pus, faeces and blood. Wound cleaned and dressed. Reapply every four hours.

'He should be fine now, nurse. Who's next, then? And could you get me some fresh water, please?'

When Tam came around, it took him a minute or two to realise that he was on a clean stretcher laid out on deck. The fresh iodine dressing was nipping at his wound, but he felt better within himself, as the smell of the salty sea air was so preferable to the stench below deck. All he needed now was a fag to keep him going. Four hours later the nurse applied a new dressing. When it was being changed the pain was excruciating, without the luxury of anaesthetics for this routine, but necessary procedure. Tam just clenched his fists, gritted his teeth and refused to cry out, for fear of appearing weak to the other men. All the wounded soldiers did the same. The nurse rewarded him with a cigarette and Tam thought it was almost worth it for that. Only another four hours until his next fag. His treatment, cigarettes included, continued for the next few days. The nurse could see that his wound was gradually improving. Although he could not yet turn round to bear weight on his backside, Tam could take his weight on his forearm, and twist his right leg a little to see something of what was going on aboard.

At midnight he was witness to a solemn ceremony. A chaplain in his robes appeared on deck and read aloud a burial service. His book was illuminated by a small paraffin lamp held by an orderly. It swayed in time to the rhythm of the waves. All the casualties on deck who were awake stopped chattering, and a silence descended. Two sailcloth-covered figures lay still beside the chaplain, a weight secured by a rope to their feet. As the minister completed the last rites, the two corpses were respectfully lifted onto the gangway board and a Union Jack was spread over them. The ship's bell rang a melancholy three times as the ships engines fell silent A final prayer and the flag was swiftly removed, the board tilted skywards, and the figures slipped into the sea with a small splash. The ship remained silent for a time and then, as the engines spluttered back into life, slowly and in at first quiet voices, the soldiers' conversations resumed.

When the ship eventually docked at Alexandria the port was no less chaotic than when Tam had first arrived. It was perhaps this perpetual chaos which led to him being transferred to the wrong hospital ship; bound, he eventually discovered to his delight, for Liverpool. He could thank an abbreviation for getting him home. Every casualty had a ticket tagged to their clothing or stretcher with the letters explaining the status of the patient. On Tam's stretcher the ticket was 'WS', meaning 'wound slight'. He should have been taken to a convalescing camp in Alexandria and then dispatched back to his company, who were still clinging on at Gallipoli. However, the Indian orderly who checked Tam interpreted the 'WS' to mean 'wound serious', and was most diligent in ensuring Tam made it to the hospital ship *Caledonia* which, despite its name, was bound for England. There the most serious cases would receive specialised medical attention. The orderly was not the first nor the last to make this mistake. Tam was unaware of the administrative blunder, but took the ship's name as a good luck sign. Nor did he look out of place onboard, as he was still stretcher-bound. By the time the medical staff had a look at his wound to assess its treatment it was far too late to send him back. When he reached England Tam's wound was all but healed. He could lie on his back again, although he walked with the slightest of limps. On arrival at Liverpool, the army deliberated about what to do with him. He could have been sent to a convalescing camp, but he was in such good condition he hardly needed that. Had Tam tricked his way on to the ship, as some desperate soldiers had been known to, then he might have spent a few months in a military prison. Instead they decided to give Tam two weeks home leave before they sent him back into action. As he sat on the Glasgow-bound train Tam began to warm to the Turkish soldier who had shot him in the backside.

'Cheers, Abdullah my boy', he said to himself as he slugged from the half bottle of whisky he had bought in a pub near Lime Street train station. He had changed his army pay back into sterling and, in true army tradition, he intended to spend every single penny of it before he returned to the front, most of it on strong drink. He hoped Kathleen would be at home when he got back and if not, then perhaps Anne would be around. Tam's luck was in, as both girls were at home, at least for the start of his leave.

*

Kathleen was growing more impatient and resentful by the day. If she was fobbed off with another condescending request to knit more socks and scarves for the boys at the front she would be fit to scream. Not that there was anything wrong with that, of course; she had already organised parcels of comforts for the boys at the front at Christmas time. She had taken part in various fundraising events for Belgian refugees and Serbian hospitals, but she wanted to do so much more. What was really fuelling her impatience was the fact that she had joined the Kirkmabreck branch of the Voluntary Aid Detachment on the Thursday after war had broken out. Along with several other local girls she had volunteered for nursing service in France or wherever the British troops would be fighting. Months went by and they heard absolutely nothing, other than dates when they were asked to participate in flag days to raise yet more funds. Her cheeks still flushed red with anger when she remembered reading an article in the *Suffragist* magazine regarding Dr Elsie Inglis. This pioneering doctor and women's rights campaigner had offered to organise a one hundred-bed hospital for war wounded in Edinburgh. Both the War Office and the British Red Cross turned her down. Kathleen knew this was because the hospital would be entirely staffed by women. But it was the response from the authorities that really made her blood boil: *Go home and sit still.*

She was sick and tired of sitting still. She no longer hid her copies of the *Suffragist* from her disapproving bank manager father, and some furious rows erupted at home. He was concerned about his position in the local community, not least because he was an agent for the local Scottish Unionist Member of Parliament. In his eyes it did not become his daughter to be involved or associated with a group of hysterical campaigners who were a disgrace to Scotland, Great Britain, and the Empire. Her mother's conciliatory attempts to explain that their daughter was allied to the moderate wing of the women's movement fell on deaf ears. She did manage to end most of the rows by reminding her husband and daughter that their four boys were fighting at the front, and what would they think if they were to witness such scenes? These comments only served to make Kathleen feel worse and even more determined to do her bit, if only the idiotic men like her father would give her the chance.

At least she had completed her First Aid certificate, which qualified her to dress cuts and grazes and bandage broken limbs. Many an eager local boy scout had served as a mock casualty for her as she completed her training. Most of the young lads were delighted when it was Kathleen who bandaged their 'wounds' and made manly comments like 'It doesn't hurt a bit, Miss,' which always made her smile.

With the Red Cross she also completed the Home Nursing certificate, which as well as medical skills, demanded that the successful candidates could fold beds properly, smooth sheets and make beef tea. She had thoroughly enjoyed the Voluntary Aid Detachment (VAD) training camps where, under the closest of supervision, they could practice on Territorial soldiers. These camps reminded Kathleen of Tam and she would always check her purse to make sure that she still had his sweetheart badge. She wondered to herself how he would be getting on and comforted herself by thinking that Tam, being Tam, he would be just fine. She also often thought about her four brothers, and of course Andrew. There were regular letters home from her brothers, but she had no idea how Andrew was doing. Probably in Canada, staying well clear of the war, she thought. At least he would be safe.

The spring of 1915 passed very slowly for Kathleen. It had an entirely different feel to it than the previous spring: it was not just that the weather was so different, but back then in the glorious hot weather she was adjusting to life without Andrew, who had left her for Canada. Now the rainy days dissolved one into the other, and her mood was as black as the thunder clouds. Only her parents were at home, as none of her brothers had been home on leave since the previous Christmas. Her continual arguments with her father echoed around the drawing room of their home. Her mother was becoming increasingly exasperated with attempts to keep the peace. Kathleen noticed how pale and drawn her mother had become. She wondered if it was the result of worry about her four sons abroad in the war. She vowed to stop the arguments with her father but at times could not help herself, given the ridiculous nature of his comments.

Kathleen had lost count of the number of letters she had written offering her services as an auxiliary nurse to any Allied country that would take her. She had heard from a friend in Dumfries who had been accepted to nurse in an army hospital in Serbia. Her father almost exploded with rage when she suggested doing likewise. This had not deterred Kathleen in the slightest, but by the time she had applied the first batch of volunteers were already well on their way. She would have to wait again for another opportunity.

She made an effort to keep herself busy at home, but it was not the same as serving overseas, and she found local fundraising so unfulfilling. Admittedly, she still enjoyed singing in public, and was always asked to contribute to concerts for whatever worthy cause, be it to help Belgian refugees or raise money for the deserving families of soldiers at the front. On one occasion she sang at the Easterbrook Hall in Dumfries and shared the stage with the great Harry Lauder himself. But even the adrenaline of singing to a packed and appreciative audience could not fill the emptiness she was feeling inside. Was her part in this great national effort merely to be singing, knitting socks, and rattling cans on flag days? There were times she despaired, and only the occasional VAD training camps lightened her mood.

Then one week in May her spirits brightened considerably. Firstly, she received a letter from France telling her that she had been accepted to serve as an auxiliary nurse near the front line. Not only that, but the letter was from the Scottish Women's Hospital at Royaumont. Kathleen had read all about the women's endeavours to set up the hospital and how they had tirelessly worked to overcome the French army authorities' perverse attempts to prevent a front-line hospital, staffed exclusively by women, being established and accepted. But overcome them they had, and now the increasing number of casualties meant they required even more staff. She was so delighted to be chosen to serve in this renowned establishment that she sat on her bed, letter in hand, and wept tears of joy.

She scribbled a quick acceptance reply, stuffed it in an envelope, and rushed along the road to the post office. Halfway along Main Street she was stopped in her tracks by the sight of a tall young lad, dressed in civilian clothes and walking with the slightest of limps.

That can't possibly be Thomas, can it? she thought to herself.

Then realising that indeed it was, she ran towards him and gave him the warmest of hugs.

Tam was almost as surprised to see Kathleen, but took his opportunity to return her cuddle. She smelled wonderful, as usual. They stood in the street looking at each other and, in their excitement, started to talk over each other, rattling off unanswered questions until Tam drew his breath and said, 'Right, Kathleen, you go first. How are you? Can I say you are looking as lovely as ever?'

Kathleen started: 'Thomas, you will never believe what I received this morning – a letter from France. I am going over there to nurse in a hospital. I am so excited! What about you; why are you home in Creetown? Are you on leave? Were you wounded?'

The pair decided they would post Kathleen's letter and then adjourn to the Ellangowan Hotel for high tea. As they sat sipping tea and eating sardine sandwiches (Tam was so glad they weren't corned beef), they caught up on each other's lives over the year and a bit since they had last met. Tam embellished his experiences in Gallipoli even more to impress Kathleen. Nor did he admit that his return home was due to an administrative mistake rather than the severity of his wound. Kathleen was delighted that he was on the mend, and reassured him that she kept his sweetheart badge and that she would take it with her to France. Tam was happy to hear that her brothers, serving on various fronts, were all alive and well. Not all families in the village were as fortunate, and the local paper relayed the sad news of another local lad's death almost on a weekly basis. They parted in the late afternoon, agreeing to meet again the following day for a walk along the shore.

The coastline at Creetown was a pretty spot. You could see across the bay to the town of Wigtown, dominated by the tall spire of the parish church. In the days before the railway line a small ferry had operated between the two towns. This time, as they walked along the sand, they talked about their futures. Tam was not sure where the army would send him next; perhaps back to Gallipoli, or France, or even Palestine. In truth, he was in no hurry to return to any front. Kathleen, on the other hand, felt the exact opposite, and was desperate to be off, in much the same way Tam had been a year before. She spent most of their time together explaining to Tam how the hospital had been set up, and how honoured she felt to be given the chance to serve with such fine women.

'Have you heard of Dr Elsie Inglis, Thomas? What a truly wonderful woman she is. She trained to be a doctor in Edinburgh, you know, despite most of the male doctors and professors being against her. So now with her colleagues she has set up a Scottish Women's hospitals in France, and also one in Serbia. Could you believe that they even tried to stop her doing that, for goodness' sake?' she asked Tam.

Tam had to admit that he had never heard of the good Dr Inglis, but he did think it was stupid to try and stop her setting up hospitals. He told Kathleen again about his wound and how good the nurses had been to him.

'At last I can be doing something useful and meaningful in the war,' she said.

Tam agreed and added, 'If I ever get wounded again, Kathleen, I hope I end up in your hospital. You would look after me just fine.' They both smiled at the thought. Andrew also came up in their conversation, but neither had heard anything about him, so they assumed he must still be in Canada somewhere. They enjoyed the rest of their walk together, their faces slowly reddening from the sea spray and sun. No further arrangements were made to see each other, as Kathleen was busying herself for departure to France, and Tam had decided to visit relatives in Glasgow before his inevitable return to the front. They parted again with a friendly hug, but Tam resisted the urge to kiss her, as he could see in Kathleen's eyes that her thoughts were elsewhere. Maybe when the war was over he could try his luck again, but for now he could not get past the thought she was just too good for him and that she had no romantic interest in him. It had first been Andrew who stole away her heart, and now it was a bloody hospital in France.

Kathleen stood admiring herself in the full-length hallway mirror. She was almost completely enveloped in a long black cloak with braided shoulder capes. It reached to within an inch or two of the ground, fittingly hiding most of her black wool stockings. She adjusted the black straw bonnet on her head, which hid most of her curly red hair, satisfied that she looked the part of a VAD nurse bound for the front line in France. She blushed slightly at the memory of the white lie she told regarding her age. The minimum age for overseas service was twenty-three, so Kathleen had added a couple of years. Fortunately, none of the authorities had demanded to see a birth certificate. She lifted her leather suitcase, had one last look at the family photograph on the wall, smiling at the image of her four brothers, and then opened the front door. There would be no pipe band to see her off, as only her mother was to accompany her to the train station. At least the previous evening her father had given grudging acceptance of her decision. Over the next few months he would tell all the customers at the bank: 'Did you know that all my four sons *and* my only daughter are doing their bit for king and country? I am so proud of them all.'

It seemed like no time at all until Kathleen found herself in London's Victoria Street Station. She found a seat in the canteen, where she could watch the world go by as she sipped from her mug of hot tea. The hectic scene was in sharp contrast to the languid pace of life back home. The hustle and bustle of the platforms fascinated her. A troop train on one platform was hissing and blowing plumes of steam, as the engineers prepared for the journey to the coast. Slowly the carriages filled with khaki-clad figures reluctantly returning from home leave. Some were accompanied by wives and children. They hugged, kissed, and spoke fond farewells publicly in a manner that would have been unheard of before the war. Other solitary soldiers made their way quietly onto the carriages, perhaps unwilling to face public farewells, or maybe there was no one to bid them goodbye. Kitbags, rifles, and backpacks were all hauled on to the train by overworked porters, as sergeants and junior officers barked out orders and took roll calls. Everyone appeared to be puffing on Woodbine cigarettes. As the large hand of the station clock clicked to three o'clock, the pistons of the locomotive groaned into movement. Handkerchief-waving women walked, then ran, alongside the carriages as the train picked up momentum. Carriage windows snapped open, with men shouting their last farewells. No longer able to keep up with the accelerating train, the women stopped running and stood to watch the train disappearing into the distance, the puffs of steam merging with the clouds on the horizon. The women returned to the station through the 'Gateway of Goodbye', doing their best to console each other. No one said it, but they were all thinking and feeling the same thing. *Would that be our last time together?* Kathleen felt a lump in her throat as she watched the women return.

Just a few hours later, emotions were reversed as joyous crowds of relatives awaited the London-bound train carrying wounded and able-bodied men home on leave. When that train made its return journey to the coast, Kathleen would be aboard a carriage designated for the nurses on their way to the front. She shared her compartment with two other Scottish nurses, bound for the same hospital, and three London nurses returning from a brief leave home. They all introduced themselves, and during their conversation she realised that she was very much the novice in terms of medical experience. And almost every experience, in fact. However, far from being overawed by this, she became more determined to play her part to the full.

On the ferry to Boulogne there was more of an opportunity to see and mix with the soldiers than there had been on the train. A matron had lectured them on what was and what was not appropriate behaviour towards the men: 'We must always ensure that they respect us.' Kathleen bristled slightly at the lecture, thinking to herself: *I am going over to nurse them, not court them.* What struck her most was how young so many of the soldiers looked; some a good deal younger than herself. She was not the only one who had fibbed about her age, then. And of course there was always the one or two who chanced things and tried to make the nurses laugh. Playing on their abbreviation, VAD Nurses, a wise-cracking soldier might say, 'I see the Very Artful Darlings are on board with us, lads.'

'Aye – their victims always die, though,' joked another.

Kathleen would never think of herself as a VAD nurse in the same way ever again. She also heard some of the soldiers' songs for the first time. Her heart stirred at how religious the boys must be, as they gathered to sing hymns. On closer listening she realised that, although the tunes were familiar, the words were most certainly new. She laughed to herself and pondered how different her reaction would have been had she heard one of the youngsters at her Sunday School attempt such sacrilege. She did, however, refrain from accepting a cigarette offered by one of the London nurses.

From the Gare Maritime in Boulogne, the nurses made the slow journey south. Kathleen was amazed at the steady flow of trains in the opposite direction. She was informed that they were the hospital trains taking fresh batches of wounded Tommies to the channel ports and on to England. Only then did she get some idea of the scale of this war. Their train bypassed Paris, much to her disappointment, and eventually arrived at the railhead at Creil, only twelve miles from the front line. What she had thought was the distant roll of thunder was the noise of German artillery battering the French lines yet again. Creil was an important rail link for the French army, and it was here most of the casualties from an extended part of the front arrived to be transported to various hospitals in the area. Two motor ambulances from Royaumont were waiting for the Scottish nurses. Kathleen was immediately struck by the fact that both drivers and auxiliaries were women. *How magnificent*, she thought.

The hospital could not afford the luxury of the petrol purely to pick up new recruits, so they had to wait for the next troop train to arrive and help the wounded onto the ambulances. Kathleen assisted in carrying the stretchers of three soldiers, two French and one Senegalese, on to an ambulance. She smiled reassuringly at the black soldier, the first black person she had ever seen. All the soldiers looked incredibly dirty and tired, she thought; there was no spark in their eyes. None of them cried out, but she knew by the field dressings that they must be in severe pain. The route to the hospital would not have made them feel any better. Journeying along the winding, potholed, single-track road was literally a bruising experience. Both drivers handled their vehicles with great skill and astonishing speed for the condition of the roads. Their priority was to get the casualties to the hospital as quickly as possible. Little time was available for small talk as the new recruits tried to take in their unfamiliar surroundings. Gradually, the noise of the guns dulled as they jolted and bumped towards the hospital. The trees by the side of the road provided dappled shade, and dust on the road rose in small swirls, stirred up by the wind and the wheels of the ambulances. They passed the occasional small village and isolated farmhouse, sometimes passing a startled pedestrian. The noise and the fumes of the petrol engine disguised the fact that the road was becoming quieter and the air clearer. The entrance to the hospital soon came into sight.

Kathleen was awestruck by the scene unfolding in front of her. In its heyday, the hospital at Royaumont had been a

Cistercian monastery. The tall, straight poplar trees lining the road to the entrance looked like they were standing to attention in honour of the new recruits. The grey masonry of the building was highlighted like marble by the setting sun; the towers and turrets stood out proudly in the low shadow. Several blue-and-white figures had made their way out of the main door and stood patiently waiting for the ambulances to draw up in front of them. Everything about this wonderful place said peace, and calm, and healing, to Kathleen. She had never been so certain in her life that she belonged in a place, even before she had set foot in it.

The nurses helped the wounded into the main entrance, where they would be assessed and taken to a ward or straight to the operating theatre, depending on the severity of their wounds. Kathleen and the other nurses were directed to the cloisters to be introduced to Matron Duncan. She found it hard to concentrate on what the matron was saying, as her attention was drawn away by the beautiful architecture of the abbey cloisters. Depending on the time of year, the cloisters served as either an external ward for recuperating soldiers, or the canteen and meeting place for the nurses and doctors. The arches and pillars were incredibly elegant. She vaguely absorbed some of Matron's lecture: the rules and regulations, what nurses were expected to do and not to do. The penalty for breaking rules was to be sent home. Kathleen sprung to attention at this last comment, determining never to break any of the rules. She could only imagine the shame of being sent home, and would ask the others to remind her of the rules again the following day. For now, the emotion of the journey had caught up with her, and extreme fatigue had set in: all she desired was a good night's sleep. Such a thing would be a rare luxury in the months ahead.

SEVEN
FRANCE

Kathleen awoke the following morning, blinking several times. Yes, she was definitely here – it wasn't a dream. A year of intense frustration was over. To have arrived in a hospital with likeminded women, all determined to do their bit for the poor wounded and maimed souls, was all she had ever desired since the war started. *I must do my best here, my very best*, she vowed.

'Good morning, Nurse Marr.' A lilting Highland voice welcomed her from the single bed shoehorned next to Kathleen's. It belonged to Mary McLeod from Inverness, who had arrived at Royamount the previous month. Kathleen replied in kind. Mary was a good three inches smaller than Kathleen, with a slight frame and her fair hair tied up in a bun. Her hazel eyes sparkled with mischief.

'Once we are dressed and presentable, I will take you down to the cloisters for breakfast, my dear.'

'Righty-ho,' Kathleen replied with a smile.

When they arrived downstairs, Kathleen realised Mary hadn't been joking. Since the refectory was converted into another ward, the doctors, nurses, and orderlies ate in the ancient arched cloisters. Kathleen felt a pleasant warm breeze on her face as she sat down at a long trestle table.

'The food is not as grand as our surroundings. Bread, jam and tea, and don't get too settled – there is no waitress service.'

Blushing slightly and mumbling a quick apology, Kathleen joined the queue for breakfast. After her modest meal Kathleen was introduced to some of the members of her unit. A unit, she discovered, consisted of seven doctors, ten nurses, seven orderlies, four ambulance chauffeurs, two cooks, two maids, a clerk and an administrator. The fact that all of these were women, bar two of the drivers, gave her a sense of great satisfaction. She smiled to herself, wondering what her dear old father would have made of it. Over time, this unit would give her a strong feeling of belonging.

After breakfast, they lined up in military fashion, nurses first, followed by the orderlies, outside the entrance to Blanche de Castille ward. They awaited the arrival of the formidable Dr Jane Simpson, or the 'Leith Livewire', as she was secretly known to her underlings. What the doctor lacked in stature, standing barely five feet tall, with cropped black hair, she more than made up with presence. Her staff were full of respect and admiration for her tremendous enthusiasm and stamina. Kathleen noticed she gave a cursory glance in her direction as she strode past and into the ward.

'Good morning, ladies. The Boche have been kind enough to take a break from slaughtering our chaps overnight, so no new *blessés* to tend to today. All wound dressings will be changed this morning and even the slightest sign of infection must be reported to me immediately. Orderlies, please remember to empty bed pans before serving breakfast. Nurses McLeod, Marr, and Johnston will accompany me on my round this morning.'

Dr Simpson's somewhat abrupt tone changed completely when she talked to the *blessés*. There was a compassionate tone to her basic French.

'*Comment ça va?*' she would ask them in turn. The soldiers usually replied positively to her questioning. She could tell as much about their condition from the tone of their voice as from the replies they gave her. The nurses were then given specific instructions for the treatment of each soldier.

'At least that was straightforward this morning,' Mary told Kathleen reassuringly, as Dr Simpson made her way to the next ward. She explained that the hospital was experiencing a quiet time, but that it would not be long until the next rush, whenever the next offensive might start.

'Just one question, Mary. What did the doctor mean when she said the *blessés*?' asked Kathleen.

'Oh, that's what everyone in the hospital calls the wounded soldiers. It's French, but you will get used to it.'

Two days later Kathleen had her first experience of a rush. A loud, piercing horn reverberated around the hospital.

This was the dreaded signal from the hall porter to warn of the arrival of the first ambulances from the nearby railhead. Kathleen and Mary left their half-finished breakfasts and dashed to the front door. A steady stream of nurses, working in pairs, lifted stretchers from the ambulances and laid them on the floor at the entrance to the hospital. Kathleen was appalled at how filthy the soldiers were and winced at the sight of shattered and broken limbs. Their first task was to wash the soldiers. Those deemed to be walking wounded went to the cleansing room, where they cleaned themselves behind a curtain. Kathleen assisted with the stretcher cases, who were blanket-bathed, their clothes removed and put in sacks to be boil-washed later. Orderlies then took the new *blessés* to a ward for the doctors to assess their wounds.

'Well done, Kathleen. You did well. I remember it wasn't easy the first time I saw gaping open wounds and limbs hanging by a thread,' said Mary, supportively.

Kathleen was pleased by the comment, as she'd to force herself to forget her own emotions to take care of the soldiers.

'Thank you, Mary. It really is very distressing, but it's why I came out here, after all.'

There was not much time to dwell on her feelings. The process of receiving patients was repeated at least another eight times in the following hours. Kathleen lost count as the day progressed, but marvelled at how well organised the whole procedure was, despite the continual strain on the hospital staff. Remarkably, all this was achieved despite language barriers. The nurses had little French and the soldiers little English to speak to the *dames ecossaises*. The sight of so many mutilated young men, with horrific wounds and limbs almost entirely dismembered, was hard to bear. Perhaps it was a blessing that she could not converse in their native tongue. Most would ask if they were about to die, or if a damaged limb would be saved. All she could do was give a reassuring smile and calm them as much as possible. One thing Kathleen never got used to all the time she was at Royaumont was the awful smell of a gangrenous wound. The sickly-sweet smell lingered in her nostrils for hours after dealing with the unfortunate soldier. Every time she had to change and apply a new dressing to a wound, she winced in anticipation of the appalling odour – a telltale sign that gas gangrene had set in. Fortunately, the hospital had an exceptional record in dealing with such cases, and the surgeons could perform near miraculous, life-saving operations.

As Kathleen settled in to her new surroundings she became familiar with the rhythm of life at the hospital. The busiest times were of course the rushes, when life was completely hectic. Their duration would depend on the intensity of any given attack or defensive action. Then, during a lull, there would be the task of caring for the blesses. A daily routine at this point involved the so-called evacuation of mended soldiers. At 6 p.m. precisely, doctors, nurses, orderlies, and the wounded soldiers who could walk assembled at the main entrance. The doctor in charge would call out the names of the soldiers to be discharged, and carefully read over their army papers which she then handed to them, in what became a kind of ceremony. The gathered crowd raised a cheer as each man was called forward. There was much handshaking and thanking of the staff by the grateful men. Some took the opportunity to present a favourite nurse with a *bagues boches*, a ring made from fragments of shell cases. Kathleen was presented with so many that she couldn't wear them all, so stored them in a small wooden box in her room, in which she also kept Tam's sweetheart badge. She always had mixed emotions when the soldiers departed for the railhead: she was pleased that they were fit and well to return, but despondent that they would soon be back at the front again. She tried not to dwell on it too much.

During quiet times there were lots of opportunities to be distracted from the horrors of war.

One bright late September morning she was greeted by an enthusiastic Mary McLeod.

'Kathleen, please tell me that you play hockey. A game has been arranged for this afternoon, and I'm short of players for the team.'

In her usual modest fashion, Kathleen explained that she hadn't played since schooldays, and there must be numerous nurses in the hospital far better than her. Mary would have none of her excuses, however, and so Kathleen found herself a reluctant teammate of Nurse McLeod. The afternoon developed into a full-blown sports event. The hospital was set in extensive grounds, and a large patch of open grassland bordered by two lines of tall poplar trees served as the playing field. A crowd of patients had turned out to spectate on the fine autumn afternoon. They made a colourful sight. Some were wearing French army regulation red pantaloons and perhaps a dark blue jacket, but most were dressed in a mismatch of army gear, hospital pyjamas, and whatever civilian clothing had been donated by locals. Tunisian soldiers wore their *kepis* and the Senegalese straw Zulu hats.

Kathleen's nerves were soothed in her merriment at the first event – a wheelbarrow race. The diminutive but ever keen Mary McLeod was teamed up with a rather larger and athletic Senegalese patient named Diarra. They looked a very awkward couple: Diarra was at least six feet tall and broad-chested, with strong shoulders and arms, one leg thin and wasted from wounds. Mary was small and wiry but very determined. She grabbed him by the ankles and heaved his legs up from the ground. As the shout to start was given, they took their time to gather momentum but, finding their rhythm, stormed past the other competitors to the finishing line, roared on by Kathleen and the other nurses. She was lavish with her praise: 'Well done, Mary; well done, Diarra. *Bon jeu!*'

The winners collapsed on the ground, smiling. 'I hope I've saved enough energy for the hockey,' was Mary's response.

Kathleen next found herself as the rear bearer in a stretcher race. Fortunately, the occupant was relatively light, and in better health than the usual stretcher cases. There was much hilarity as the soldiers rolled or were tipped out of the stretchers and on to the ground when the overenthusiastic nurses ran too fast with the stretcher. Kathleen's team finished a credible second. Both nurses declined the invitation to take part in a tug of war, wanting to prepare for the hockey match. Even more fun was had in the potato race, with soldiers and nurses competing against each other, trying to balance the prized vegetable on soup spoons borrowed from the kitchen. The soldiers thought it very amusing that such a valued food as the potato was used in this way, confirming their belief that British nurses had an eccentric side.

And so to the final event of the day; the nurse's hockey match. Kathleen discovered that the side had been chosen, not by ward or unit, but by their political affiliation to the prewar women's movement. Mary and Kathleen were in the National Union of Women's Suffrage Societies team – the Suffragists – playing against the Women's Social and Political Union – the Suffragettes. No quarter was given, and the allegedly more peaceful suffragists gave as good as they got. Kathleen received a few heavy dunts, which bruised badly, but she really enjoyed herself. Her spirits were high after the earlier events and she managed to make a few important blocks as well as having a shot on goal. The match finished in a three-all draw, to rapturous applause from the crowd of soldiers. One *blessé* shouted, 'Sisters, I want you beside me next time I charge the Boche!' The doctors joked they would have to spend more time treating the injured hockey players than they had the patients from the last rush. Everyone returned to the hospital in fine fettle and enjoyed a simple supper before bed. To complete the holiday atmosphere of the day, the soldiers were given an extra ration of their Pinard – a rough red wine which the French Army authorities had deemed suitable for wounded soldiers. For just one light-hearted afternoon, the war had seemed like a distant event. Kathleen was delighted to see there had also been a mail delivery to the hospital, and that she had a letter from home. *What a perfect way to round off the day*, she thought, smiling. Her eager hands tore open her mother's letter. She sat perched on the edge of her single bed and began reading.

Dearest Kathleen,

I hope my letter finds you well and that you are being looked after in France. I received your letter last month and enjoyed finding out about the valuable work you are doing out there. Even Father agrees you are performing a very valuable service. Life here in Creetown is much the same as always, although so very few young people are around and there is not so much food in the shops presently. I think I saw that young man you know, Thomas Murdoch, recently. He must be home on leave.

Kathleen, my main reason for writing is to inform you of the tragic news we had about your brother Edward…

Kathleen felt a knot tighten in her stomach as she read on. Edward was her oldest brother and had always looked out for her in their childhood.

…It is over a week since we had the telegram and I can barely bring myself to write now. I suppose, my dearest, all families must make sacrifices for this great effort, but it is so hard to bear. It must be God's will, I know. Your father tells me that is the case. I just pray for it all to end soon and for you to return home safely, along with your other dear brothers.

Kathleen let the letter drop gently on to the floor. She began sobbing quietly. She considered all the young men here in the hospital she had help save from death, and wondered if, had she been close by, whether she could have helped save the life of her dear brother, who had always looked after her. Floods of tears interrupted a broken night's sleep. Mary, her roommate, who was on night duty, had not returned until the early hours of the morning, so was unaware of her bad news. When she saw a red-eyed Kathleen the following morning, she immediately knew something was wrong. She suggested they approach the ward doctor and ask for the day off. Kathleen had also considered asking for home leave to be with her mother. However, even before breakfast was finished the dreaded horn sounded, signalling the start of the next rush. To some extent Kathleen was grateful to be occupied that day, helping wounded French soldiers as they flooded into the hospital. Although exhausted come the evening, she found time to kneel at the end of her bed and pray to God to protect her mother and father and her three remaining brothers. She added the names of Andrew McDowall and Thomas Murdoch, too.

*

Corporal Andrew McDowall had become surprisingly used to army life, and flourished as a soldier in the second Canadian division. Their training camp at Shorncliffe in Kent was home for the summer of 1915. Each day followed a familiar routine. At 5.30 a.m. reveille sounded, to prepare the men for the day. After much scrambling to find uniform and kit, his section gathered round an iron stove as the water boiled for mugs of tea, before assembly on the parade ground at 6.30 a.m. On a fine day the sun would be up, and the men squinted to see Sergeant John Briggs, standing to attention next to the flagpole. Briggs was an intimidating figure, around six feet tall and almost as broad. His glistening bald head was already sweating in the early morning sunshine. He had the required booming voice, and being a religious man, started each day with the Lord's Prayer. He then bellowed:

'What are the three duties of a soldier, boys? I will tell you. They are, number one: Obedience! Number two: Cleanliness! And number three: Honesty and Sobriety!'

The soldiers followed the sergeant's cue and repeated the duties rote fashion. 'Sobriety' was shouted the loudest, the sergeant perhaps unaware of the soldiers' sense of irony. Andrew thought that made four duties, but dare not point this out to the sergeant, for fear of breaking duty number one. Over an hour of drilling and fitness followed before breakfast.

They could see the steam rising from the field canteen and the oaty aroma of porridge wafted across the parade ground. Each section lined up behind a wagon to have their mess tins filled, balancing a thick slice of bread and jam on top, and carrying a mug of strong hot tea in the other hand. In good weather they sat outside the hut to devour the food. Yet more drilling followed for the rest of the morning. Andrew's section became competent at forming fours. He noticed how over the weeks his boys improved, and how much fitter they were than when they had left Canada. Anders, the Norwegian Canadian, excelled at route marches, always in the front line and never slow to encourage any others in his platoon who were lagging. Long route marches of up to twelve miles, in full kit and with rifles and bayonets attached, became the main afternoon activity.

Evenings, in contrast, were quieter, unless a soldier was detailed for fatigues or a work party. Cleaning kit and polishing boots out of the way, the boys in his platoon would gather round the large wooden table that formed the centrepiece of the room. Some would play cards or checkers. Andrew still called the board game draughts, which raised a smile among the Canadians. As Sergeant Briggs was such an unapproachable figure, the lads tended to confide in Andrew. Despite being only a few years older than most of them, he soon became a father figure. Perhaps because he could not quite shake off his schoolteacher manner, he referred to them as his boys.

There was a YMCA hut in the camp, which had a small library. In a few quieter moments Andrew would borrow a book and buy some tobacco for his pipe, a habit he had recently acquired. On one occasion he was delighted to find a short story by Saki, which he enjoyed enormously. As summer ended, his platoon advanced through field movements, night operations, and weapons training. One afternoon in early September, as the men practised trench digging on a nearby hillside, word spread that the regiment would embark for France the following day. The camp was so near to Folkstone that they would be there in less than twelve hours. Andrew knew this was what all the training had been for, but still felt a mixture of dread and excitement. His greatest hope was that he would perform well in action and look after his section as best he could.

His regiment did not go straight into action when they arrived in France. They were transported from the port of Boulogne to the nearby Étaples army base camp, which had originally been a quaint fishing village popular with landscape artists for the quality of its light. They had painted on the beach, which was known as Paris Plage. This area was out of bounds to non-commissioned officers and soldiers as it was the preserve of the senior officers, or 'Red Tabs' as the soldiers called them. Military police patrolled the area at night to keep it out of bounds. The war, however, had taken its toll on the surroundings. The village was overcrowded, and its narrow streets were grubby and worn down. It had recently become the target of German Zeppelin raids, which had inflicted substantial damage to property. The camp itself was a vast, sprawling mass of wooden huts and canvas tents. Dotted around the camp, which stretched for three miles, were larger hospitals for the war wounded. In the middle of the camp was the infamous 'bullring' – the parade and drilling ground. Soldiers would assemble at Étaples if, like Andrew's regiment, they were fresh and raw recruits. But battle-hardened troops, or wounded soldiers deemed fit to return to active service, were also mustered here. Irrespective of their origin, all soldiers were put through intense and gruelling drills by the instructors. Andrew noticed a more sadistic approach than he had experienced while training in the south of England. When one lad in his platoon, John Halliday, was constantly picked on by a burly sergeant major, Andrew found it increasingly difficult to contain himself. The lad had collapsed during a particularly long forced march. As he lay exhausted, the sergeant major had launched himself at him and, with heavy boots, swung a vicious kick into the prostrate soldier's ribs.

'Get the fuck up on your feet, you fucking Canadian faggot. Why did you bother coming all the way here to lie down and let Fritz have his way with you? Useless cunt!'

Andrew felt every muscle in his body straining as he fought his instinct to attack the sergeant major. Instead, with the help of Private Anders Halvorsen, he helped the aching and disorientated Halliday back to his feet, and supported and encouraged him back to camp

Over the next few days, the new recruits were introduced to and drilled alongside more experienced Canadian troops from the first division. It was army practice to move new and battle-hardened regiments to the front at the same time. The soldiers from the First Canadian Division were either regular soldiers or reservists before the war, and had arrived in France in October 1914. They had seen action, most notably in the second battle of Ypres. Not surprisingly, they tended to make fun of the newly arrived troops, much of which was light-hearted. The new troops were rather overawed by their veteran colleagues.

The same sergeant major who had assaulted Private Halliday was roaring his instructions to the men.

'Imagine an ugly Hun is standing right in front of you. Stick it to him hard, boys, go on!' he roared as they bayoneted the swinging straw dummies.

Dissatisfied with the level of the troops' enthusiasm, he barked, 'Look at Sergeant McAllister over there – that's how to do it, boys!'

Quick as a flash McAllister replied, 'That's because I was thinking it was you, Sergeant Major, sir.'

The enraged sergeant major leapt towards McAllister and stood toe to toe with him. The others looked on in total silence. They stood eyeballing each other for over a minute. Something in the sergeant's steely, determined eyes convinced the sergeant major to back down.

'Squad dismissed,' he shouted, finally.

The soldiers headed towards their tents and huts. Andrew was wearing a huge grin.

'I meant it, by the way. I could swing for that bastard – never been near the front or fired a shot in anger,' confided McAllister.

Andrew struck up a friendship with sergeant Hugh McAllister from the 16th Canadian Infantry, otherwise known as 48th Highlanders. He was of Scottish extraction, explaining to Andrew that his grandfather had emigrated from the island of Mull to Canada at the time of the Clearances.

'It makes me smile to think that my ancestors fought and died battling the redcoat British Army, and now here am I fighting alongside them,' he joked. 'My grandfather would turn in his grave.'

'You Highlanders just like a good fight,' suggested Andrew.

In the large wooden canteen where the Canadian soldiers ate, someone had procured an upright piano and a fiddle. When McAllister boasted that, as a Gael, he had the finest of voices and knew his way around the piano, Andrew took up the challenge and said he would accompany him on fiddle. After some over-elaborate tuning and several false starts, the pair gave the assembled troops a fine rendition of old favourites, including 'Highland Laddie', 'the Skye Boat Song', and 'Bonnie Mary of Argyll'. McAllister had a powerful tenor voice. Andrew could not help but remember how Kathleen was such a fine singer. He wondered what she would make of him as a soldier. The evening sing song had at least provided light relief to the tension of the afternoon.

The bullring was packed with soldiers in full kit the following morning. The sergeant major strode pompously into the centre. Standing tall with chest puffed out, he announced:

'God help you miserable wretches, but at 11.00 hours you lot are up the line to the front. Back here in thirty minutes for a march to the railhead.'

'Look on the bright side – last time we'll see his ugly face,' McAllister responded.

There was only enough time to gather up the remainder of their belongings and then head back to the muster point. Andrew had purchased a Kodak Brownie box camera in England. He gathered his section together to organise a photograph. He placed Anders in the middle, as he was the tallest, with the rest of the section in descending order of height flanking him. He clicked the button just at the point when all twelve lads gave bright, innocent smiles together.

EIGHT
HOME FRONT

Glasgow, the second city of the Empire, was a hive of industry. Into an already growing population poured thousands of men and women from across Scotland to bolster the workforces of the shipyards, steel works, and munitions factories. The overcrowded tenements burst at the seams with the new arrivals, providing a rich opportunity for exploitative landlords. Over a quarter of Glasgow's sons had heeded the call to arms in 1914, but as the war lengthened, resentment and anti-war feeling grew over harsh living and working conditions. There was a whiff of sedition in the air.

Tam Murdoch's nostrils were mainly filled with soot as he stepped off the locomotive at St Enoch station. He had joined the great migration to the city, albeit for a short period of time. There were sufficient days left of his medical leave from the army to visit his cousins, Iain and Mary, who had moved to Glasgow from Galloway at the turn of the century. Their father, Tam's uncle, had died of pneumonia several years before, and now his Aunt Ina was poorly with consumption. Tam thought this might be his last chance to see the old lady. They lived in a room and kitchen tenement in Parson Street in the Townhead district of the city. Iain worked as an engineer in the Beardmore steelworks at Parkhead. As it was a Saturday afternoon, Iain had some precious hours off work, and was at the station to meet Tam. The two young men shook hands warmly. They could have been mistaken for brothers, possibly even twins, given their strong family resemblance. What distinguished the two tall, sandy haired young men was Iain's wire-rimmed spectacles.

'Guid tae see you Tam; yir looking grand. I missed the fitba this afternoon to come an' get ye, so ah hope you feel honoured.'

'Ah well, I got my arse shot off defending you stay-at-homers, so I wouldnae expect anything less,' retorted Tam.

'I think we need to mark the occasion wae a pint, then. Is there a pub on the way to the house?'

'Aye, just the twa dozen.'

'A pint in each, then. Sounds fair.'

They made their way to Fingal's Bar on Buchanan Street. It was a refined establishment by Glasgow public house standards. A large brewer's mirror, which dominated the back wall, made the interior appear more spacious than it was. Over the first pint they caught up on the health and happiness of each other's families. Iain didn't think his mother would last much longer. He was annoyed at his sister, Mary, who had applied for a job as a tram conductress when the Glasgow Tram Company controversially opened positions to females.

'I suppose they have tae. No' enough men for aw the jobs need doin', but she might have waited until our old ma passed away. She has always been a strong-willed one, ma sister Mary.'

Tam agreed with the sentiment. He was aware of how strong-willed some young women could be. At their next stop, the Cosy Den on Cathedral Street, another two pints of weak beer were consumed. The conversation turned to the war, and Tam was confused by Iain's attitude.

'Who do you think you're fighting for, Tam?' Iain queried.

Before he could even consider a response, Iain continued:

'Ah will tell ye. It's those bastards that own the factories and the greedy landlords that are making a fucking fortune oot the war. Oor soldiers hae mair in common wi' the German soldiers than the likes o' them. Ah tell ye, Tam, it's them you should be firing at and stabbing wi' yir bayonet, no some boy fae Berlin that's just the same as us.'

Tam shivered at the memory of the young Turkish soldier he had killed. He still had recurring nightmares about him. Reluctantly, he explained what had happened at Gallipoli to Iain.

'I was only defending myself and my mates. If ah didn't I wouldn't be here now.'

'Ah'm no' getting at you, Tam, but we need to spread the message and end this fucking mess.'

Tam's memory of the final pub, the Glebe Bar, was hazy to say the least. They had started drinking 'hauf and haufs' – a half pint of beer with a whisky chaser. Iain introduced him to his pals in the Independent Labour Party – at least, the ones who weren't in the Temperance movement. Under the terms of the Defence of the Realm act, all public houses had to close by 9.00 p.m. The landlord, however, allowed his regular loyal customers, of whom Iain was one, the pleasure of a 'lock-in'. It was the early hours when the pair staggered around the corner to the tenement flat. Tam vaguely remembered agreeing to attend a meeting on Sunday morning at Bath Street to hear someone called John McLean, or something like that, give a speech about the war.

The whistle of a boiling kettle woke Tam from his pull-out bed on the kitchen floor. Mary was preparing a breakfast of tea and porridge on the small cast iron range. Iain had already folded away his recess bed and was in the parlour talking to his mother.

'Morning, Tam. How's the heid?' asked Mary cheerfully.

'Been better, Mary, been better. Should you no' be away driving a tram somewhere?'

'No' before ah make ma favourite cousin his porridge. Mind and say hello to Ma – she fair perked up when she heard you were coming.'

Tam took his mug of black tea and sat at the bottom of his aunt's bed. The frail old lady enjoyed his company. She reminisced about summer Sunday walks, when all the Murdochs would get together to stroll along the banks of Galloway's River Cree.

'It was so peaceful, and the air was so clean. Nothing made me happier than watching all you bairns playing together.'

As her eyes became heavy, Tam took his leave and returned to the kitchen. Iain, unshaven and looking as rough as Tam, urged him to get a move on, as John McLean was due to give his speech in thirty minutes. McLean, a Glasgow schoolteacher and Marxist, along with other revolutionary speakers and small left-wing parties had made the Sunday public meeting a regular occurrence. This was despite the efforts of Glasgow Town Council, the local police, and the Conservative and Unionist Party supporters to disrupt them.

They arrived at the outdoor meeting just as McLean was about to speak, having to settle for a place at the back of a crowd, which numbered over a thousand. A line of stern-faced policemen stood close by. Tam thought McLean looked an impressive figure, quite tall and broad and very well dressed in shirt and black suit. He bore more than a passing resemblance to his old friend Andrew McDowall. His voice was loud and accustomed to public speaking. Tam found some of his speech quite difficult. There were a lot of 'isms'– imperialism, economism, syndicalism, and socialism. He did agree that the workers were being forced to work overlong hours by the government, and it was wrong that families were being threatened with eviction because they could not afford the rising rents. The enthralled audience had not paid much attention to a smaller crowd of protesters who had gathered on the other side of the police line. That is, until they started to hurl abuse at McLean:

'Coward bastard!'

'You want the Kaiser ruling us?'

'Hun spy!'

'You need hung, McLean.'

McLean took it all in his stride, but when he remarked that the war was murder of fellow workers, the police inspector thought it seditious and ordered his men to charge the tea-chest stage and arrest him. Mayhem ensued. His supporters turned to face the charging police. One officer made a wild swipe with his baton, catching Iain on the nose and sending his blood-spattered spectacles flying into the crowd. Instinctively, Tam delivered a hefty punch into the policeman's groin, and as the constable bent double in pain, he followed up with a fierce uppercut which knocked him out cold. Iain was on his feet again now, so Tam grabbed him by the arm and they ran with the rest of the quickly dispersing crowd into a narrow side street. Out of breath, Tam enquired:

'Are you awright, Iain?'

'I'll live,' he replied through a blood-soaked handkerchief.

'Tell you what though, Tam, you will be in line for a Victoria Cross noo.'

'How come?'

'Well, first a Johnny Turk and noo a Glasgae polis.'

In the cold light of the following morning, Iain and Mary agreed that it would be best for Tam to leave Glasgow and head back to Galloway.

'They bastards look after their own and will be making enquiries about ye. They have informers everywhere.'

Tam thought their advice was sound, and had a final chat with his aunt before heading south.

'See you after the Revolution!' Iain declared as they parted.

Tam didn't know what to think as he mulled over the events of his weekend in Glasgow. He had never given much thought to why he had joined up or what the war was about. As a Territorial, he knew he would be called up as soon as a war started, just like the rest of his pals. He was told they were defending gallant Belgium against the Kaiser, whose armies had to be stopped to save civilisation. Until a few days ago he had not heard any criticism of the war. He hoped the policeman he knocked out would recover, even though he had deserved a good wallop. That was the last he expected to hear about the incident. The prospect of returning to the army did not exactly fill him with enthusiasm, but he did wonder how all his friends were doing, still out in Gallipoli. Sergeant Irving would be taking good care of them, no doubt.

Back at his parents' house in Newton Stewart, his mother had some intriguing news. The Major had heard that Tam was home and requested that he visit him as soon as possible. He had absolutely no idea why the old man would want to see him. The following day Tam presented himself, in full uniform, at Kirroughtree Estate house. A four-legged streak of lightening bolted down the avenue to greet him. 'Well, you know how to welcome a man, don't you, boy?' he said to Sammie, as the dog jumped up to lick him. Nothing much had changed on the farm, other than it seemed quieter, with fewer workers around. Mrs McKnight was still there and opened the door for him. She was now housekeeper and cook, as so many of the younger female staff had left for war work.

'Himself will see you in the drawing room. Just knock and go in,' she indicated to him. The last time Tam had been in that room was when he was twelve and accompanied by his mother. He had met the Major, who took him on as a shepherd boy. So, somewhat apprehensively, he knocked on the mahogany door, turned the brass handle, and entered. The old man was sitting in the far corner at a writing desk. He gestured to Tam to come in and take a seat.

'Come in, Thomas. Sit down, please.'

Wondering what was coming next, Tam sat down. The Major had never referred to him as anything but Murdoch.

'You are looking well, my boy. I'm so proud of the old regiment, you know. What a frightful business out in Gallipoli, but I believe they are holding on well. Far too many have died, though, and I do not see an end in sight.'

Tam thought the old man looked thinner and paler since he had last seen him. Perhaps that explained his war-weary comments, which were so different from his gung-ho approach to the beginning of the war.

'I lost too many good comrades in the South African War, and I don't like to see it happening again with your generation.'

Tam remembered when his regiment were stationed in Edinburgh and Sergeant Irving had taken them to Northbridge to see the memorial to the King's Own Scottish Borderers who had fought in South Africa. Tam had remarked on how impressed he was by the sculpture, but that none of the four figures were as close to handsome as him. 'Do you think they will build one for us?' he had asked Irving.

'More than likely, son, and everyone will walk past and ignore it, just like this one.'

The Major continued to go on about the war for some time.

'It is not easy back here either. I have lost so many of you young workers to the services that it's hard to keep the estate in ship shape. I know I encouraged you all to go, and was so proud when you did.'

Finally, he came to the point of the meeting.

'I still have some influence in the regiment, you know, and the Member of Parliament here owes me a few favours. So, Thomas, I have here a letter of exemption for you. All you must do is sign and you will be relieved of your military duties to return and work here on the estate. It's necessary work, you know, and it will be more than just shepherding, too.'

Tam was dumbfounded and sat in silence for some time. The prospect of not returning to the army had a certain appeal, but he was struggling to understand why the Major would do this for him. It was so out of character.

The Major broke the silence: 'Please read the letter; it is all above board. As I say, all you have to do is sign at the bottom.'

Tam respectfully asked if he could take the letter home to consider his decision. The Major thought that was a splendid idea, but that he would require Tam's answer the next day. Back home, Alexander, his younger brother, read out the letter to Tam and his mother. It read just as the Major had explained. His mother was overjoyed and pleaded with Tam to sign it straight away. 'You would be daft not to, son. How many lads out in the trenches just now wouldn't jump at the chance?'

'Ah know, Ma, but why would the old Major do that for me? I don't understand.'

His mother indicated to Alexander to make himself busy elsewhere. She sat next to Tam and continued: 'You know the Major is a widower, right? Well, it was tragic, as his young wife died in childbirth. The baby, too – it was a boy, apparently. It nearly broke him, they say, but he got through it eventually. And if gossip is to be believed, he became very fond of one of his young maids – Christine Dewar – she was about ages with me. A few years later there was a big scandal when she got pregnant and had a son; she wisnae married or anything. I'm told it was the Major's. You might mind him – Alan Dewar. A right quiet wee lad.'

'I do mind – he joined the merchant navy, did he no? But what's all that to do wi' me?'

'Well, the week we heard you had been wounded at Gallipoli, Christine got a telegram to say Alan had been killed. His ship was sunk by a U-boat. I think its preying on the Major's mind, that's all.'

The following morning, he presented himself to the Major, letter in hand, complete with his scrawled signature. He would see out the remainder of the war in the peace and quiet of Galloway while trying to keep the estate in good order. He thought about asking the Major to write a similar letter to the Red Cross to excuse Kathleen Marr from nursing duties. Then he realised that Kathleen was so headstrong she would probably rip it up. He consoled himself with the fact that Anne Gillespie might still be working and living locally.

On his first Sunday from work, he made the short train journey south to Wigtown where she lived. It was the county town of the area. An impressive town hall, which included a court and jail, looked out on a wide main street lined with trees. Anne lived with her mother and sister, in a modest cottage in one of the vennels just off the main street. As it was the Sabbath, all the shops, hotels, and public houses were closed. Tam had decided it was no longer appropriate to be in uniform, so was wearing his Sunday best black suit, which fitted rather tightly around his frame. Quick-witted as ever, and trying to hide her excitement at unexpectedly seeing Tam, Anne greeted him:

'Tam Murdoch, come away in. I was just reading over all those letters you wrote me from France!'

He smiled apologetically. 'You know me, Anne. Was never a great one for writing, so I asked the field marshal if I could come home, just to see you.'

'Well, I am glad he let you,' she responded, kissing him lightly on the cheek.

Pleasantly taken aback by her show of affection, Tam blushed from head to toe.

'Don't be getting any ideas, mind. You're the first lad under fifty I've seen all year.'

Tam gave a hearty laugh, remembering how funny Anne could be. Her joke, though, was founded in fact. She was employed at the nearby Bladnoch Creamery, where all the young male workers had left for war service. The farmhands who delivered the milk were either old men or women.

'On the bright side, Tam, I have had three proposals of marriage ... but the youngest was seventy!'

Tam laughed loudly again. 'Maybe you will be luckier next time, Anne.' He winked.

'Not that I want to give you a swelled head, Tam, but I am just happy to see you again,' she shouted from the scullery as she readied some tea and bread with jam. 'It's homemade, and the good thing about the creamery is, I always have a bit of fresh milk.'

She sat next to him on the couch as they reminisced about childhood and the latest news about mutual friends who were serving on various fronts. It was mainly depressing news of deaths, missing, and wounded. Anne took his hand and asked, 'Did you think it would turn out this way, Tam? I had no idea.'

He liked the feel of her soft hand in his, and squeezed it gently. 'No, I never, Anne. Thought it would be over by now. I'm lucky, I suppose, because of the old Major, but my pals might all be dead soon, the way it's going.'

'I know. I hate to think of all the young men dying over there – just boys. Never seen anything of life, really.'

He looked at Anne intently, realising how attractive she was. Her hazel eyes were welling, but he was unsure what to do next. As he fumbled in his trouser pocket for a handkerchief, she leaned forward, kissing him lightly and briefly on the lips. He smiled at her and gingerly returned the kiss. This playful exchange continued for some minutes. He awkwardly pulled her closer, placing both his arms around her shoulders, as her hands slipped around his waist. They kissed deeply and for longer. Tam enjoyed her lavender scent and the softness of her touch. He was becoming aroused, and just for a brief second thought that maybe the first taste of whisky was not the best feeling in the world after all. At that, the front door handle clicked as Anne's mother and sister returned from visiting relatives at the other end of town. The pair bolted upright and distanced themselves to either end of the couch. Anne fixed the ribbon in her long dark hair and Tam straightened his tie. They looked sheepishly towards her mother, who scolded Anne.

'You never told me you were expecting a gentleman guest, Anne, but now I see it's Thomas Murdoch.' So that's where Anne got her sense of humour, he thought. Tam apologised for his unexpected arrival, which appeared to satisfy the older woman. A fresh brew of tea gave Tam time to regain his composure. As he was being shown to the door, he turned to Anne and said, 'Thank you for a pleasant afternoon. I hope I can see you again soon.' Anne gave an exaggerated smile and replied: 'I expect so, Thomas.'

Her mother added a final question. 'Have you heard from your friend Andrew, or that lovely girl of his who was a beautiful singer?'

'No, I haven't, Mrs Gillespie.'

NINE

ONWARDS

A ndrew and Kathleen may have been at different parts of the front, but they shared at least one common experience during the winter of 1915 – the biting, unrelenting cold. Andrew's regiment was moved to the front on a quiet part of the line between Ploegsteert Wood, or Plug Street as it was called by the British soldiers, and St. Eloi, south of the infamous town of Ypres. The area had already witnessed heavy fighting, but the winter months were generally quieter due to the adverse weather. Andrew despised the cold, wet weather. In Canada he had become accustomed to freezing temperatures, but it was dry, crisp cold, for which he was equipped with layers of fur. Here in Flanders it was the combination of biting winds and heavy rain that were draining his enthusiasm away by the day. How different his section's attitude had been when they first marched along the communication trenches to their position, belting out the words of 'Boys from Canada':

'We the boys from Canada
Glad to serve Britannia!
Don't you hear them?
Well then, cheer them!
Send a loyal, loud Hurrah!
'Tis the Maple Leaf they wear,
Emblem of their country fair,
Proud to send them
God defend them
Boys from Canada.

They still sang it now, but not with the same gusto. The prospect of an assault on the German lines, or holding back a counter-attack, had filled them with a mixture of fear and exhilaration. But, as neither had happened yet, despondency had taken over. Daily life in the trenches was a dull business of shoring up dugouts, filling sandbags, bringing up rations and trying to keep weapons clean and in working order. And then there was the never-ending rain and cold, for which their standard khaki uniforms were inadequate.

Andrew tried to hide his feelings from the lads in his section, to keep up their morale. After one particularly heavy drenching he turned to Private Halliday and said, 'Don't worry, son – your uniform might be soaking, but your skin is still waterproof.'

'Don't know about that, Corporal. Even my bones are wet.'

At least the terrible weather kept the German regiment of Saxons opposite them subdued as well. Most casualties were the result of sniper fire, at which the Germans seemed particularly accurate. A moment's lack of concentration, when a soldier's head might raise above the parapet, the single crack of a rifle shot, and another fatality. The company captain, on visiting the trenches one morning, decided it was time the Canadians hit back. He asked for the best marksmen in each section to come forward. Those with experience of hunting tended to be the best sharpshooters, so most were native Indian. In Andrew's section, though, it was Anders Halvorsen. Using a short magazine Lee Enfield rifle, and with Andrew sometimes working as his spotter, he killed at least six unsuspecting Germans over the next few weeks. There was something exhilarating about hours of patient spotting, looking for weak spots in the German trenches or the telltale signs of steam rising from a billie can brewing coffee. Anders had nerves of steel, breathing deeply and slowly, holding the rifle steadily and then giving a single squeeze of the trigger.

'Did you get him?'

'Of course – as easy as a hitting a muskrat, except the Hun was uglier.'

A mad dash followed to change position before the inevitable German retaliation, as they tried to calculate their sniping location.

The late November weather changed from heavy wind and rain to hard frosts. There was something beautiful about the way the white frost covered the battered landscape and hung from the limbs of shattered trees. On the first of December, the repeated toll of church bells was carried in the wind from the nearby village of St. Eloi.

'Do you think the war is over, Corporal?' asked a hopeful Halliday.

'I very much doubt it, son, but wouldn't it be grand to be out of here by Christmas?'

Andrew later heard the villagers were celebrating their patron saint's feast day. As Christmas approached they were still in the trenches. A seasonal greeting from the new commander in chief, Field Marshal Douglas Haig, was conveyed to all the Allied troops on the Western Front.

His communication made it clear that any troops who engaged in fraternisation with the enemy – as had been widespread the previous Christmas – would face the severest of consequences, i.e. execution by firing squad.

On a bitter cold Christmas Eve, Andrew's section huddled together in a dugout and discussed the merits of a ceasefire the following day. One soldier remarked: 'I was speaking to an English lad who told me there was a right party going on last year at Plug Street Wood. Singing carols, exchanging gifts – German cigars are very good, he told me – and there was even a bit of a kickabout.'

'I didn't come across the Atlantic to play fucking football with the Hun,' retorted Halvorsen.

'That's because you're rubbish at football, though.'

The section was split on what they should do the following day. Halliday suggested that a brief truce would allow both sides to collect their dead from no man's land, without fear of being killed themselves. As the section had lost two men whose bodies had not yet been recovered, most agreed with the idea. Andrew had the last word. 'Let's obey orders, lads.'

Christmas morning dawned peacefully. The German positions, barely a hundred yards away, were very quiet. There was none of the usual sporadic rifle or machine gun fire. Sergeant Briggs arrived and wished the men a merry Christmas. He gave out to each a small Red Cross parcel, which included a card, chocolate, and cigarettes. He returned quickly with a mess tin full of rum. This was administered via a metal tablespoon. When Andrew went to move on after he had received his ration, Briggs said, 'Wait, one more spoon for the baby Jesus.' He gratefully gulped the second spoonful, unsure if the sergeant was joking or not. The spirits of the section were literally lifted after this unexpected show of generosity. Very shortly afterwards there was a shout from a sentry: 'Corporal, come and listen to this.'

Andrew strained at first, but then recognised the air, if not the words. The Germans were singing 'Stille Nacht'. When they finished, the Canadians applauded.

'All right; our turn,' said Andrew, wishing he had a fiddle to hand. He sang the first line of 'Good King Wenceslas' and the others joined in. It was then time for the Germans to show their appreciation. After more carols were reciprocated in this way, a German officer appeared over the parapet, unarmed but waving a white flag.

Sergeant Briggs turned to Andrew and said, 'I am going over to meet him, but keep me covered.' Andrew saw two figures shaking hands, and lots of gesticulating and signing. Briggs returned, to announce: 'We have agreed a two-hour truce to retrieve our dead. I think they are genuine, so absolutely no firing first, boys.' Both sides were as good as their word, and no man's land was cleared of corpses. Artillery fire from behind the lines put paid to any further fraternisation. In the darkness of Christmas night, singing continued from both sides.

*

Singing also featured prominently in Kathleen's Christmas of 1915. It was the culmination of a bitter, cold winter at Royaumont. The hospital was probably the best organised and equipped on the entire front, but it was not immune to shortages. Coal and other fuel were scarce. This in turn meant that electricity, provided by the hospital's own coal-fired generator, was severely rationed. Only the operating theatres had a guaranteed supply. Kathleen became used to finding her way around the wards and the nurses' quarters by candlelight. Jokes about the Lady with the Lamp wore thin. The hospital incinerator consumed large amounts of coal, but for hygiene reasons was given priority over heating. In the autumn, eating in the cloisters had been delightful. In winter it became something of a trial. Kathleen and Mary put on layers of whatever warm clothing they could find before venturing down to breakfast. They tried to be near the front of the queue, as any warm food would swiftly drop in temperature in the chilled morning air. The evergreen ivy, which wrapped itself in great clumps around the stone pillars of the cloisters, provided the only colour to a drab winter setting.

Suppers could be charming, however, especially on a clear night, as the grey arches reflected the moonlight onto the long white tables where the food was served. The doctors and nurses. wearing furs and sheepskins, eagerly discussed what dish might be presented by the wonderful Michelet. The hospital had had the good fortune to admit him as a *blessé*. His skills did not become apparent until he wandered into the kitchen during his convalescence and asked to help. The British cooks were very impressed by his culinary technique and enquired about his life prior to the war. He explained that he had trained and worked at one of the most prestigious Parisian restaurants. The hospital made the most of his expertise, until his inevitable recall by the army. He may have been unable to make a silk purse from a sow's ear, but he could turn it, or any other humble ingredient. into a palatable and tasty dish. His contribution to the morale of the patients and staff was immeasurable.

Visits from dignitaries also had a good effect on staff spirits. Miss Ivens, the chief medical officer, pulled off something of a coup when she sent President Poincaré and his wife an invitation to visit the hospital, one they accepted. Kathleen was impressed by how long the couple stayed, taking time to talk to each *blessé*. As Christmas approached, plans were hatched for the staff to provide entertainment for the patients. Each ward was given the task of providing an act.

'I have heard you are a good singer, Kathleen?' Mary asked idly one December morning.

'I like to sing, yes, but who told you that?' she replied.

'Just a little birdie.' She smiled. No more was said about it until later that evening at supper. 'I spoke to Dr Simpson this afternoon and you are to be the ward's entertainment at the Christmas party!'

Ordinarily, Kathleen would have been annoyed if she was volunteered for something without her consent, but the opportunity to sing and entertain again was a pleasant prospect.

'Thank you for that, Mary,' she said, in a tone which left her best friend guessing as to whether she was pleased or not.

Christmas morning dawned bright and cold. The two nurses performed their usual pre-breakfast routine. With a thick frost encrusted on the window of their small room, the girls wasted little time washing and dressing. They piled on as much outdoor clothing as possible and made their way to the cloisters for breakfast. Everyone cheerfully bade each other a merry Christmas, as they sat at the wooden tables with a warming bowl of porridge and a mug of steaming black coffee. The hot food and drink helped them find the energy to complete a ward round with Dr Simpson, who was her usual indefatigable self. At 11 a.m., all the *blessés* who were mobile made their way to the cloisters to hear Christmas Mass, given by the remarkable hospital chaplain, Monsieur l'abbé Rousselle. The local priest was already a hero for saving his village, Asnières, and the abbey from the advancing Germans during the Battle of the Marne in 1914. His brave and calm negotiations proved a better defence than the one offered by the retreating French army. The devotion he showed to the patients and staff of the hospital was impressive. Every day the nurses would see the small, grey-haired old man walk from the village to the hospital, his pockets full of cigars, cigarettes, and sweets for the *blessés*. It made no difference to him if they were Catholic, Protestant, Muslim, or anticlerical. He treated them all with his same quiet and selfless compassion. He was the only Catholic priest Kathleen had met, and like the other nurses she was full of admiration for him. He made her doubt the extreme divisions between the Christian faiths she was accustomed to back home.

Although the wonderful chef Michelet had returned, temporarily, to the French army, the hospital cooks provided a Christmas lunch of which he would have approved. There was no turkey or goose, but roast chicken and pheasants provided the centrepiece to a table groaning with boiled potatoes, cabbage, stuffing, and gravy. They had even acquired some very decent red wine, a gift from local villagers. The afternoon entertainment matched the high standard of their meal. In fact, it would not have been out of place in a Paris theatre, given the wealth of talent amongst the staff. It began with a scene from a play, written and performed by an auxiliary. One of the first things Kathleen had noticed on arrival at the hospital was how well spoken and refined many of the auxiliaries were. Mary had explained they were from wealthy, privileged backgrounds, but had been denied the chance of any medical education or training. That had not prevented them from volunteering to take on all the menial jobs at the hospital.

A piano recital followed, and then it was Kathleen's turn. Two mugs of red wine had helped steady her nerves. She gave a wonderful rendition of 'Keep the Home Fires

Burning', followed by 'Annie Laurie', and, for an encore, 'Ae Fond Kiss'. The *blessés* responded with warm applause, whistles, and cries of '*Encore, encore!*'. She was thrilled by their reaction, enjoying the adulation.

Mary complimented her. 'I didn't know you were that good, Kathleen,' she said. Daphne Chambers, another auxiliary, approached her, saying, 'Wonderful, simply wonderful, Kathleen. I have theatre contacts back in London. Whenever the war is over I must introduce you to them. That talent is too good to keep to yourself, dear.'

Kathleen thanked her and smiled at the prospect of a career on the stage; something she had never considered before.

The day's entertainment finished with the *blessés* singing to the staff. They had been sternly warned by Miss Ivens that they were not to include anything *pas covenables* –inappropriate or indecent! They were as good as their word. 'La Madelon' was belted out with great gusto and then, touchingly, 'It's a Long Way to Tipperary'. Parisians, Basques, Bretons, Corsicans, Arabs, and Senegalese had all made the effort to sing the words in perfect English. Kathleen thought she detected a tear in Mary's eye. 'My lad is in an Irish regiment,' she explained.

Kathleen was exhausted but elated by the end of the evening. She concluded her evening prayers with an additional request. 'Please God, let this be the last Christmas at war.' She dreamt of singing in the Alhambra on Leicester Square.

*

The early months of 1916 passed quietly for Andrew and his regiment. The dull routine of trench life continued. However, his section of the line was plagued with an infestation of lice.

'I think I hate them more than the Huns,' a demented Anders cried. The body lice were particularly active at night as the men huddled together for warmth and comfort. It was hard enough to get more than a few hours' sleep in the trenches without the constant irritation of the little pests feeding on their hosts' blood. They were particularly keen to live in the soldiers' trouser seams at the crotch, and on the stitching on the back of their shirts. 'Chatting', the practice of running a candle along the seams to pop the lice eggs, or using a sharp fingernail to do the same, would while away an hour or two in the trenches, but was largely ineffective as each female louse could lay ten eggs a day. Relief only came back at the reserve lines, where delousing stations boiled and steamed uniforms while the men had hot baths and washed with carbolic soap. A couple of days back in the front line and the sorry cycle repeated itself.

A lot of the men in Andrew's section came down with 'five-day fever', which he experienced himself. It started with painfully aching shins, and then flu-like symptoms – a high fever, headaches, dizziness, and muscle pain. As the name suggested, it tended to subside after five days, but had a very annoying habit of recurring. With severe cases, soldiers had to report to the army doctor. Unaware of the fact, until near the end of the war, that it was an infection spread by the lice, the medical staff would prescribe 'M and D', or 'medicine and duty'. Soldiers were given a pill and sent straight back to the front. It was a standing joke that whatever ailment a soldier might have, he would be returned to the trenches with Pill Number Nine – which was little more than a laxative.

When John Halliday returned from a visit to the doctor, Andrew enquired about his wellbeing.

'I still feel like shit, Corporal, and I still scratch like mad. But by God, am I getting fit running back and forwards to the latrine.'

Andrew smiled at the thought that sometimes it was only the lads' sense of humour that kept them going.

Winter gave way to a new spring, but with the same old miserable weather. The Allied High Command were planning the next offensive, and soon Andrew's battalion were involved in the action. The Germans had created a one hundred yard deep and a six hundred yards wide salient on the front line, close to the village of St. Eloi. The British and Canadian generals determined that it would be taken in the spring. Six tunnels were secretly dug under the German lines and packed with explosives. At 3.30 a.m. on 27 March, the mines were detonated. Although several miles from the explosions, Andrew was awoken by the deafening noise as the ground shook underneath his feet. His section, terrified it might be the start of a German attack, sought reassurance from their officers. 'It is Judgement Day,' said the ever-religious Sergeant Briggs.

They couldn't hear each other because of the ringing in their ears.

Down the line, six massive craters were blown into the German front line. Any soldiers present were blown to pieces. Experienced British troops poured into the gap, taking heavy casualties to secure their position. By 4 April the first Canadian divisions were sent in to relieve the British, in what was becoming an increasingly fluid and confusing action. Every massive crater was bitterly fought over, with next to no protection for the troops. Very early on the morning of 6 April it was the turn of Andrew's battalion, the 27th, to relieve the hard pressed 29th. A confused situation became one of utter chaos. Andrew led his section up the communication trenches in the pitch black, everyone with a full pack and bayonets fixed to rifles, and wearing the newly issued tin helmets. They were an ungainly sight, trying hard to keep noise to a minimum. A steady stream of battered, bruised, and wounded soldiers from the 29th passed them in the opposite direction.

'Good luck, lads: you will fucking need it.'

'Is it far to the front line?' asked a rookie from the 27th.

'Front line? There is no front line, son!'

At that, a barrage of German artillery shells exploded around them, scattering earth, wire and body parts in all directions. Andrew and his section scrambled to the lip of a massive crater, its size not yet discernible in the gloom. He buried his head in the soft earth, trembling as another volley of shells burst close by. Halliday was next to him.

'Tin fucking suits are what we need, not helmets.'

Finally there was a short respite. Andrew, his nerve restored, gathered what was left of his section. Three were unaccounted for, but he grouped the rest in a semi-circle on the edge of the crater. They noticed shadowy figures passing between them and the neighbouring crater.

'Must be the rest of the 29th.'

The sharp-eyed Anders whispered, 'Then why are they wearing German uniforms?'

'Are you sure?

'Pretty sure.'

Andrew peered, but could not be certain himself until rifle fire was aimed in their directions. The Germans were trying to punch a hole between the two Canadian occupied craters.

'Fire!' he bellowed at his section. A withering volley of Lee Enfield bullets ripped into the advancing Germans, cutting them down. A round of Mills bombs, thrown by the prostrate Canadians, inflicted further damage on the Germans. They regrouped quickly when they realised they were caught in a crossfire. Every yard of mud was bitterly fought over. Two more of Andrew's section perished as they were pushed deeper and deeper into the crater. As dawn broke, both sides were completely exhausted. The Germans had succeeded in pushing into the gap, but there were still pockets of determined Canadians holed up in the craters. A further barrage of German shells pummelled the Canadian positions. The earth shook and rippled underneath them in shallow waves. Red-hot fragments of shrapnel burst above their heads, and all the time the utterly deafening noise washed over them.

'How the fuck did we survive that, Corporal?' Halliday asked.

'Wait and ask me again, John, if we ever get out of here.'

The shrill blast of a whistle gave the signal to retreat, so Andrew led the remnants of his section back towards their own lines. A further German infantry counter-attack was less than five hundred yards away. Machine gun fire raked the retreating Canadian soldiers. Andrew, Halliday, and Halvorsen made a lung-bursting dash to a smaller crater for shelter against the hail of bullets. They could hear the exchange of fire and screams and moans around them, but dared not look up for fear of being hit. As night fell, the cold and hungry three were still in their isolated position.

'We will hole up here tonight, boys, and see what's what at dawn. Two hours' watch each will see us through the night,' decided Andrew. The April evening was chilled as the sun set. Andrew took first watch while Halliday and Halvorsen crouched close together for some heat. He had no idea whether any of the rest of his section were alive, but he vowed to make sure the two lads sleeping next to him would make it through safely. When it was Halliday's turn to relieve him, Andrew was grateful for the heat and comfort of Halvorsen's already warm body and fell into a deep sleep of his own. Just before dawn, they made their move by slithering out of the crater, and in fits and starts moved towards their own trenches. They passed over the bodies and body parts of dead soldiers, grimly pushing severed limbs out of the way, as their own trenches came into sight. A shouted exchange of information about name, rank, and battalion with an alert sentry allowed them back safely without being shot at.

'Don't worry, boys – the whole division was called back. The Germans have taken back all the craters. What a fucking waste that was.'

With his hands cupped around a hotly brewed mug of tea, a shivering Andrew was close to tears.

He was grateful to be back safely, and glad his two privates had survived with him – they were the only ones to have done so. The first real action for his division had been a humiliating, demoralising experience for them all. 'I will never, ever again retreat in the face of the enemy. Nor will I let any of my section do so, so help me God,' he said to himself. Then he fell asleep exactly where he stood in the trench.

TEN
THE LULL

Tam sat at the kitchen table eating hot porridge, followed by toast and jam, washed down by a mug of hot tea. He sat back on his chair with his feet perched on a stool, pointing them in the direction of the warm Aga range. The sweet, smoky smell of burning logs was very comforting. Sammie, his sheepdog, lay patiently in the corner, sprawled on the stone floor but with an attentive eye on his master, waiting for him to make a move. Mrs McKnight refilled his mug with more hot tea, served from an enormous cast iron teapot. She left a parcel of sandwiches beside him for lunch.

'Your supper will be ready by the time you're back tonight, Tam. I'm making a big pot of Scotch broth.'

'Thanks, Mrs McKnight. You're my other Ma.'

The old lady smiled as she went about her business.

I surely made the right decision to stay at home, he thought contentedly, as he drained the dregs of his tea.

Outside it was a crisp winter morning, with just a hint

of spring from the weak sunshine. A few brave snowdrops were blooming in the frosted grass. His first job of the morning was to take feed to the sheep, which were penned on the lower ground near the estate during the winter months. Sammie trotted in front of him as he pushed the barrow of hay and turnips towards the animals. The ewes bleated in anticipation as he approached with their fodder.

When he returned, the Major was waiting for him with instructions for the rest of the day. The old man enjoyed their conversations together. Tam would update him on repaired fences or fallen trees that needed chopped for firewood and, more recently, on how close the ewes were to lambing. It would not be long until the busy lambing season started. The Major continued to address him as Thomas, which still slightly perplexed Tam. The old man had certainly mellowed, and no more so than when Tam asked for time off to attend his aunt's funeral in Glasgow. Before the war he would have been refused his request, or at best made to work longer hours in exchange for time off. Now the Major simply said, 'Yes, and I am sorry for your loss.'

His Aunt Ina had been a very determined soul, but the cold winter months had finally seen her succumb to the illness that blighted the overcrowded tenements of Glasgow: tuberculosis.

Tam accompanied his mother to Glasgow. Ina had been her older sister, and his father stayed at home in Galloway to look after his younger brothers. Iain, Tam's cousin, had paid into his union's burial club, so his mother was given a decent send-off and spared the ignominy of a pauper's grave. After the church service and interment at the city's Necropolis graveyard, the funeral party returned to the room and kitchen on Parson Street. Mary busied herself making pots of tea for the women while Iain poured the men halves of whisky from a bottle donated by the landlord of the Glebe Bar.

Iain proposed a toast to his departed mother, after which the conversation centred on anecdotes about her life and family. The small flat was crowded with extended family. Everyone remarked on how Tam had been her favourite nephew, and how pleased they were for Tam that he was out of harm's way now, working on the estate. His mother's cousin Ella remarked:

'You have landed on your feet there, Tam. I never knew that old Major had any kindness in him. Funny what this war does tae folk, don't ye think?'

Then, turning to his mother, she continued: 'Agnes, did you no' work for that auld brute when you were young?'

'Oh, just for a wee while, Ella. I suppose he's just getting softer wi' age,' she answered, before quickly changing the subject.

Iain poured Tam another whisky and sat next to him.

'It's getting serious noo, Tam,' he said. 'The war is complete slaughter, and just as we expected, Lloyd George's government have introduced conscription. But you will know that anyway. He came up here on Christmas Day to tell us the Munitions Act was the workers' friend. Workers' friend! Bloody cheek o' the man. He's diluted the skilled jobs, like mine, and we cannae even strike because it's against the Act. There was nearly a riot in St. Andrew's

Hall and he left the stage early, wi' about a hundred polis around him.'

'I've joined the No Conscription Fellowship – in fact I'm secretary of the Glasgow branch. The movement's growing – there's bound to be a branch near you. I think I'll get arrested soon, Tam. Some of the lads who refused to serve are already in military prison, and there's talk some might be executed as an example.'

'I don't think they would do that, Iain.'

'I wouldnae be so sure, Tam. But look, you are safe down in Galloway. Just make sure you keep oot o' it, do you hear?'

'Course I will, Iain. Whit would I want to be going back to that for? And I'm courting a nice lass called Anne, too.'

'That's great, Tam. Maybe they will let me oot o' prison for your wedding.'

'Right you are, Iain. Mind and send us the address for Barlinnie, then.'

Tam was indeed courting Anne, although the opportunities to see each other were limited. There were few social functions organised by that stage of the war, as so many of the younger folk were away. Any time Tam visited Anne at her house, her mother made a point of being at home. They had a brief time alone together after Sunday tea when they would walk down to Wigtown harbour and look out over the bay. On a late May evening it could be a very romantic spot, with views across the estuary and spectacular sunsets. If no one was around Tam would steal a kiss and try to pull her close. Anne had, however, something not very romantic to tell him. She had been waiting for the right moment to break the news to him.

'Tam, there's something I need to tell ye, but yir no' going to like it.'

He studied her worried face carefully. Alarm bells started ringing in his head and his heart rate raced. He felt his mouth go dry.

'Are yi in the family way, Anne?' he dared to ask, bracing himself for her reply. Anne's reaction told him everything he needed to know. She burst into a fit of loud laughter.

'You daft big lump, Tam Murdoch! And how, can you tell me, would that have happened?'

Tam reddened with embarrassment, but at the same time was very relieved.

'If every time a lad kissed and cuddled his lass there was a bairn at the end of it, we wouldnae be able to move fir wee yins at our feet.'

She continued to laugh for a while as Tam sat fidgeting with an awkward smile on his face.

At least when she told him her real news it was slightly more palatable.

'I'm moving to Gretna, Tam, to work in the munitions factories. Thousands of girls are doing it. I saw an advert in the Galloway Gazette. I can make at least twice as much as I am at the creamery.'

Tam had heard of the massive factory, built by the Ministry of Munitions to overcome the scandal of the shortage of shells for the front.

'Aye, but cream and butter won't explode in your face like cordite, Anne,' he warned.

'Listen, Tam, I'll be able to put a lot of money away, and the war won't last for ever. You will still be here when I come back, won't you? I should get home now and again. It's no' that far and I can get a train all the way there. You could come visit me, too.'

Although he was disappointed with her news, Tam could see the sense in what she was doing. He thought of what might be after the war. If he kept on the right side of the Major, he might make him estate manager, and he and Anne could rent a nice cottage on the estate. It would be a fine place to bring up children.

'Well, I suppose you have made yir mind up anyway, Anne.'

'Aye, I have. It will be for the best, Tam,' she said, planting a kiss on his cheek.

Her hazel eyes widened in mock panic as she joked with him: 'Oh no, Tam, what if I'm with child now?' The couple laughed their way back to her mother's house.

Life certainly became more monotonous for Tam after Anne left for the munitions works at Gretna. She wrote to him about once a month, letting him know that she missed him, but that she was fine. The work was hard and unpleasant, and her living accommodation was just like an army barracks, but the pay was good, so she would stick it out. She never mentioned the accidents or the illnesses the women came down with, for fear of worrying him.

*

'Thomas,' the Major instructed him, 'I want you to take the horse and cart to Wigtown and pick up four shirkers. They will be working here for a month or two to help on the estate. At least they might be useful for something.'

Tam took the low road to Wigtown, along the Cree estuary, passing farms with crops ripening nicely on one side and the River Cree meandering slowly on the other. The run of summer salmon, or grilse, was on, so he made a mental note to go fishing at twilight. Sammie sat upright on the back of the cart, taking in his surroundings and barking at startled geese in the fields. He was heading to the Home Office Committee forestry camp for conscientious objectors. It was the first of its kind in Scotland, and an attempt by the government to find an alternative to prison for the growing number of religious and political objectors who refused service in the armed forces.

Tam handed over a letter from the Major to the camp commander. Within five minutes he was barking at four young men:

'Boag, Miller, Johnstone, and Spiers: in the back of the cart. Now! Private Murdoch is taking you to Kirroughtree Estate, and I hope he works you till you drop.'

And then, to Tam, 'Don't spare them, son. They're no' fit to share a cart with the likes of you.'

Tam wondered what exactly the Major had written in his letter.

The conscientious objectors, or 'conchies', were very quiet as Tam drove them back to the estate. Their quarters were an old outhouse without any heating. Mrs McKnight had acquired four old mattresses, which lay in the corners of the stone floor. A few well-worn wooden chairs completed the furniture.

'Home sweet home, boys,' Tam joked, as he showed them inside. Then he added, 'There's a standpipe round the back where you'll get water to wash.'

'Thanks, Private. Anyway, this is like the Ritz compared to Wormwood Scrubs,' said Joseph Boag, who Tam guessed was their leader.

'Food is better too,' continued Tam. 'You'll meet Mrs McKnight, our cook, soon. She will leave you out a can of porridge in the morning, by the kitchen door.'

The Major refused to meet or acknowledge the objectors, but gave Tam daily details of their work. He slowly got to know them, especially Joseph Boag. A lot of what he said about the war was very similar to what he had heard from his cousin, Iain; mainly political stuff, with lots of 'isms' again. Tam wondered if the countries they were fighting, including Germany or Turkey, had men like Boag who refused to fight. The objectors said they did, and that was the point – if more men on all sides refused to fight, the war would be stopped. That made some sense to Tam, but he couldn't see it happening. There was one lad, Alex Spiers, a Quaker, who was against the war because of his religious beliefs. He told Tam it was wrong to kill under any circumstances. Tam learned there were two types of objectors: 'Absolutists' and 'Alternatives'. The former refused any type of work instead of military service, so remained in prison. The latter. like Boag's group, were prepared to take part in Home Office schemes, so long as it did not relate directly to the war. The more Tam learned about the men and how they had been treated by the army, and whilst in prison, the more he came to respect them. They also happened to be very good workers, and were company for Tam. When he had no money for the pub, he would sit with them in their bothy, listening to their discussions. He could not, however, take them with him to the pub on a Saturday night, for fear of reprisals by the locals. Tam even got some grief for associating with them.

On one such Saturday evening, Tam had just settled into his favourite spot at the bar of the Queen Victoria when in walked the sorry-looking figure of John Glendenning. His boyhood friend and fellow KOSBs territorial looked smaller and older than Tam remembered him, but what was even more noticeable was the cheap suit he wore, with a limp and empty right sleeve. Tam tried to hide his shock and bit his lip to prevent asking John how he was. Instead he offered to buy him a pint, before saying, 'It's good to see you, John.'

'Good to see you too, Tam and I'll manage that pint with ma left haun nae bother.'

For the next hour or so John gave him a potted history of the regiment since he had been wounded at Gallipoli.

'It didn't improve any after you left, Tam. A fucking Turk mortar did for ma arm. Just a week before they evacuated Helles too. Just ma luck.'

Tam started to ask how the other Creetown lads had fared. John welled up when he talked about his brother, Kenneth. 'He's dead, Tam. I'm sure of it.'

'But ah never heard anything about that in the paper, John. The old Major keeps me updated.'

'No, you won't have. Officially, he is missing, him and Sergeant Irving. They were out in no man's land one night, placing decoys, and never came back.'

'Might have got off on another ship, John,' Tam suggested hopefully. 'Might be in Alexandria or somewhere?'

'Don't see it maself. Gallipoli was chaos. There were bodies everywhere, rotting in the sand. But you know whit? They might be the lucky ones. What use am I now, without this? No chance of getting ma job back, so I'll have to live off the parish; nae girl will come near me either.'

Tam rose to the bar to buy another drink, but his brain was in overdrive. He returned with the drinks and asked John, 'Are you staying at your mother's for now?

'Aye. She doesn't like leaving me out of her sight. I hear her crying at night over Kenneth and she has a hundred and one questions about him during the day. I've no' got the heart to tell her that I know he's dead.'

'Well, finish your pint and get home to her. I'll call round and see you tomorrow night.'

Tam did not sleep very well that night, but in the morning his mind was completely clear on what he was about to do. When Mrs McKnight served him breakfast, he asked her if it would be possible to see the Major right away.

'Well, he likes a bit of a lie in on a Sunday morning, but I will ask him when I bring up his tea.'

Around 11 a.m., Tam had a long discussion with the Major in his drawing room. Over an hour later, as the meeting concluded, Tam emerged with another letter in his hand. The old man shook his hand warmly and said, 'I am so very proud of you, Thomas.'

ELEVEN
THE PUSH

The 1916 New Year celebrations may have lifted the spirits of everyone at Royaumont, but they did nothing to raise the freezing temperatures. The most welcome sight of the week was the return of the overworked hospital lorry from Rouen, with a precious load of coal. It had to be used very sparingly, so Kathleen and Mary kept themselves well wrapped up in warm clothes, even when they went to bed in their cold and dark room.

The hospital was quiet in the early months of the year. The number of *blessés* gradually decreased, as most were ready to be invalided home or deemed fit to return to the front. There was even space for some local civilians to be treated in the wards. The front line did not remain quiet for long, however. In February, Falkenhayn, the German chief of general staff, launched a huge offensive on the fortress city of Verdun, to 'bleed the French white.' The long months of bitter struggle which followed resulted in large number of casualties on both sides. When the fighting finally subsided in December, the front line had hardly moved from its original position. 'Attrition' became a favourite word of the military strategists.

Despite the appalling French losses, the battle of Verdun did not impact directly on Royaumont, as the wounded were sent to Paris or Lyon. However, Miss Ivens did not allow the hospital or the staff to sit still, as she constantly sought ways to improve. She used the spring months for meticulous preparation and the capacity of the hospital was increased from 250 to 500 beds. A new oil-fired electricity generator was installed, as was a second X-ray machine. She reorganised the staff to that ensure every department was headed by an experienced and talented doctor. A fresh group of auxiliaries were recruited from Britain, to help deal with the increased capacity. Existing staff were given leave to rest and recuperate before the next inevitable big rush. An excited Mary broke the news to Kathleen one fine May morning.

'You'll never guess, Kathleen. I've just heard from Dr Simpson that we've been given four days leave, starting Tuesday. Can you believe it?'

'Wonderful,' replied Kathleen. 'But it is hardly enough time to think about going home, so what shall we do?'

'Oh, I've thought of that already. Let's go to Paris!'

'Yes! Let's.'

The following Tuesday the two nurses hitched a lift on the hospital truck and boarded a train for Paris at the railhead. The short journey took them to the Gare de l'Est. They disembarked alongside hundreds of refugees from war-torn areas of France, who were making their way to the relative safety of the capital. Thousands of French soldiers lined the platforms for the outbound trains, heading to the front at Verdun. All around was noise, bustle, shouts, cries; the whistles of locomotives and the screech of carriage brakes. The two girls looked at each other and smiled excitedly. Lifting their carpet bags from the train, they began their journey on foot towards their sleeping quarters. The two-mile walk did not seem long in the pleasant sunshine as they took in the sights of the 9th and 10th arrondissements. At the halfway point of their walk, Kathleen noticed a sign for the Folies Bergère.

'What exactly is that, Mary – do you happen to know?' asked Kathleen innocently.

'I think it is one of those French music halls. I heard some of the *blessés* whisper about it as they passed around postcards of the dancers.'

'I should like to see French dancing, then, if we have time.'

'I don't think it will be the type of dancing you would approve of, Kathleen.' Mary laughed. 'Although the French and British officers on leave enjoy the entertainment, I believe.'

'Why, that's improper, then!'

'I think that's the point, Kathleen.'

'Really!' tutted Kathleen.

The two girls looked at each other and Mary laughed at Kathleen's disapproving look. Kathleen smiled back at her.

Closer to their destination they passed the Palais Garnier, an opera house.

'Now that looks like a place where we might enjoy a decent evening's entertainment, don't you think?'

'Oh certainly, yes,' replied Mary. 'If we could afford the ticket prices. After the war, Kathleen, you'll be singing in places like that, so don't forget to invite me along.'

'Don't worry. I won't forget,' said Kathleen, grinning.

'I hope we won't have to walk much further; my arms are getting tired carrying this heavy bag,' complained Mary.

'Well, the directions Dr Simpson gave us suggest we should be almost there,' responded Kathleen, encouragingly.

Royaumont had connections with several military hospitals in Paris. Doctors exchanged visits to learn about best practices and methods, which were advancing all the time. Dr Simpson had kindly arranged for Kathleen and Mary to stay in the nurses' quarters at the Grand Palais. The building had only been open since 1900, to house the numerous artistic events for which Paris was renowned. It had been requisitioned by the French army in 1914 as a transport depot but was shortly after refurbished as a hospital.

'We cannot possibly be staying there!' exclaimed Mary. 'There must be a mistake, surely?'

Kathleen surveyed the building in front of her with a sense of foreboding, in much the same way as she had on her first day at Royaumont. If the medieval abbey was testament to France's past, then the Grand Palais was a statement of the modern French Republic. It was an enormous structure of stone, glass, and steel, designed in a blend of classic and baroque styles. Were it not for the soldiers and staff who milled about the impressive entrance, the two girls would have been convinced Dr Simpson had played some sort of elaborate joke on them. A jovial staff nurse who spoke good English escorted them to their quarters. 'Bonjour, mesdames écossaises. We have been expecting you. This way, s'il vous plaît.' She led them through the steel and glass domed nave, all 240 metres of it.

Kathleen remarked to Mary that the entire abbey at Royaumont would fit inside this massive room. The hospital had made very good use of the space to rehabilitate soldiers. Across the area, therapists and masseuses were working on the latest techniques to help the men become fit again.

When the nurses finally made it to their quarters, they saw that even their humble room was well decorated, with iron Art Nouveau bedsteads. They lay talking until late, discussing how they would spend the next day sightseeing in Paris.

The following morning after breakfast they headed towards the Eiffel Tower, joking with each other that they couldn't possibly fail to find their way to the tallest structure in Paris. It did not quite have the grandeur of its peacetime appearance, surrounded as it was by barbed wire with French soldiers patrolling its perimeter. Anti-aircraft guns were installed at its corners to protect against Zeppelin attacks. Because of its role as an important radio transmitter for the French military, civilians were denied access for fear of sabotage. Disappointed that they could not get on the lifts that would have taken them up the tower, the girls consoled themselves with an afternoon trip to the *grands magasins* of the city. They were, after all, in the haute couture capital of Europe.

As they sauntered down Boulevard Haussman, Kathleen reminded Mary:

'We agreed last night, if you remember, that we would restrict ourselves to window shopping only. We couldn't possibly afford the prices of clothes here, and besides, when will we ever have the chance to wear something fancy?'

'I suppose you're right as usual, Kathleen,' Mary agreed half-heartedly, as her gaze fixed on the entrance to the Galeries Lafayette. They noticed that the very smartly dressed concierge at the entrance was a woman. She smiled at the girls and wished them '*Bonjour*' as she held open the door of the Art Nouveau building.

'Did you notice how short her skirt was, Mary? I am not sure I would dare to wear that.'

'It's the fashion now, Kathleen; don't you keep up? Let's try some on and see how we look,' she laughed.

'I suppose that wouldn't do any harm.'

'We are on leave, remember. Let's enjoy ourselves.'

Before they could peruse the rails of the latest Paris fashions their attention was diverted to the magnificent dome of the building, adorned with gloriously colourful stained-glass images of nature. They were transfixed, gazing with upturned necks at the artwork, so much so that they became dizzy from spinning around. They laughed at each other's antics. A rather prim and proper sales manager spotted their behaviour, and somewhat haughtily asked in French how she might help them and what items of clothing they were intending to buy. Not fully understanding what the woman had said, but judging her stern facial expression, they decided it would be best to apologise and leave the store.

'Well, that was fun.' They giggled to themselves.

'Yes,' said Mary, 'but we still haven't tried on any French fashion. I think we should find another store and behave ourselves this time.'

'Agreed.'

Their next destination was the more reasonably priced Printemps store, which they arrived at via its own Metro station. They enjoyed taking the elevator to the women's fashion department, resisting the temptation to ride up and down on it repeatedly.

'We said we would behave, remember?'

The staff appeared altogether friendlier, and an elderly shop assistant was most helpful, especially when she discovered they were 'white angels' – nurses from the front. She chose a crinoline suit for Mary to try on, and a dress and three-quarter-length coat for Kathleen. Both girls hurried to the changing rooms to try on their new creations. Kathleen was more than a little disconcerted to find that a shop assistant was to help her undress and put on the new clothing. Mary reassured her from the neighbouring cubicle. 'It is the French way, Kathleen. When in Paris, do as the Parisians do!'

They emerged from the changing room at the same time and stood admiring each other. Mary spoke first:

'Oh, you look very refined, Kathleen. It really, really, suits you,' she commented, admiring the elegant style of the black coat her friend was wearing and posing in.

'And you look very smart indeed, Mary,' Kathleen replied, as she eyed her up and down. 'The hemline is rather short, though.'

'I thought you might say that!'

The shop assistant hurried off for a minute and returned with a pair of flesh-coloured stockings and black-buttoned half-boots for each of them.

'To complete your outfits, *mesdames. Très belles.*'

The assistant had good taste and the accessories complemented their new clothes. Kathleen was pleased that the boots covered her exposed ankles and lower calves.

'We simply have to buy these, Kathleen. When might we get a chance to go shopping again?'

Kathleen could barely convince herself, let alone Mary, that they had agreed simply to window shop. The assistant's offer of a discount for the 'white angels' broke what was left of her willpower. They emerged onto the sunny Parisian streets, laden with bags, smelling sweetly of the French perfume they had sampled and with a spring in their step.

'I can't wait to show the others back at Royamount how fashionable we are now.'

'Don't be in such a rush to get back, Mary,' joked Kathleen.

'How shall we spend this evening?'

They had found a pleasant and reasonably priced family-run restaurant close to their quarters, lured by the smell of roasting chicken and pork in the first place. Over a well-cooked meal of chicken with broad beans they discussed their plans for the evening. They finally decided to attend the music hall where the great Gaby Deslys was performing. She was as popular in France as Mary Pickford or Harry Lauder was in Great Britain. Her popularity was proven by the fact they had to queue outside the hall for over an hour to get in. The audience was fifty-fifty servicemen and local Parisians. A fog of bluish-grey smoke hung over the stall seats, with the slightly acrid smell of French cigarettes. It helped disguise the stale scent of body odour and cheap perfume which pervaded the well-worn seats. To one side of Kathleen and Mary sat three soldiers, whose facial stubble suggested they had come straight from the front. Kathleen caught a sniff of aniseed *pastis* from their breath as they graciously stood aside to let them take their seats. To their other side sat a pair of older women who offered them a sweet from a large bag, speaking very quickly and with thick Parisian accents.

'Weren't the French soldiers very gallant, Kathleen?'

'Yes, and probably quite handsome if they had a bath and a shave.'

'I think everyone is here to have a good time,' suggested Mary.

'You're right, of course, and I hope we do too,' responded Kathleen.

The crowd enjoyed the first act – a comedian who told bawdy jokes, judging by the reaction of the men in particular. Some acrobats, a juggler, and a rather

incompetent magician were tolerated as the anticipation
for the main act built. From the back of the stalls, a chant
of *Gaby, Gaby!* started quietly at first and grew in intensity
and volume, reaching a crescendo as the audience in the
circle joined in and stamped their feet. Mary chanted
enthusiastically too, but Kathleen, somewhat mesmerised,
preferred to observe the crowd. The din died down as the
houselights dimmed and the stage curtains opened slowly,
revealing the star of the show. A single spotlight picked
out the silhouette of a slim, diminutive figure. As she half-
turned to face her audience Gaby beamed a smile, which
lit up the theatre. Her costume was spectacular. A vivid
green cloak draped down her back as far as her ballerina
pumps. She wore a flared pink skirt which daringly
stopped at the knee, revealing flesh-coloured stockings.
Her headdress, sitting on top of her dark, ringleted hair,
consisted of green and pink ostrich feathers. Most of the
men in the theatre were on their feet applauding even
before she started to sing or dance.

'Have you ever seen the like?' Mary asked Kathleen.

'No, I most certainly haven't!' confirmed Kathleen.

Gaby signalled for her male dancing partner to join
her on stage, then whispered softly to the conductor.

'Maestro, *la musique, s'il vous plaît.*'

She delighted her audience with a dancing performance
which included the trademark 'Gaby Glide'. She positioned
herself in front of her partner, her back slightly towards
him. She draped her bare left arm up and around his neck
to settle on his head. Her right arm she held straight out
at shoulder length and, lifting her right leg to above knee

height, the glide effect was achieved as the couple moved to the music. The term 'bringing the house down' could have been coined for the crowd's reaction. Even Kathleen and Mary found themselves on their feet applauding loudly. Hearty wolf whistles pierced the clapping.

A brief interlude followed, then Gaby reappeared in a complete costume change, this time with a simpler, white, narrow-fitting dress and a long pearl necklace. She sang 'Tout en Rose' and 'Philomene' before appropriately encoring with' La Parisienne'. Her voice was melodic and tuneful, enhanced by her accent and on stage mannerisms. It was not, however, as pure or strong as her own, thought Kathleen. As they stood again for a ten-minute ovation, Mary turned to her and shouted over the noise, 'She is quite the performer, is she not? But I don't think she is as good a singer as you, Kathleen!'

They finally made their way out amongst the jostling crowd into the warm evening. Kathleen turned to Mary, saying, 'I hope you don't think I am immodest Mary, but I do agree with you.'

What stayed with her most, however, about their evening's entertainment was the sound of the audience's appreciation for Gaby. She talked about her performance on the train back to the hospital the following day, and for the first two weeks of their return to Royaumont, she would lie in bed with the window open. In the still of the night she could recall the clapping of hands, stamping of feet, and shouts and whistles of the crowd. The hospital was so quiet at this time, with only five patients remaining, all others having been cleared in anticipation of the next great offensive which had become an open secret. From 25 June the incessant booming of artillery guns could be clearly heard in the hospital. The front was only twenty-five miles from Royaumont. At breakfast the staff would speculate as to when the attack would begin and if it could possibly lead to the end of the war. Kathleen was of the opinion that it would, but deep down she actually had serious doubts.

At dawn on 1 July, Kathleen was awakened by the rattling of her window as the whole room shook from the even more thunderous roar of the guns. The cacophony continued for two hours before an eerie silence descended. The great push to end the war had started. The sense of excitement and anticipation was palpable throughout the hospital, and staff were kept busy preparing and checking equipment. Kathleen and Mary were part of a group sent to count gauze and bandages. They were assigned to a new emergency ward of eighty beds, situated in the refectory.

No hospital could have been better prepared for what was to follow. Everyone was drilled and drilled again about procedure for the arrival of large numbers of wounded: 'Absolute readiness and haste without speed.'

'I wonder how the poor lads are faring,' pondered Mary.

'We all are, Mary, but even if they are successful, we will still have to deal with all the wounded,' replied Kathleen.

'I think the best thing we could do for now is have an early night and get as much rest as possible.'

It was exactly what they did, and it proved a very wise decision.

The following morning started quietly enough in the heat of midsummer. The four ambulances headed to the clearing station at Creil to pick up the first casualties. A telephone message gave warning that they were returning with sixteen very seriously wounded soldiers, known as *grands blessés*. The shrill whistle of the porter signalled their arrival, and the hospital sprang into days and weeks of unending action. The dreaded gas gangrene was the most serious threat to life and around 90% of cases over the next few months were infected. Speed was of the essence. As soon as soldiers were stretchered into the receiving area, their wounds were swabbed and taken to the bacteriologist, so cases could be prioritised. Kathleen and Mary spent much of the day rushing between rooms, helping with this vital task. Over 100 patients were received on the first day. The hospital reached its 500-bed capacity within the first week, and still the cases kept arriving.

Kathleen and Mary were ordered to rest at 7 a.m. on the morning of 3 July, having worked throughout the night. They resumed at 11 a.m. the same morning. The spirit of cooperation in the hospital was incredible. The day shift worked longer to overlap with the night shift, who reciprocated. The six senior surgeons had the least sleep, but junior doctors would take on the less complicated operations. Orderlies and nurses did their best to clean and sterilise the operating theatres between procedures. Kitchen staff and clerks doubled up as supplementary stretcher-bearers. The ambulance drivers worked on a rota, but barely had more than three hours' sleep a day.

'Have you ever felt so tired in your life, Kathleen? How much longer do you think this will go on?'

'I've no idea, Mary. I think I'm living in a dream – well, a nightmare, really. Hopefully not much longer now. I would hate to make a mistake. It is so hard to concentrate.'

'I know if I was a surgeon, I would probably saw the wrong leg off,' joked Mary.

The two descended into a fit of hysterical laughter and tears ran down their exhausted faces. Ten minute later the porter's whistle shrilled again. They splashed their faces with cold water, sorted their uniforms, and made their way to the entrance hall.

*

The battle continued throughout the summer and into the autumn. In September Andrew's division were brought into action at Flers-Courcelette. The summer of 1916 had passed relatively quietly and peacefully for Andrew and his platoon, as they formed part of the reserve corps. This had involved the tedious task of manning and repairing reserve trenches, in between drilling and training a safe distance from the front line. With the mounting casualties on the Somme, however, the British High Command decided to move the Canadian corps to the front line to take part in the third great offensive of the battle, ever hopeful that the elusive and decisive breakthrough could be achieved.

'Remember all that time ago, when we were daft enough to sign up in Canada and the recruiting officer said we would see the world as we fought for king and Empire?'

'You don't need to remind us, Sarge,' responded a weary Andrew. 'Seems like a lifetime ago.'

'Well, he wasn't lying, lads. First, we had the delights of the bullring in England, then all this lovely mud in Flanders. So now the army is spoiling us by sending us to France for a swim in the River Somme.'

'Fucking excellent, Sarge,' chipped in Anders. 'Can't wait.'

Andrew had heard about events at the Somme and was not too surprised at the latest events. At least the new lads in his section had bonded well with the survivors from 1915, like Anders and John Halliday. He felt they were prepared for front line action. The days before the attack were filled with the usual rumours and speculation, to which Anders was to add another. He had been chatting with a gunner from the British Royal Artillery, who had heard a new weapon was to be unleashed on the unsuspecting Germans. No one paid much attention to his comments until the morning of the attack.

Officers were briefed that the artillery were to lay down a creeping barrage of continuous shellfire ahead of the infantry as they launched their attack. There were also 'corridors' free of artillery fire to give space for the new weapon to be deployed.

'OK, lads. Don't wait for the guns to fall silent before we go over – they are going to keep firing ahead as we attack. Listen for my whistle, and if all else fails, just make sure you follow me pronto.'

'Eh, just how far ahead of us will they fire, Sarge?'

'Far enough, Halliday, but don't run too fast, just in case.'

Their objective on the first day was to clear the road to the village of Courcelette.

Over the noise of their own fire and the rattle of German machine guns, Andrew's section advanced towards the German lines. The barrage was doing its job, as they made it to the first line of German trenches with everyone intact for once. Andrew dropped into the enemy trench and signalled Anders to join him. They reached the edge of first bay in the trench unopposed. He lobbed a Mills bomb into the bay and, as it exploded, he heard a yell. Anders dashed past him and fired several rounds into the German soldiers, who were dazed and wounded by the grenade. Checking none were left alive, they moved to the next bay in the trench and repeated the process. This time both Anders and Andrew used their bayonets on the stunned Germans. Neither stopped to think about how ferociously they had killed their foe. All along the line, others from his regiment were carrying out the same manoeuvre to secure their position. As they awaited the orders to proceed to the next line of German trenches, Andrew lay still, at once both exhausted and exhilarated.

'Well done, lads, well done,' he shouted to those around him.

His congratulations were drowned out by an unusual loud lumbering noise.

'What in the name of all that is holy is that fucking thing?' exclaimed Halliday.

From his prone position Andrew could see the steel rhombus-shaped vehicle steer slowly towards the German lines, with a group of British soldiers huddled behind for shelter. It spewed thick black smoke from the rear, and thin red flames spurted intermittently from its side-mounted machine guns. In front of the mechanical monster, German troops were fleeing towards their reserve lines.

'That, Halliday, is what they call a land ship, I believe,' concluded Andrew.

'Whatever it is, I'm glad it's on our side,' responded Halliday.

The remainder of the day went well for the division. Aided by the few tanks that did not break down, they achieved most of their objectives, gaining over two kilometres of ground.

'Have we won the war then, Corporal?' the ever-optimistic Halliday asked.

'I think the Huns might still have something to say about that first.'

As if on cue, the Germans launched an artillery barrage as a precursor to a counter-attack. The bombardment was as ferocious as any he had faced previously, but Andrew was becoming so used to them that he huddled against the side of the trench with his head bowed deeply, almost breathing the dank earth in. When the heavy guns stopped, he directed his section to hold fire until they could see the advancing Germans. On his command they fired a hail of bullets at the advancing foe, cutting them down mercilessly. By the end of the day they had repelled another two German counter-attacks, and as night fell both sides stopped, completely and utterly exhausted.

At around 3 a.m. the following morning Andrew was startled by a tug on his arm.

'What the fuck!' he exclaimed, as he instinctively reached for his Lee Enfield rifle.

'There will be no need for that, Corporal,' replied a vaguely familiar Highland voice.

'Well, I'll be damned,' said Andrew. 'What brings you to this neck of the woods, Sergeant McAllister?'

'I heard you boys were helping out around here and thought it would be rude if I didn't visit you lot. Have a swig of this; it's not whisky, but good stuff all the same.' He passed Andrew a half-finished bottle of French red wine.

He gratefully accepted and took a long gulp. The liquor was quite coarse and harsh as it hit his stomach, but he appreciated the warming glow.

'I've left a case for your boys back at the dugout. We acquired a good few boxes from the village café before the Hun artillery blew it to bits, the stupid bastards.'

They spent what was left of the night swapping stories and getting progressively more drunk.

It might have been the drink, but Andrew was starting to feel that he actually enjoyed being a soldier, fighting in this war. Just before dawn they brewed a billy can of strong-smelling coffee to sober themselves up before stand-to. Sergeant McAllister had already staggered back to his platoon, hoping that the German artillery would be kind to his hangover.

TWELVE
THE RETURN

Tam was working up to an impressive hangover, sitting with his new mates on a troop train heading towards the English south coast. His journey from Newton Stewart station had none of the pomp and ceremony of his original departure back in August 1914. Only his weeping mother had seen him off earlier in the morning, disturbed by her son's decision to return to the war. Tam, however, was pleased with himself. He was particularly happy that the old Major had agreed his invalided pal, John, could take his job at Kirroughtree Estate. He was further grateful to the Major for speeding up his return to the local regiment, The King's Own Scottish Borderers, although this time he would be serving with the 6th division in France.

Once Tam was settled in his compartment, he reached into his breast pocket and took out an envelope. He removed the lavender-scented letter inside and held it to his nose. It was handwritten by Anne. In his head he memorised the content, as read to him the previous week by his younger brother. She started with her usual complaint that he never wrote to her. She went on to describe her barrack-style living accommodation, which she shared with seven other women, four from Scotland and three from the north of England. What intrigued Tam the most was Anne's description of what happened when the fiancé of one of her roommates had visited. The rest, including Anne, had made themselves scarce so the couple could be alone for a few hours. Anne had even hinted that the others would do the same, if Tam were ever to visit her at the munitions works. That thought, plus the scent from Anne's letter, made Tam sit rather uncomfortably in his seat. As the train stopped at Castle Douglas station, he strategically placed his kitbag across his lap, in case anyone should sit beside him.

Any romantic thoughts and notions soon disappeared when Tam spotted his old running foe, Jim McRoberts, board the train. He took great pleasure in plonking himself down next to Tam.

'Well, if it isn't young Murdoch! I heard you were shirking the war, hiding up in the Galloway hills wi' yir sheep for company. Whit are ye doing here in a soldier's uniform?'

'Fuck's sake, Murdoch. You're a bigger pain in the arse than the Turk who blew half of mine away at Gallipoli. Where were you then? Standing in the pub, scrounging pints and boasting to your mates?' replied Tam, angrily.

'Naw, ya halfwit. I'm in the 6th division in France in the mud, while your lot are sunning themselves in Palestine.'

'So why are you no' in France now, big man? Had enough?' Tam couldn't remember anyone who could annoy him quite so quickly as McRoberts.

'Personal reasons, Murdoch, personal, if you must know.'

'Aye, is that right? Such as?'

McRoberts lowered his voice. 'Well, if you must know, the wife was working at Gretna when there was a big fucking explosion. Killed her and two others stone dead. I got leave for her funeral, but they never let me see her body. Coffin was nailed down.'

Tam's anger dissipated in an instant, and he immediately offered his sympathies. He wished that he had bitten his tongue and been more civil to the older man.

'Ma mither is looking after the three bairns, so hopefully that will stop her fretting about me back at the front again.'

Tam searched in his kitbag and produced a half bottle of Highland Stag whisky. He opened the cap and offered it to McRoberts. They exchanged gulps as the conversation between them became more affable. They talked about mutual friends and acquaintances in the regiment. It suddenly dawned on Tam that Anne might have been involved in the accident at the munitions work. He tentatively asked, 'The other women in the accident – were they local lassies?'

'No, Tam, they were from the north of England, I think. Why do you ask?'

Somewhat relieved by this information, Tam opened up to McRoberts.

'I know a girl who works there, and I hope she is all right. Were there many injured, do you know?'

'Just a few, I think – something about faulty detonators on the assembly line where the wife was working. I'm sure your girl will be fine.'

'Sorry, Tam, but I need a sleep now,' murmured McRoberts as the whisky began to take effect.

Tam was even more determined now to get off the train at Gretna to check that Anne was all right. Hopefully, she would be fine and they could spend some time together, and if that time was alone, then even better. Afterwards he would catch the next train south. For now he would take a wee nap and dream of being with Anne.

The clatter of the carriage door slamming roused Tam from his drowsiness.

'Well, if it isn't two of his majesty's finest,' said a lilting Irish voice.

'You don't mind if I join you boys, do you?' said the stranger as he sat beside them, before either could respond.

He was of average height but quite stockily built, with a shock of black hair and piercing blue eyes. He was wearing an army uniform, but Tam couldn't make out his badge.

'Allow me to introduce myself: Thomas Lennon of the Army Service Corps, or Ally Sloper's Calvary, if you prefer. Although I drive a 3-tonne lorry, not horses. My friends call me Tommy, but to become my friend we need to have a drink together.'

As Tam and Jim McRoberts came to their senses, they drowsily introduced themselves to their new companion.

The Irishman produced a full bottle of fine brandy and shared it out generously. Tam was impressed by the smoothness of the liquor.

'This is good stuff, Tommy; where did you get it?'

'Oh never mind, lad, but stick with me and there will be plenty more where that came from.'

'That would be just fine and dandy, Tommy, but I need to get off at Gretna to see my girl.'

And then, emboldened by the brandy, he added:

'I am on a promise.'

At which point McRoberts burst out laughing.

'I don't think so, son!'

Tam looked indignantly at him. 'Whit, do you no believe me? I told you about Anne earlier.'

McRoberts pulled himself up straight in his seat, clearly enjoying the moment, and with a big grin on his face continued. 'Oh, I believe you all right, Tam. Agreed, the lassie must have taken leave of her senses, but there is no accounting for taste. Still, you'll no' be seeing her the night.'

Tam's perplexed face made him laugh out loud again.

'Oh for Christ's sake, Murdoch, Tommy here got on the train at Carlisle. Just like me, you slept through the stop at Gretna, so unless the train driver puts us in reverse for an hour, you are well and truly fucked, my boy!'

'Or not, just to be exact,' interjected Lennon, as the two men howled with laughter. He added, 'Don't worry, Tam. I'll sort you out when we get to France. I'll introduce you to some *mademoiselles* who will guarantee you'll go back to the trenches with a big smile on your face.' He offered Tam another swig of brandy and a Woodbine cigarette.

'Here, this will take your mind off her for a while.'

A sheepish Tam meekly accepted, and eventually settled down to listen to Tommy Lennon tell tale after tale about his exploits in the war.

'I can't wait to get back into the action after I had to take some unplanned leave at his Majesty's pleasure. I didn't think much of his accommodation and the food was awful, but I'm raring to go again.'

It took Tam a while to realise that Lennon was talking about a six-month jail sentence for theft.

'A week before I was nicked, we were at the Somme front delivering supplies on the three-tonner. It was the first time I had seen a dog fight in the sky. A Hun plane chased and hit one of our observation planes, and it burst into flames – must have got the fuel tank. The poor bastards jumped from the plane and their bodies smashed into the road not far from us. We knew that they must be goners, but you have to check just to be sure, don't you?'

He paused to take breath.

'I suppose you do,' replied Tam.

'They were dead all right, smashed to pulp on the ground. But do you know what was really strange about it?'

Again, he stopped, this time for effect, until Tam encouraged him.

'No, Tommy. So tell us.'

'Well, when the medical orderlies scraped away what was left of the poor buggers, there were two perfect outlines of their bodies, arms and legs spread wide, forced into the cobbles on the road. I swear to God, the force of them hitting the earth must have forced the stones about a foot into the ground. Once news got out, boys were coming from all over to have a look.'

'Fuck's sake; that was grim. I thought those pilots had an easy time, too.'

'Not a pretty sight, lad, not a pretty sight. I've seen some sights in this war, believe me. Here, have another brandy and I'll tell you another.'

*

Tam leaned over the railings on the deck of the troopship and retched violently again. He couldn't decide if his condition was sea sickness or a consequence of an almighty hangover. He made a mental note to avoid brandy and stick to whisky in the future, just to be on the safe side. At least the sea spray stinging his face was keeping him awake. He didn't want to be asleep when he finally docked in France.

Although Tam wasn't to know, his next month was to be very similar to Andrew's experience when he had arrived in France the previous year. From Boulogne they were transported to the same training camp at Étaples. They endured the same extreme drills and exercises at the bullring, and had to put up with the same sadistic sergeant major. Tam, however, did not mind the long, forced marches and, unlike Andrew, was not familiar with the rest of his platoon. As he was now part of a different division, he did not have the comfort of his old comrades and school friends. Jim McRoberts was the only soldier he knew, so it took him some time to become familiar with the others. Most of them were older married men and it amused Tam that the main topic of their conversation of an evening in the barracks was sex. He mainly kept quiet on the subject, but smiled and laughed at the comments or nodded his head, as if knowingly.

Through the fog of French cigarette smoke and the odour of stale sweat, the men liked nothing better than reminiscing about the fairer sex back in Blighty.

'Sunday morning – that was me and the wife's time together. I was a gardener before the war and worked bloody hard for six days a week. Never was a religious man though; I have no time for all that church malarkey. So on a Sunday morning, she would bring me my tea and toast in bed, and then we would have our fun,' remembered Archie Peebles, an affable man from Dumfries.

'So you sowed your seeds during the week and then sowed your oats on a Sunday, Archie, you lucky bugger,' teased another soldier.

'That's right; every Sunday without fail. Tell you what though, I would settle for a kiss and a cuddle right now,' conceded Archie.

'Well, I don't think you will find many volunteers for that the night, Archie, although if you had a shave I might consider it,' taunted Ewan Fraser, the joker of the platoon. He went on, 'But tell you what, I'll tell another tale.'

'With my last lot, we were in a quiet position in the reserves, not far from a wee French village. Cannae remember its name. Very cushy, it was, and not much action at all. But every now and then our sarge would disappear for an hour or two. Not that we minded, as it kept him out our hair. This must have been happening a few times a week for well over a month and curiosity started to get the better of us. We would talk among ourselves about what the fuck he was getting up to. One lad decided he would keep a close watch on him. He was an observant boy, so he worked out that every time the sarge vanished, it happened the same time a French wifie hung oot her washing in a nearby farmhouse. Turns out that was his signal that her man was away, and the sarge could go back to get his leg over – dirty bastard!'

The group descended into howls of laughter, with one lad spraying his table with the mouthful of tea he had been about to drink. Just as they were regaining their composure and yet another story had started, who should make a grand entrance but none other than Tommy Lennon. He placed three bottles of French red wine on the table and told the lads to 'wire in', sitting next to Tam and Jim McRoberts.

'You're wondering what I'm doing here, but I always keep my promises to my lads. I bring glad tidings, too. A little birdie told me you lot are about to get two days leave before you're up the line to the front. I have the three-tonner outside, so tomorrow the three of us are having an excursion to Rouen. They have a very special class of French ladies there, Tam. So drink some wine, and have a wash in the morning before I pick you up. Prepare to join me on the road to ruin, as it were. Night, lads.' And he took his exit. Tam went to sleep in his lower bunk bed with a rather large smile on his face.

As the truck rumbled over the cobbled road to Rouen the following morning, Tam had an incessant number of questions for Tommy Lennon.

'So how come you knew we were getting leave before anyone else did?'

'Let's just say I have friends in high places.'

'Fair enough then ,Tommy; you are some man. But why are we going to ruin, or whatever you call it?'

'Because, my lad, Rouen has the best *maisons tolérées* in all of France.'

'Maison whit?'

'He means whorehouses, ya eejit. You know – brothels,' interjected McRoberts.

Tommy Lennon was enjoying being the font of all knowledge.

'Well, when I say the best, I mean the best *lumières rouges*. What with being a simple soldier myself, I have no idea what our respected officers get up to in the *lumières bleues* – they are not for the likes of us.'

'Can you stop talking French and use the King's English? I'm confused enough as it is,' remonstrated Tam.

McRoberts took a deep sigh and explained. 'Why do I feel like a fucking interpreter when I'm with you, Tam? I'll keep it simple. Two types of brothels – blue lights for the red tabs, and red lights for the likes of you and me. Got it?'

'Aye. I think so.'

'Only an hour or two now lads, then we'll have our fun. It's good for your health to get your end away, did you know that?' asked Lennon.

'So long as you don't get a dose of the clap, it is,' cautioned McRoberts.

'Well let me tell you, I know lads who would pay a girl good money if she could give him a dose. At least two months in hospital and away from the trenches – a price worth paying, maybe?'

'You know what? I would rather fight every Hun from here to Berlin than face my departed wife, God rest her, if I went home with the clap.'

'Well, I can see your point there, McRoberts, but don't worry. The girls in the house I'm taking you to are inspected by army doctors, so you should be safe enough.'

Two hours late, Tam, McRoberts, and Lennon joined a long queue outside a popular *maison tolerèe* in Rouen. As they slowly waited their turn, Tam could indeed see a bright red light in a lampstand outside the building's entrance.

'Fuck's sake,' said McRoberts, 'the last time I stood in a line this long I was waiting to get into Rugby Park to see Kilmarnock play Hearts in the third round of the Scottish Cup.' That comment got a laugh or two from the soldiers within earshot. Most were in very good spirits, fortified by alcohol from the nearby inns and boasting of their sexual prowess.

'I hope you boys have all read good old General Haig's leaflet, *Things a Soldier May Avoid in France*?' shouted a corporal at the back of the queue. 'So why don't you all bugger off and let me get near the front of the line?'

'Oh, I read it all right mate, and it came in handy for wiping my arse,' replied a private.

'You're going to have a long wait, whether you like it or not, Corporal. Because when I get in – let's put it this way – me and Madame Fifi, we will be taking our time.'

Finally, they reached the front of the line and Tam, Lennon, and McRoberts were ushered inside as a small group of Royal Engineers made their exit. There was a heavy scent of cheap perfume and tobacco. The ground floor was dimly lit by gas lamps and flickering candles. Popular French songs were playing on an old gramophone in the corner. In the centre of the room three large sofas were arranged in a semi-circle, with a table laden with drinks in the middle. Tam could make out five attractive, dark-haired girls, seated or lying on the sofas, half-dressed in lace chemises and high heels.

Tommy Lennon whispered, 'They always have the prettiest girls out at the front as bait, or waiting for the Aussies or Canadians who pay more. Have a drink of wine and then, if you're still interested, take your place on the stairs to the rooms above. It's pot luck up there, mind – you could get a nice young thing or an old hag just as easily.'

'So are you going up yourself, Tommy?'

'Oh no, not me, son. I'm here on business rather than pleasure. I need to sort out the wine supply for the Madame – she drives a hard bargain.'

Tam discovered later that, as a result of the shortage of civilian transport and the petrol ration, Tommy could arrange a 'detour' with his lorry to pick up cases of wine and brandy to deliver to the *maison*.

A petite girl with short black hair, wearing only a sheer silk white blouse and panties, brought them glasses of wine while smiling half-heartedly at them. Tam admired the paleness of her skin and the contours of her physique, visible through her minimal clothing. When she stood close to him, he was drawn to her light hazel eyes. What struck him was the deathly look they conveyed, the very same expression he'd seen in the eyes of colleagues suffering from battle fatigue at Gallipoli. They were expressionless, blank and empty, perhaps open in appearance but closed to the world outside. Tam shuddered and wondered what might have happened to the girl. He felt uneasy, so took another gulp of wine.

'Time for a bit of love and laughter,' said Jim McRoberts as he summoned up the enthusiasm to leave his cosy seat and join the queue of soldiers waiting on the stairs.

'Come on, Tam, let's go.'

Tam stood apprehensively behind the older man as he waited his turn. At the top of the stairs was a corridor leading to a row of five private bedrooms. Standing in front of the first bedroom was a tall, formidable-looking older woman, dressed in a long black frock, her grey hair tied up behind her back. She held a hazel stick in one hand.

'Eh, who is that?' asked Tam nervously, fearing she may be the one he would end up with. A laughing voice in front of him explained:

'For the benefit of the uninitiated here, that lovely lady is the cock examiner. You have to whip your thing out for her to inspect. Any sign of the clap and she will kick you downstairs quicker than you can say *bonsoir, Madame.*'

That information was more than enough for Tam. He turned around and hurried downstairs, muttering to himself. He sat at a table and the petite girl, whom he discovered was called Louise, served him another glass of wine. They chatted for a while and she told him that her mother and father had been killed in a German bombardment at the start of the war. Her two brothers were in the French army, but she had not heard from them for a while. After the war she intended to open an inn with the money she had saved working in the *maison*. Tam gave her an abbreviated account of his life story and promised he would visit her inn after the war. When his two friends had completed their business, they all made their way back to the lorry for the return trip to Étaples.

'So how was it, McRoberts?' asked the ever-inquisitive Tam.

'If I'm being honest, much the same as tugging on your thing, but having someone to talk to and laugh with at the same time. Not worth the wait or the money, but you know I miss the wife for that sort of thing.'

'Now don't you worry, lads. I have one more evening's entertainment lined up for you, and it won't cost a pretty penny,' Lennon informed them.

'Hope it's better than tonight's,' said a deflated Tam.

'Now that might just depend on your tastes, young Tam, but anyway, we're going to a concert party. There's an entertainment troupe touring the training camps.'

The makeshift wooden stage had been erected at the front of the parade ground. It was festooned with Union Jack bunting and an upright piano sat to one side. In front of the stage the soldiers were positioned, sitting squat. Most were smoking heavily. Tam and his friends were halfway back, with a decent view of the stage. The usual party of variety acts performed, to a mixture of laughter and good-natured heckling. No particular act stood out in the first half of the performance. The whole of the crowd was anticipating the star act of the second half: none other than the great Harry Lauder himself. In his trademark costume of tartan kilt, Harris tweed jacket and matching tartan shawl swept over the shoulder, completed with an oversized tam-o'-shanter, he took to the stage. The soldiers, to a man, stood up to show their appreciation. He waved back to them with his *cromach*, a crooked walking stick. He then did a roll call of all the regiments present, raising the loudest cheer from the Scottish units. He told jokes and sang his well-known favourites, such as 'I Love a Lassie' and 'Roamin' in the Gloamin'. He finished the evening with a song he had written recently, called 'Keep Right on to the End of the Road'. Tam enjoyed this immensely, and found himself humming and singing the words he could remember over the next few days as his regiment made its way to the front, close to the town of Arras.

THIRTEEN
DEADLOCK

Kathleen and Mary had come to the end of the road at Royamount. Out of the blue they were summoned to Miss Ivens' office, unsure of what to expect. Like everything else concerning Dr Frances Ivens, her office was very modest. Sitting behind a simple wooden desk, she beckoned to the two friends to take a seat.

'I expect you are wondering why I summoned you here this morning, Nurse Marr and Nurse McLeod?' she said, peering over her rimless spectacles.

'We really have no idea,' replied Kathleen.

'I am in somewhat of a quandary myself, nurses, as I cannot decide if I am the bearer of good or bad news. Let me get straight to the point: I can assure you this is through no fault of your own, but you have overstayed your time at the hospital.'

Kathleen and Mary stared at each other in disbelief.

'How can that be, Doctor?'

'An administrative error, I am afraid. What with all the

pressure we have been under lately, it was only yesterday that the hospital Committee had a chance to review nurses' and orderlies' contracts. You may not be aware, but our maximum time for a nurse is one year, and you have both served considerably longer than that.'

Kathleen was trying to deal with the heartbreak of this very unexpected news. She attempted to remember the content of the letter of appointment which had caused her so much excitement back home, but could not recall anything about the duration of her service. Dr Ivens was, however, correct, as always.

'You have both performed admirably here and we will be very sad to see you go. Dr Simpson always speaks very highly of you. As you do not strike me as the type of girls who wish to return to domestic duties in Scotland, I have taken the liberty of writing a letter of recommendation to a very good sister I know who is in charge of a British Army casualty clearing station near Gommecourt. They are crying out for experienced nurses like yourselves.'

The girls were still in such a state of shock that the best they could do was give a garbled reply of appreciation. As soon as Dr Ivens dismissed them, they quickly made their way to the nurses' quarters to console each other.

'I don't know what to think, Mary. It is all so sudden and unexpected. What do you make of it?'

'I haven't had time to let it sink in yet. I mean, I love working here – all the staff, the *blessés*, you … At least we will still be together if we go to the clearing camp. It does sound very exciting.'

Kathleen crossed from her own bed and, taking Mary's hand, sat next to her.

'Yes, it does indeed, and very necessary work too. As you say, we will still be together, so that's something.'

'Of course. I know I could not bear the thought of us parting. As we have been through so much together.'

'You're right, Mary, and I suppose we don't really have a choice. I think I might ask Dr Simpson if we can leave when the next batch of *blessés* are being released.'

'That's a wonderful idea, Kathleen. It would be nice to head off with some of the boys we have cared for, although I don't think I will be able to keep a dry eye.'

'Me too, Mary, me too.'

Their final week at Royamount passed in something of a blur. They attended to the daily routine of checking and changing dressings and assisting with the arrival of new patients, albeit with heavy hearts. Following Dr Simpson's pleading, Miss Ivens had agreed they could have their send-off at the same time as the evacuation of the fit-again patients.

On a clear, frosty evening in mid-December, Kathleen and Mary said their farewells. Dr Simpson was on duty to roll call the names of the dozen or so soldiers who were returning to the front. The two nurses stood on the top stair of the hospital entrance and applauded each man as he received his service papers. The doctor paused before reading out the nurses' names, to allow the mobile patients from the ward to file outside to form a guard of honour. Covered in blankets and shawls to protect them from the cold, the French, Arab, and Senegalese patients gave them a passable rendition of 'Auld Lang Syne' as they made their way, hand in hand, to the ambulance transport. For the previous week the men had been holding impromptu and secret rehearsals under the supervision of Dr Simpson.

'I thought I could make it without crying, but this is too much,' confessed a sobbing Mary, as the many-accented singing faded into the still evening. Biting her bottom lip, Kathleen struggled to reply. She mounted the single step into the back of the ambulance and held out her hand to help Mary climb aboard. As the engine sparked into life with a throaty roar, their spirits lifted a little. They waved a last goodbye, taking a final look as the abbey hospital faded into the background.

'Well, that song was the last thing I expected,' admitted Kathleen. 'I expect Dr Simpson was behind that, but isn't it wonderful how quickly the *blesses* can learn our tunes?'

'Yes, Kathleen, and quite appropriate really, as it will be New Year soon enough. A new year and a new beginning for us both, I suppose. Let's hope it is the last year of this awful war too.'

'Let's hope so. But we said that last year too, didn't we?'

If life at Royamount had bordered on the Spartan at times, it was comparatively luxurious compared to the conditions at the casualty clearing station, where they had been eagerly accepted. Situated a few miles from the front line, it could best be described as a tented village. Sister Agnes Crewe, a tall, elegant woman with short, curly fair hair, gave them the grand tour. Eight large marquee tents, including two which served as emergency operating theatres – the remainder were used as wards for the soldiers – formed the centre of the station. Dotted around were numerous smaller bell tents, which provided accommodation for the doctors and nurses. It was unfortunate their arrival coincided with the coldest winter in living memory. The bell tent offered very little in the way of protection from the elements. They did, however, acquire some sandbags, which they built up igloo-style inside their tent, and these at least provided some insulation from the biting cold.

The clearing station was a multi-functional operation. It provided emergency operations, including amputations for soldiers who otherwise would not have survived a journey to the nearest hospital. Minor operations were also completed, to allow soldiers to return to the front quickly. That winter the weather was responsible for nearly as many casualties as the Germans. Soldiers arrived with lacerations to their legs, caused by ice forming in the freezing wet trenches as they stood through the night on sentry duty. Mary assisted at minor operations where fingers and toes were amputated as a result of frostbite. Fatalities included pneumonia, brought on by continued exposure to the severe weather. Kathleen was assigned to the moribund tent, where she learned that soldiers who were beyond help were looked after until their inevitable death. Despite such traumatic conditions, she excelled in her new role. She would sit beside the beds at night, keeping the soldiers company; even, on occasions, singing softly to them. Once or twice she was asked to write a letter home to a loved one. James Young, a Scottish soldier in the Gordon Highlanders, on hearing her accent, asked if she would write to his mother. Kathleen was happy to oblige and scrounged some paper and a pencil. In a faltering voice he dictated:

'Dear Mother,

It is with a heavy heart that I write you these lines tonight. I am wounded but being looked after very well in an army field hospital. Unfortunately, Frank did not fare so well. After a bombardment by our artillery, we mounted the parapet amidst a hail of bullets and shells bursting above our heads. We went forward calmly and by this time the machine guns were spitting out their terrible hail of bullets. We were in the open and looked for shelter. Frank was just in front of me when he was struck by a bullet. He fell into my arms and I could see he was hit below the armpit. I put a field dressing on the wound, but it was of no use. He died in my arms, lasting only about three minutes.'

He stopped for a minute, sobbing. Kathleen fetched the soldier a glass of water. 'Frank was your brother. That must have been so difficult for you, James.'

'I'm not finished; can we go on, please?'

'God did not keep him in agony, and he had a noble death. He opened his eyes as if to say *I am finished*, then he closed them again and went quietly in my arms. I was glad to be there beside him because he had a peaceful end. I am sure his soul has gone to heaven, as he never was a bad boy out here. The shellfire started up again and that was when I was hit. They tell me it is a 'Blighty one', so when I am able, I will be transported home to Scotland and will see you and Father again. I pray that God will give you the strength to deal with this shocking news.

Your loving son,

James.'

'You write very well, James,' said Kathleen as she quietly folded the letter into an envelope for posting home. He smiled at her, said a simple 'Thank you, Nurse,' and fell asleep. Kathleen dropped the letter into the British Army Postal Service mailbag on the way back to her tent.

The following afternoon, when she was back on duty in the moribund tent, she was not entirely surprised to hear that James had passed away during the night. She didn't have much time to contemplate the fate of the young Gordon Highlander and his brother, but she was very moved by the strength of his Christian beliefs and vowed she would attend the next chaplain's Sunday service. She admitted to herself that she had become quite lapsed in her religious observation. Kathleen also decided she would write home to her mother that very evening, to inform her of their new surroundings.

The cold weather resulted in the nurses dealing with as many frostbite cases as wounds. Mary paid careful attention as Sister Agnes demonstrated, on a grateful private, how to treat the condition.

'Look at this poor fellow's feet: pure white, swollen, and most likely dead. Still, he hasn't lost any toes yet, so let's hope we can save them.'

She proceeded to massage, quite vigorously, warm olive oil into his feet for around ten minutes, then produced a rather large hat pin which she stuck in various parts of the soldier's feet to ascertain where he had feeling left.

'Do you feel anything at all, lad?'

'Sorry, Sister, but there's only an ache in my heels.'

'Nurse McLeod, you will take over this case from this evening. Massage every morning and evening until feeling comes back. Right, lad, put on your fisherman's socks and keep those ice blocks of feet warm until then.'

Just as they were about to leave, a cheer rang out from the opposite bed. A relieved patient had felt the pain of a pinprick, so feeling was returning to his foot.

'It's our custom here to give a little cheer when that happens, as it's very good for morale. He will be on his feet again with the aid of crutches quite soon – but that's actually the most painful part of the recovery,' explained the sister. She gave a little wince as they made their way towards the bronchitis tent. There was an overwhelming fishy odour from the linseed poultices used to treat the condition. The routine here was similar to the one in the frostbite tent, as poultices were applied day and night with patients monitored between times.

At dinner time Mary and Kathleen would catch up with each other in the mess tent.

'Have you noticed how awful the tea is here, Kathleen? It doesn't seem to matter who makes it, but it always tastes disgusting.'

'That's because it's made from chlorinated water. Army regulations, I'm afraid. It stops us getting any nasty infections.'

'Well, it's actually stopping me from drinking anything. I have the most painful headaches now. Oh, and how I miss the food at Royamount, too,' she added wistfully.

'Tell you what Mary, when we have a day's leave, why don't we walk into town and have a proper lunch with good coffee at a café?'

'That's cheered me up, Kathleen; thanks. Yes, let's do that, and perhaps a handsome officer will be gallant enough to pay for our meal. Or is that against Army regulations, too?'

'I do believe it is,' laughed Kathleen.

'But who's to know?' winked Mary.

The following Wednesday afternoon they had their first opportunity to visit the nearby town. On the edge of the camp they noticed a medium-sized tent, with two armed sentries standing to attention outside.

'How very strange,' said Mary. 'Do you think there are wounded German soldiers in there? Let's go over and find out.'

Before she could argue otherwise, Kathleen was yanked by the arm in the general direction of the mysterious tent. The two Royal Military Police officers smiled at their approaching female visitors.

'Beg pardon, nurses, but this is a restricted area. Only designated medical staff are allowed past us.'

'Oh, I didn't realise. Is the Kaiser being treated in there?' asked Mary, cheekily, as Kathleen raised her eyes to heaven.

'Well, only if he has shot himself, Miss. This is the SIW tent and you are still not getting in,' he said, rather more sternly.

Kathleen explained, 'Self-inflicted wounds – it's for the boys who shoot themselves to get out of the trenches.'

'The poor souls; imagine being desperate enough to do that.'

'Poor souls indeed, Miss, but they are cowards and shirkers – wasting bullets meant for the Boche. I would leave them all to bleed to death, and only treat the lads who were wounded in battle. They are the real heroes, not the scum in this tent.'

Kathleen thought to ask the sentry how long he had spent in the trenches, but stopped herself.

'We had better be on our way before the café closes. Good day to you.'

'Don't accept a lift from any of the officers in their swanky staff cars – it's against regulations. Me and Dick here, see, we wouldn't want to arrest you, now would we?' he said, half-jokingly.

'They would have to catch us first,' whispered Mary as they headed off down the road.

Much to their disappointment, no officer's car passed them on the way into town, but the snow-covered fields had a simple, still beauty which they appreciated greatly, and the long walk gave them a healthy appetite. After an hour of walking on the frozen road they finally arrived in Gommecourt. The only vehicle which had passed them was a farmer's cart bringing eggs and milk to the town.

At least when they entered the Café de Flore there were a number of British Army officers seated at some of the linen-covered tables. The café they chose was warm and cosy from a wood-burning stove, upon which sat a large metal pot of strong coffee, its rich aroma pervading the room. The red-checked tablecloth completed the sense of homeliness. An elderly French waiter showed them to a small table by a side window. Both girls were aware of a hush and stares directed towards them as they took their seats. They both ordered the *soup du jour*, which provided a talking point as neither could decide which vegetable was the main ingredient. The ham omelette which followed, they both agreed, was very tasty. The highlight of the meal was without doubt the pot of rich dark coffee.

'No chlorine in this brew, that's for sure,' purred Mary.

'It is even nicer than the coffee we had in Paris. I think I might walk here every day for a cup,' added Kathleen.

As they were reluctantly finishing their last cup of coffee, the elderly waiter arrived with two glasses of local cognac.

'Compliments of the captains,' he said, in broken English.

The girls looked across towards the table opposite, where two dapper-looking officers smiled in their direction. The taller of the two walked towards them, saying, 'I hope you don't think us too forward, but in our line of duty we rarely get the chance to converse with such charming ladies as yourselves. May we join you?'

Once the four had sat together, he introduced himself as Captain David Brown of the 2nd Battalion Cameronians, and his shorter but better-looking companion as Captain Denis Wilson of the 6th Battalion King's Own Scottish Borderers. Kathleen's interest was piqued as much by the fact his regiment was local to her home in Wigtownshire, as by his fair good looks. She was disappointed to hear, however, that he was only newly dispatched to France from

England, and was yet to meet up with his men. Any news about local lads, including Tam, would have to wait. Their conversation, however, was most enjoyable, and Kathleen was slightly thrilled by the fact that what they were doing was strictly against protocol. They were the last group to leave the café, but headed their separate ways –the nurses back to their camp and the officers to their barracks in the town. Back in their cold tent, the girls debated for well over an hour who was the most charming and debonair of the officers. They both agreed that a brew of chlorinated tea before bed would only spoil what had otherwise been a highly enjoyable day.

*

Corporal Andrew McDowall, on the other hand, would gladly have accepted the brew just so long as it was hot. He was shivering in a trench not so far away, close to Ancre Heights, the scene of a battle towards the end of the previous year. His battalion had earned their nickname, 'Tobin's Tigers', after their first commanding officer and their fearsome attacks during the battle, all of which had proved futile in the end. The entire division had lost close to 20,000 men for a gain of 400 yards of muddy trenches. As usual, all of Andrew's men had come through largely unscathed. His long-serving and God-fearing sergeant, John Briggs, was seriously wounded and removed from the line. He was replaced by a Sergeant John Dewar, another Canadian Scot, with an already impressive war record. He gained Andrew's and his men's immediate respect.

'No more religious bullshit, thank God,' Anders Halverson had commented about their new sergeant. Andrew laughed as he pointed out the unintended irony in Anders' remark.

Now they required all their brave determination to fight the appalling cold of the bitter winter weather. Christmas 1916 had passed without ceasefire or truce. The mood had changed to one of bitterness and bloody-minded resignation, as both sides had lost too many men to be charitable to their enemy, even at Yuletide. The weather had even held up the delivery of cans of Christmas pudding, which Andrew's section finally received the day after Boxing Day. Right now, he would have been more than grateful for a mug of steaming hot tea to wrap his mittened hands around. He could not remember the last time a canteen of even lukewarm tea had made it to their trench. It wasn't unknown to open the canteen and break through a thin layer of ice to get to the beverage. His face was permanently red with the cold; other than his thick black moustache, he tried to keep as clean shaven as possible. Anders had shown him a trick he had used when out hunting in the frozen Canadian wastes, which involved filling a Capstan cigarette tin full of snow and then melting it by placing a candle underneath. A reasonable temperature could be reached, which helped produce a lather for shaving. Such a small comfort in difficult surroundings helped to keep his spirits up. The men had been issued with the standard Canadian Army seven-button greatcoat to keep out the worst of the cold. Andrew had also procured a sheepskin jerkin from a

British soldier, in exchange for his wooden pipe and some tobacco. Old newspapers, and even field dressings, were wrapped around arms and legs for extra insulation.

At least the bitter cold had caused a lull in the action. The previous day, Andrew had witnessed the bizarre sight of a random German shell hitting a frozen shell hole, only to bounce on the ice and skip over the top of the trench, much as a pebble skimmed over a loch would do. All who witnessed it found it very amusing.

'Well, I'll be damned. If that hole hadn't been frozen, we would all be blown to bits by now,' reflected Andrew.

'Suppose that's true, Corporal, but I'm still bloody freezing,' chittered John Halliday.

'Better to be cold and alive, son, than cold and dead. You're a long time dead, and you would never warm up again.'

'Never mind – another two days to bear, boys, and we are back down the line. Just think – a warm soapy bath, hot tea, and a tot of rum,' said Sergeant Dewar encouragingly.

'That sounds splendid, Sarge. I'm warming to the idea already. Any chance of sleeping on a warm *mademoiselle*'s pillow, and can she bring me tea and toast in the morning?'

'Dream on, my boy, dream on. But not until after you do the first four hours' sentry duty tonight. No sleeping then, mind you.'

'No chance of that, Sarge; it's too bloody cold,' replied Halliday.

At 2 a.m. the following morning, Andrew left his makeshift dugout and, bleary-eyed, made his way to relieve John Halliday. A bright full moon illuminated the snowy trenches, making visibility far clearer than normal. As he turned the corner towards the sentry post, there was no sign of Private Halliday.

Where in the name of God has that boy gone? Andrew thought to himself. *Probably having a piss at the back of the trench, but he's not so thick that he doesn't know an officer would have him done for that.*

'Halliday, where are you, boy? It's Corporal McDowall. Show yourself, son, and pronto!'

Andrew traversed the trench for around 100 yards, retraced his steps, then did the same in the opposite direction. There was still no sign of the missing private. He had no choice but to inform Sergeant Dewar, who did not take kindly to being disturbed. Immediately he switched to professional mode and assigned another soldier to sentry duty. Meanwhile, the two NCOs scanned the first- and second-line trenches with no success. They returned to the sentry post, and with a trench periscope, surveyed no man's land in front of their position.

'He can't have headed that way, as he'd be a sitting duck for any Hun sniper. It's just too clear tonight,' suggested Dewar.

'True, Sergeant. So what do you think has happened to him? He's always been a reliable lad up until now.'

Dewar thought for a minute and then said, 'Best thing that could have happened to him is that he was nabbed by a Hun patrol. They'll beat the shit out of him to get any information about our lines, then pack him off to a prison camp in Germany, where he'll eat turnip soup for the rest of the war.'

'You said "best thing"?'

'Yes, because if the stupid young bastard couldn't wait for his hot bath and scarpered down the line, then Halliday is a dead man walking.'

'No question about that, Sarge, and would serve him right,' agreed a grim-faced Andrew.

FOURTEEN
RETREAT

Tam huddled into the bottom of a sodden trench, raindrops dripping from the rim of his steel helmet. He was vainly trying to light a Woodbine cigarette. At least his misery was shared by the rest of his section.

'Let me see if I've got this right, Tam. You actually chose to come back here, you mad bastard?' mocked Joe Flannigan, a recent 'draftee' addition to the section.

'Aye, well, some of us didnae hide for two years, waitin' to be forced here. Actually, it was worse than that, Joe. I had to pull strings to get back here, for fuck's sake. Right enough, I thought I would be heading to sunny Palestine with my old mates, but no, here I am, right enough.' He laughed out loud.

'Just what the fuck was I thinking of? I could be back in Galloway with ma girl. Christ, I would even go back to Gallipoli for the dry and the heat rather than ...' He waved his hand in exasperation. '... this.'

By March 1917, the freezing weather had given way to

an unexpected and rapid thaw. Trenches filled with rain and melted snow, roads became quagmires, and supplies to the front became all but impossible. Horses struggled in the deep mud to carry wagons which disappeared in the sludge. The soldiers struggled on because there was nothing else they could do. Morale was not particularly high, and rumours of a new spring offensive were not met with any enthusiasm.

Having finally managed to light his cigarette, Tam imagined himself back home, sitting in the Bladnoch Inn with Anne by his side and a pint of beer in his hand. Chances were, Anne would be buying him pints, because of all the money she was making in the munitions factory. How good would that be? Somehow, Anne had found out he had been sent to the Western Front. Tam suspected old Major Black had spilled the beans. As a result, one of her letters had found its way to him via the Army postal service. She had told him off in no uncertain terms for not visiting her before his return. Happily, she had come through the explosion at the factory unscathed. She finished the letter by promising to wait for him until the war was over. To Tam's shame, he was yet to reply to Anne. Maybe this next rumoured offensive would win the war and he would be home by the summer.

Joe Flannigan couldn't help teasing Tam some more.

'So what in hell made you come back? Did you get some poor lass up the duff and scarpered before her father found you?'

Tam scowled and shrugged his shoulders, saying, 'Truth is Joe, I hated being a shepherd. I was out in all weathers, hail, rain, or shine. I missed the comfort of the army too much.'

'You're madder than I thought, Murdoch.'

As Tam was about to chain smoke another Woodbine, the platoon sergeant, Harry Simpson, appeared and jokily shouted: 'Look lively lads, I am the bearer of two bits of good news.'

'Great – must mean we are all going home and it's going to stop raining tomorrow?'

'Wrong on both counts, Murdoch. No, the new captain has arrived, and he'll do a tour of inspection tomorrow. Make sure you are all spick and span. and for fuck's sake keep your rifles clean.'

'Would you like me to polish the mud too, Sarge?'

'No, you won't have time for that, Murdoch, because you just volunteered for night patrol with smiler Flannigan here. That was my second bit of good news.'

'Thanks, Sarge, but why do we need to do that? It's been really quiet here this last wee while. Even Fritz would rather keep dry in his deep trench than risk getting his helmet rusty.'

'Nice try, Murdoch, but orders are orders. You will report to my dugout at 2 a.m. and I'll brief you then. Stand down for now.'

Their mission was straightforward enough. Gather what information they could when they got close to the German lines: position of machine guns and gaps in the barbed wire, for example. And if they were able to surprise and overcome a German sentry they were to bring him back, or cut off shoulder straps, or grab a cap to identify the regiment. Tam blackened his hands and face with soot, then pulled a woollen balaclava over his head. He removed his greatcoat and all his heavy equipment, before tucking his bayonet into his belt. He hauled a haversack full of Mills bombs over his left shoulder and stood shivering as he listened to the sergeant's last-minute orders. He could feel the veins in his forehead stand out under the balaclava as the adrenaline pumped through his body. His heart beat hard as he realised tonight would be his first serious action since he was wounded at Gallipoli.

At least the poor weather was in their favour, for once. Any German sentry would have great difficulty spotting them in the lashing rain. Tam followed Joe Flannigan up the ladder and slithered on his belly out into no man's land. To their left and right, four more Tommies from the neighbouring platoon joined them. It took over thirty minutes of edging forward on all fours to reach the first line of barbed wire. Previous artillery bombardments had thrown the wire in all directions, creating a tangled mess with very few gaps. Flannigan used hand signals to tell the others he would cut a path through the wire. With each snap of the heavy wire cutters they waited breathlessly for a reaction. When none came, they cut again, and repeated until they were within yards of the German trenches.

Suddenly a light burst above them, illuminating the landscape for a few moments. Tam instinctively threw himself face down into the mud, breathing the sweaty, earthy smell deep into his nostrils. He sank his hands into the wet ground to stop them from shaking. A trace of machine gun bullets ripped above his head, then stopped abruptly. It was dark and quiet again, other than the sound of the rain. The six lay completely still for over ten minutes. Eventually, Tam dared to whisper, 'Flannigan, are you all right?'

'Think so. How about you, Tam?'

'Scared shitless, but otherwise OK.'

' Good, Tam. I think the other lads are sound too. Did you realise that burst of machine gun fire came from behind us? It came from our side.'

'Fuck's sake – strafed by our own lads. The Sarge must have kept quiet about our raid, the stupid bastard!'

'Surprised it didn't wake up Fritz, too. Still heard nothing from them.'

'Suppose we'd better push on.'

'Might be bloody safer in the German trenches.'

Another twenty yards on, and they clambered over the sandbags in front of the first German line and dropped down quietly into the trench. They formed into two groups of three – a grenadier and two riflemen in each. Tom led his group to the edge of a bay in the trench. He quickly pulled the pins and tossed two Mills bombs, in quick succession, around the corner. As they exploded, the two riflemen leapfrogged past him to mop up any stunned casualties. There were none. Even more surprising was the fact that there was no reaction at all along the front line. They repeated their well-rehearsed manoeuvre twice, and each time they rushed a new bay, it too was empty. When the two squads regrouped at the head of a communication trench, it became clear that the other lads had not encountered any Germans either.

'Well, what the fuck do we do now?' asked Flannigan.

'Call it a night and get back to our trenches, pronto,' suggested one of the boys.

'Only problem with that is, if we go back empty-handed the Sarge will think we fell asleep in no man's land and then slunk back to our trenches,' cautioned Tam.

'Never thought of that, right enough.'

'I think the Hun thought there was an artillery bombardment coming and they have buggered off to safety behind their lines. Only way for us to find out is to keep on going.'

Slightly emboldened, they walked along the communication trench and then crouched down again as they approached the second-line trench. They could see in the half-light that the trenches were very well-constructed, but there was still no sign of life. Dugouts were empty of men, equipment, weapons, ammunition, food, or anything else. Only the stubs of cigarettes and cigars, stamped into the duckboards on the bottom of the trench, showed any hint of occupation.

'Fuck me, this is so strange. Have we missed something? Is it the Kaiser's birthday and he's laid on free shags at the brothels?'

'Very funny, Flannigan, but why do I get the feeling the entire German army is going to be on top of us at any minute?'

Dawn was approaching, and the group decided that it would be far too risky to push on to the third line. Instead they retraced their steps back to the German first line. They climbed out of the trench and, again on all fours, slowly made their way through the wire and safely back to their own trenches.

Tam was dreading the prospect of telling Sergeant Simpson about their evening's exploits, as he was sure that they would all be put on a charge of failing to obey orders. In a nervous voice he explained in detail exactly what had happened.

'Do you lot expect me to tell that pile of crap to the new captain? He's going to be so impressed with this platoon, now isn't he? I hope this isn't your idea of a joke, my lads, because as God's my judge I'll take a bayonet and fillet each and every one of you up the arse,' exploded Simpson.

Tam spoke up for the group again. 'It's like we said – not a sign of a German anywhere. We can't explain it. They just weren't there.'

The bewildered sergeant put the six soldiers on fatigues, instead of letting them rest, as he stormed off to report to Captain Wilson. He returned an hour later in a rather more forgiving mood.

'Seems you were right enough all along, boys. Captain said similar reports have come back all along the line. The Germans are retreating but didn't have the decency to tell us. You can go get that rum ration you missed this morning.'

'I think he just said "sorry" to us,' whispered Tam, with a relieved smile on his face.

The Germans were indeed retreating. The German High Command had decided that their strategy for 1917 would be defensive on both fronts. In the west, unknown to the Allies, preparations had begun the previous winter,

A shortened, well-defended line would allow the German army to make use of its dwindling manpower, given their losses at Verdun and the Somme the previous year. So, work had started on the *Siegfriedstellung*, later to be known to the British troops as the Hindenburg Line. Three lines of defences were constructed, with deep ditches, reinforced dugouts and concrete blockhouses, all connected by tunnels. The whole system was protected by dense thickets of barbed wire, up to fifty feet in depth. Operation Alberich was the manoeuvre that withdrew German units back behind the new defences. This was all completed within a week in March, which the Allies failed to spot until it was almost complete.

*

Andrew's Canadian division was one of the first to advance into the deserted positions. Their progress was hampered by fierce German rear guard resistance and appallingly bad weather.

'Boys, we are moving out, or should I say moving on. Message from High Command says the Germans are retreating along the line and we must give chase. Get your kit sorted quickly. We're on the move in twenty minutes,' shouted Sergeant Dewar. Andrew gave a wry smile. He had been looking forward to a few days well-earned leave behind the lines. But now the prospect of leaving the trenches and pushing forward over open ground excited him. Anders Halvorsen was equally enthusiastic as he scrambled to gather his pack and round up the others in their section. Andrew Halliday, however, was still missing. No one had seen or heard sight nor sound of him since his mysterious disappearance.

Climbing out of the trench into no man's land was an unnerving experience. Andrew instinctively cowered and crouched, half-expecting a shell to burst or a machine gun to rake across their path. Instead there was silence, except for the chatting of the men and the barking of orders from the officers. The command came to slope arms as the men marched on, doing their best to avoid the deeper, rain-filled shell holes. They passed the last old German line completely unhindered, and assembled at a roadside leading towards Neuville-Vitasse. Any chance of a swift advance ended there. The scene was one of absolute chaos. Artillery regiments had been ordered forward and their gun carriages with teams of horses clogged up the breadth of the road. Advancing infantry spewed out onto either side of the road in their eagerness to catch the retreating Germans. Struggling in the opposite direction were a detachment of military police, vainly trying to escort bewildered German prisoners of war back behind the lines.

As they passed Andrew's unit, Anders singled out one German prisoner and smacked a strong left hook into his jaw. The soldier crumpled to the ground but was helped to his feet by his weary comrades. A military policeman scowled at Anders, then moved his prisoners on.

'Why in God's name did you do that, Anders?' asked a shocked Andrew.

'Because I felt like it, Corporal,' he replied coldly.

The others simply shook their heads at him.

'Well, it was for Halliday – I'm sure they got him, and it made me feel better.'

By evening they had made very little progress, and so they were billeted in a small French village. Or, to be more precise, what was left of it. Most of the houses had been gutted by fire set to their roofs, and furniture and clothing was littered everywhere on the streets. Following orders from the High Command to enact a 'scorched earth' policy, the retreating Germans had ransacked and destroyed as much as they could. At least there was plenty of wood for firemaking, and Andrew had sent two privates to collect as much as they could. They returned with a handsome pile of table and chair legs and the remains of a wine barrel.

'Don't suppose there was any wine in that when you found it, boys?' asked Andrew.

'No chance, Corporal, but we did come across a wine cellar that the Boche had smashed to pieces, the bastards. I tell you, if I was the French innkeeper, I would be sending them the bill after the war.'

'Well, wine would have been safer than water, because the wells are all full of horseshit, so steer well clear of them. Streams or rivers are your only option now until our water supplies get through. Make sure you boil it, too. Once the fire gets going, someone get a brew on the go.'

'Wonder what horseshit water tastes like?'

'Be as good as your rotten tea.'

They had found a small roofless barn, so built a large bonfire in the middle. A few tarpaulins were acquired and hastily put up against one wall, where they crouched together out of the rain. Anders had also been on the scrounge and returned, grinning from ear to ear, with a large green bottle in one hand and a bow and fiddle in the other.

'I had a good day hunting, boys.' He had been the only one brave enough to lift the musical instrument from a ruined house, as other soldiers had been convinced it was a *pickelhaube* – in other words, a German booby trap. Even better was the bottle of green liquid which he held high in his other hand. 'I am told this stuff will help us all sleep tonight.'

As the fire took hold and became hot enough to brew strong tea and to warm tins of Maconochie's stew, Andrew's section bedded down and listened to Anders' tale. He had wandered around the village chatting with other Canadian soldiers. 'You lot might have thought I was hard on that Hun prisoner, but he got off lightly compared to what some of the Indians in our Calvary did. Used them as target practice for their lances. Now, that was brutal. MPs just stood around and let them get on with it. Anyway, I found this old bottle of hooch and the seal is still good, so let's have a nightcap.'

Anders pulled the cork and took the first swig. A bitter, herby taste attacked his tastebuds and the liquor set fire to his throat.

'Damn, lads. This is worse than moonshine, but get it down you anyway.' He passed it on to Andrew, who wiped the top and took a gulp. He summoned up all his effort to avoid coughing it back up in front of his men, but once it was down, he felt warmed and relaxed. He examined the label on the bottle, part of which, he saw, read *Absinthe Verte*, before passing it on. By the time the nearly empty bottle passed him the second time, he had already taken up the fiddle to play old Scottish songs. Anders was attempting to sing the words while two of the others were dancing a demonic version of a Highland fling. They were all roaring with laughter. Completely exhausted and with the bottle emptied, one by one they fell asleep. Andrew lay next to Anders and in his vivid dream he was back in the Canadian Rockies with his two alpine guide friends Hans and Nils, sitting around a campfire, exchanging stories again. The following morning, he was convinced the liquor had been poisoned, such was the ferocity of his hangover. His head thumped to the sound of a massive artillery bombardment and he was sweating heavily. The others felt much the same. One weak-kneed private was retching painfully in a corner.

'Just where did you get that stuff, Anders?'

'I can't remember exactly. One lad did say it was powerful stuff. The French have banned it.'

'I can see why. Someone get a brew on, before we all die.'

*

Kathleen and Mary, on the other hand, felt they might die if they were to drink one more cup of chlorinated tea. After months of drinking the stuff, they both felt the taste was absolutely disgusting. Since the start of 1917, there had been a lull in the number of casualties treated at the field hospital. Most of their time and energy had been devoted to keeping warm through the bitter cold winter. Now, just as at Royamount the previous year, the two nurses realised that they were once again preparing to deal with the consequences of a new offensive.

'You know, Mary,' Kathleen sighed wistfully, 'I used to smile when I saw the first snowdrops blooming. It was a sign that winter was almost over and spring was just around the corner. It fairly cheered me up to see banks of the little flowers cover our local churchyard back in Creetown.'

'Sounds very bonnie,' agreed Mary.

'Yes, but after last year, I see the white of their petals and all I can think of are the rolls and rolls of white bandages we prepared for weeks on end to treat the hundreds of wounded. And here we are again, doing exactly the same thing. I don't think this will ever end.'

Bandages, disinfectants, and surgical instruments were stockpiled and additional canvas tents appeared around the edges of the camp, empty for now, but likely to be full of wounded when the spring offensive began.

Unlike the previous year, there was to be no leave for the nurses, as no one could say with any certainty when the big attack would begin. The girls were disappointed at the news, as they still talked fondly about their visit to Paris and the fun they had had there. At least a concert party had been organised to take their minds off the monotony of their daily routine. And for once Kathleen did not need to be coaxed into singing a song or two. She had become more determined that after the war she would try her hand as a professional singer. Mary had offered her unbridled and enthusiastic support to her idea.

'You know, Mary, I really don't think I could go back and live in Creetown after this awful war is over. It would just be too dull and drab after everything we have been through here. It's so funny, but before the war I was looking forward to settling down with Andrew and having lots of children.'

'Well, that is funny, because I could never picture you like that at all. Did you ever hear from Andrew after he emigrated?'

'I did once or twice, but nothing since the war started. I have no doubt that he will have signed up with the Canadian Army. Andrew always did have a very strong sense of duty.'

'Ach well, what's done is done. You never know, Kathleen; we might meet those two nice officers again and they will sweep us off our feet.'

'Ha ha. You're such a dreamer. But there is no harm in that.'

The concert party proved to be a rough and ready affair, for several reasons. The small makeshift stage could only be accessed by climbing up on four precariously balanced tea chests, which wobbled underfoot. This proved to be a source of amusement to the audience as each new act stumbled on to the stage. An accordion player, whose enthusiasm far outweighed his musical ability, was the only accompaniment. Not that it mattered too much, as the audience, made up mainly of soldiers from neighbouring camps, lustily joined in all the songs, even providing alternative lyrics to some well-known tunes. Emboldened by the fact they were soon to be sent over the top, the lads were determined to enjoy themselves.

Kathleen was beyond the point where such things would have shocked her. Even when she mounted the stage, somewhat inelegantly, to a shrill of wolf whistles, her reaction was to smile and wave at her admirers. Pushing back her long red hair from her face, she launched into a gutsy rendition of Harry Lauder's 'Roamin in the Gloamin', which was met with wild enthusiasm. Following another couple of uptempo crowd pleasers, she felt confident enough to end her set with a slower, but heartfelt, rendition of 'Keep the Home Fires Burning'. The boisterous crowd showed her the greatest of respect by falling silent as she sang, and then erupted into loud applause when she finished. Kathleen stood centre stage, her heart pounding, but with a broad smile on her face. She was joined on stage by the other acts to lead the singing of 'God Save the King.' As the soldiers stood to attention, Kathleen thought she heard the beat of a loud bass drum. However, the noise continued well after the last verse ended, growing louder all the time. A massive Allied artillery bombardment was underway.

FIFTEEN
ARRAS

By the spring of 1917, all roads for the British and Colonial troops led to the northern French town of Arras. A keen student of history, such as Captain Wilson, would have known that in Roman times Arras was called Nemetacum, and in true Roman tradition, many roads led there. It was already established as a main base of the British Army, but in 1917 featured in the main British diversionary attack for the French Nivelle Offensive which, once again, the Allied High Command hoped would be the final, decisive battle of the war.

Tam Murdoch had an excellent view of the army's preparations as he sat at the back of a three-tonne Dennis army truck which trundled and bounced his platoon along the congested cobbled road towards Arras. They had been given very little information about their task, but everyone knew that this was a big offensive and the 6th KOSBs had to play their part. There was much nervous chat as they made their way to the front, with the noise of the artillery bombardment growing ever louder as they approached the town. On the outskirts they noticed a group of sappers busily digging behind a tree-lined road.

'That's a bit far from the front to be digging trenches,' Tam suggested. 'We must be hedging our bets on a retreat, if the attack goes arse-up as usual.'

'Look again, son; that's graves they're digging. What a joyous sight,' said Jim McRoberts.

'That's just what we need to boost our morale.'

'Do you think if we asked the driver to stop we could nip over and choose our plot? You know, like you would do at the kirkyard at home?' said Tam, half-joking.

'Tell you what, Tam, why you don't try? But I bet you would be in that grave quicker than you think, if you did.'

Everyone laughed. 'Aye, that driver is a big bugger right enough,' conceded Tam. 'Bet he can't wait to get rid of us and scarper back to safety.'

Further along the road there was a new village of recently built Nissan huts – over 4,000 across the front, to provide temporary accommodation for the troops about to take part in the battle. It was here the truck stopped and a sergeant on duty pointed them in the direction of their hut, where they all collapsed and fell asleep for the evening.

The following morning, after a standard British Army breakfast of tea, bread, and jam, served from a mobile canteen, Tam, Jim McRoberts, and Jim Flannigan decided they would scout the local area in pursuit of alcohol.

'Right, Murdoch, we'd better get our bearings here. How will we tell our hut from the thousands of others, especially if we come back steaming?' said McRoberts.

'Good point,' agreed Tam, as he looked around him to see row after row of huts in every direction. He scratched his unshaven chin and suggested, 'Maybe we could get the other lads to burn something copper on the stove and we'll see the green smoke for miles.'

'Oh, we're quite the scientist now, are we, Tam? Better get them to put the kettle on now and it might melt down in a month,' said McRoberts, dismissing his idea.

'I've a better one,' chipped in Jim Flannigan. 'Get the lads to fire off a Very light just at curfew and back we go!'

'Aye, right you are, just in time for every Hun gun to blow us and the hut to kingdom come. Am I really going over the top with you two dimwits any day now? God help me!'

Rather more sensibly, they decided to take an immediate left turn and walk up a makeshift road between the long line of huts, in the general direction of the town.

Ten minutes later they had reached the limit of the hutted village.

'Tell you what though, that lass of mine has been busy,' enthused Tam.

'What the hell are you talking about this time, Murdoch?' said an exasperated McRoberts.

'Remember she works at the munitions in Gretna – oh shit, that's where your wife was killed. Jim, I'm really sorry. I forgot,' blurted Tam, wishing he had never opened his mouth.

McRoberts simply shrugged but said nothing.

Nervously, Tam continued, 'I mean, have you ever seen so many guns and ammunition in one place?'

They had reached a line of heavy 18-pounder guns, which were grouped very closely together and which extended like a dotted line over the horizon. Crate upon crate of high-explosive shells were stacked high by each gun emplacement. There was a smell of cordite in the air.

'I'm so glad we won't be on the end of that little lot,' remarked Tam. 'Surely to God that will blow the Huns to pieces before we have to go over the top.'

'Aye, we thought that at the Somme, Tam, but fat lot of good it did the poor bloody infantry,' cautioned McRoberts.

'I don't know about the Somme, Jim, but I think we mean fucking business this time.'

The High Command would have agreed entirely. Part of General Allenby's plan – he was known to his troops as 'The Bull' due to his stocky build and fierce temper – was to unleash a five-day continuous bombardment of the German defences. Firing twenty-four hours a day, day and night, the objective was to destroy German artillery positions, trenches, and dugouts. And back home, with the government setting up a Ministry of Munitions, thousands of women like Anne were working long hours to supply all the weapons and shells required. It also placed tremendous strain on the British gun crews, who had to work on twelve-hour shifts throughout the onslaught. In addition to the heavy concentration of artillery, the gun crews were also supplied with a new type of shell with a fuse which detonated immediately on impact. This was designed to destroy the thick entanglement of barbed wire in front of the German lines.

'Well, I hope it works this time before we go over the top,' repeated Tam, feeling the butterflies kick in his stomach.

'All this talk is making me hell of a thirsty,' said Flannigan. 'Is there any sign of a pub yet?'

'Don't know about a pub, but I think I must be drunk already. I've just saw a couple of black-and-white double-decker buses over to our left there.'

Sure enough, the other two looked in that direction and saw Tam was correct.

They stood, slightly baffled, for a minute and did not notice a military policeman approaching them.

Despite his huge, athletic frame, the MP appeared friendly enough.

'Right, my likely lads, I hope you are not eyeing up our carrier pigeons for your supper tonight.'

The others laughed loudly when they realised the strange vehicles were home to messenger carrier pigeons.

'No bother at all; we wouldn't want to miss out on our bully beef, now would we? But tell you what, if you could point us in the general direction of a fine French inn selling good wine and women, we will be on our way,' joked McRoberts.

'Strange you should say that, lads, but I have here a message from one of those pigeons for you.'

Taking the bait, Flannigan asked the MP what it said.

Clearing his throat, with relish the MP replied, 'Ah yes, I remember: it said no other ranks allowed in the town, so fuck off back to your Nissan hut like good lads!'

The deflated trio returned to their hut and spent the evening chatting, smoking, playing cards, and drinking tea. Some used their spare time to write letters home to loved ones. 'Just in case,' as one private put it. When McRoberts asked him if he would write to Anne, Tam said no, explaining that he thought it bad luck and that he fully intended to come out of the upcoming battle alive.

'What I wouldn't give for a decent pint of beer right now,' he added.

'I know; where is Tommy Lennon when you need him? I half expect him to burst in any minute with a crate of beer and say something like "Now, you didn't think I would forget you boys, did you?"' said McRoberts, hopefully.

'That would be bloody marvellous,' agreed Tam. 'I wonder what the toerag is up to now? No damned good, no doubt.'

The following morning, as the bombardment intensified, Tam and his platoon could feel the ground shake beneath their flimsy hut, and a noise like continual peals of thunder filled the air. For the next few days the noise never abated, day or night. Tam developed a ringing noise in his ears and an almighty headache, as bad as any hangover he had experienced. He found it increasingly difficult to sleep over the next two nights. One by one the infantry divisions were ordered from their billets to march up to the front line. Finally, it was Tam's division's turn. His platoon decided to pool their army wages, leaving it with a camp orderly to distribute to the survivors on their return. There was the usual joking and bravado on the approach to the battle zone. The weather had turned unseasonably cold, not something General Allenby had foreseen, having ordered the infantry to discard their greatcoats for fear of slowing down their attack. Tam attributed his constant shivering to the inclement weather.

On Easter Sunday, the day before the infantry attack, church services were held along the line for soldiers of all denominations. Even Tam found himself at an open-air Anglican service, not quite knowing why he was bothering other than to kill some time, as the waiting was making him jittery.

The padre blessed them, prayed for them, and reminded them that God was on their side, but Tam's mind drifted back home to the conscientious objectors he had worked with on the estate. He remembered one earnest lad who had argued it was wrong for a Christian to kill, under any circumstances. After communion, Tam whispered to McRoberts. 'Jim, do you believe in all this stuff, you know, about God and Jesus and Heaven?'

'Well, the way I like to think about it,' started the older man, 'is if I'm blown to tiny little pieces tomorrow and my entrails are scattered all over no man's land for the rats to eat, well, hopefully that's not the end of it. You know, maybe there is a Heaven, somewhere better than this for sure. Maybe I'll meet the wife again there, too.'

Tam resisted the temptation to make a joke about McRoberts' last remark because he noticed his comrade was becoming emotional.

'I wish I could feel the same, Jim, but I just can't believe any of that. It's a good story though.'

'Let me put it another way, then. I look on it as a kind of insurance policy, like you get from the Cooperative.

Keep paying into it by keeping on the straight and narrow, going to church at Christmas, Easter and Harvest, and then if Peter is at those pearly gates, I'm sure to get in,' said McRoberts, brightening up.

The service ended with the hymn 'Abide with Me'.

'That's just what we needed to cheer us up,' said Tam forlornly, lighting up a cigarette as they trudged towards the reserve trenches where they would spend the evening. It was a thoroughly miserable night. Falling temperatures and squally sleet showers compounded their discomfort. Even an impromptu singsong to lift their spirits was out of the question, owing to the strict orders to remain silent.

'Bloody daft if you ask me. The Hun would never hear a full-piece orchestra above the din of the guns, let alone us croaking out 'Tipperary,' whispered Tam as he drew deeply on his last cigarette.

'Out of fags now, too. Bloody typical.'

At 1 a.m. the Army Service Corps finally made it to their section of the trenches with a meal and tea. Tam held out his mess tin for the cook to ladle in two gloopy soup spoons of lukewarm stew. He gratefully scoffed the lot.

'Oh man, was I starving. Any of you lads too nervous to eat, just pass it along here. It'll no' go to waste.'

Sadly for Tam, he had no takers. At least the hot sweet tea put a grin on his face. He cradled his tin mug in his cold hands to warm them. The tea seemed to have the same effect on the rest of the platoon, who came to life for a moment or two, joking and encouraging each other.

'Pipe down, lads, it's our turn now. We're moving up the line. Keep in single file and grab on to the belt of the man in front if you can't see where you're going,' ordered the sergeant. It was still pitch dark, so Tam could only see a couple of feet in front of him. He lined up behind McRoberts and told Jim Flannigan to follow him. In the distance, the night sky lit up with the glare of exploding shells and then fell into complete darkness again. Their column stop-started as each salvo flew over, causing the men to adjust their eyesight from the brightness of the gun flashes back to darkness again. From above they resembled a drunken caterpillar.

Tam let out a 'fuck' as his left foot slipped off the duckboard and plunged into a foot of icy water. The cold seeping through his boot made him wince. The noise of the guns was now overwhelmingly deafening. It sounded like a deranged orchestra, with each calibre of gun out of tune and time with each other. Just before dawn, they reached their assault trench and rested briefly by leaning on ammunition boxes piled high behind them. When the sun came up Tam could see a row of what looked like chimney pots dug into the barren earth at a forty-five-degree angles. Before Tam could utter a word, McRoberts had responded to the quizzical look on his face.

'Livens Projectors, Tam, that's what they are. I expect they'll lob gas and liquid fire at the Huns just before we go over.'

'Christ, I don't want to be near any gas, even if it is ours. I'd rather take a bullet; fast and clean.'

'Right enough, Tam. Your arse would know all about that.' They stifled a laugh.

Ahead of them the battle had started. The first wave of infantry headed towards the German positions. Visibility was very poor due to the sleety showers. In the distance they could just make out matchstick men spread out across no man's land, slowly moving forward, smoke billowing in all directions. The rat-tat-tat of machine guns joined in the cacophony of noise. A salvo of high-explosive shells burst on the land, causing the earth to move like waves on the sea. Tam could feel his legs swaying in the aftershock.

'Thank God they are getting a pounding. I hope Fritz scarpers before we go over,' Tam said, hopefully.

At that moment they were ordered to advance into the forward trenches which poked out into no man's land.

'This is one time I don't care if you beat me, McRoberts,' said Tam, trying to put on a brave face.

'Just so long as we make it over. I'll settle for that.'

'Agreed, Tam. So long as we make it to the Hun line in one piece, I'll be happy too. They're not giving out prize money today.'

Flannigan looked bemused. 'What are you two on about?'

'Ach, we used to race each other back at home. This young bugger could never beat me no matter how hard he tried. Isn't that right, Tam?'

'Aye, that's right. Just remember to use your sharp elbows on the Hun as well as you did on me and they'll have no chance.'

'You two save your energy for them, then, and I'll just tag along behind you picking up the pieces,' suggested Flannigan.

The rum ration interrupted their bickering. Tam took such a large gulp that some of the alcohol reached into his lungs, making him cough violently. Through streaming eyes he joked, 'That did me a pile of good.' Next came the order to fix bayonets. A round of smoke shells whizzed overhead and burst close to their position.

'Over we go, boys. Look sharp!'

For fifty metres they had a clear view of the devasted and shell hole-pocked landscape. They slipped and slid over the thin film of sleety snow covering the ground, trying to avoid the deep shell holes and the mutilated bodies of those stuck down in the first wave of the attack. Tam was frustrated that he couldn't gain any momentum to his run. His feet repeatedly gave way beneath him. Others collapsed to the ground and struggled to get back up again under the weight of their packs. Their own smokescreen engulfed them, causing chaos. Tam coughed and spluttered. He rubbed his stinging eyes, trying to keep them half open.

'Keep going forward, just keeping going forward, follow the man in front,' barked an NCO.

Tam, the two Jims, and the rest of his platoon tried to do just that. The smokescreen, however, did prevent the Germans from having a clear sight of their enemy, slipping and stumbling in their direction. At any minute they expected a deadly volley of machine gun fire. Fortunately for them they made it to the safety of the first line of German trenches, which had been taken at great cost by the initial wave of attackers. British and German bodies lay together, testimony to the bitter hand-to-hand fighting which had just occurred. They held their position unopposed until the captain arrived with fresh orders.

'The artillery boys are putting over another barrage just in front of us. As soon as they do, we've to make for the second line of trenches.'

'Just our luck; I thought we were finished for the day too,' muttered McRoberts sarcastically.

'No, the fun's just starting, Jim,' replied Tam.

They were heading for the second objective of the morning, which High Command had identified as the 'blue line.' It ran along the front of the Arras to Lens railway line and was expected to be a formidable obstacle. However, the artillery had given the area such a pummelling that there was little resistance. Streams of German prisoners from a Bavarian regiment were already heading back as Tam and his mates reached what was left of the German trenches, most of which had been flattened. Their immediate task was to dig shallow trenches in case there was a counter-attack.

'Bloody typical,' moaned Tam. 'We were meant to be in the middle of a great offensive and here we are digging trenches again. I've used my shovel more than my rifle today.' Privately, he was more than delighted that he had had it relatively easy so far.

They had only been digging for half an hour when, as if by fate, a pistol shot whizzed past Tam's ear. To his front, a soldier fell, hit by two rifle bullets, and then a machine gun sprayed across their path, sending them all scattering for cover. A group of German soldiers, led by an enthusiastic officer, had emerged from a sunken dugout behind them and decided to fight on rather than surrender. They had hastily assembled a machine gun and it was causing havoc on the unsuspecting British soldiers. Captain Wilson, who had been supervising the digging party, assessed the situation quickly. 'We need to outflank the machine gun nest and get in behind them.' He selected six privates to put down covering fire and sent Tam and McRoberts to work round the Germans' flank. 'I hear you two are fast, so let's see what you can do.'

Tam grabbed a haversack of Mills bombs and McRoberts his Lee Enfield rifle.

'Good luck, lads,' said Flannigan, who was mightily relieved he had not been picked for this arduous task. The two runners slithered to the edge of the trench that had been dug earlier, then bolted for the first shell hole in front of them. A volley of rifle shots ensured that the Germans kept their heads down. Breathlessly, the two checked each other was all right, before they dashed to the next hole about twenty yards away. So far, the Germans had not spotted them as they drew level. Tam could make out the officer and a group of about four men, two of whom were manning the lethal machine gun.

'Stupid bastards. Why did they not surrender like the rest of their fucking regiment?' said Tam, under his breath.

'Well, they're about to regret it, Tam, is all I can say,' replied McRoberts. 'See that shell hole to our right on that rise of ground? If we make for it, we'll be in a good position to give them stick.'

Another volley of rifle fire from their comrades gave them the chance to reach their goal. They crouched at the top of the hole with their backs against the crater, waiting to recover their breath. They were fifteen yards behind the German position. McRoberts edged his rifle over the lip of the shell crater and slowly pulled himself up to take aim. The Germans were still unaware of their presence, concentrating as they were on the Tommies in front of them, firing a burst of bullets whenever a soldier broke cover. He lined up a shot at the unsuspecting officer.

'I think I can take the officer out, if you're ready to follow up on the machine gunners,' he whispered to Tam, who had already taken several Mills bombs from his sack.

'Just say when,' responded Tam, grimly.

'As soon as I fire, run like fuck and blow them to bits. I'll be right behind you, son.'

He took three deep breaths to steady his aim, then firmly pulled on the trigger. The shot hit the officer on the shoulder, knocking him clean off his feet. As the officer's men turned to attend to him, Tam bolted from the shell hole, throwing two grenades as he ran. The first fell just short but caused panic and confusion; the second scored a direct hit on the machine gun, splinters maiming the faces of the crew, who screamed horribly, writhing in pain. Another soldier trained his rifle on Tam but fell to his knees after another shot by McRoberts, which caught him square on the chest. The remaining soldier fumbled to take aim with his rifle, giving Tam the chance to launch himself, rugby tackle-style, at him. His momentum bowled over the standing German and the two grappled ferociously on the ground. Tam managed a few sharp jabs to the ribs but took a strong punch to the face. He was knocked cold for a second or two. When he came round, he was struggling for breath. Two hands were firmly clasped around his neck, pushing down heavily to cut off his air supply. He writhed and kicked in an effort to shake off the strong German, but to no avail. The grip around his throat suddenly went limp. Tam felt a warm liquid trickle down his face and panicked when he tasted blood. McRoberts had forcefully rammed his bayonet through the back of the German's neck, killing him almost instantly. He kicked the dead man off Tam, who was coughing and rubbing his bruised neck, while wiping the German's blood from his face.

'Are you all right, son? The blood's no' yours, by the way,' enquired an exhausted McRoberts.

Tam raised a weak smile but remained lying on the ground until he got his breath back. By now, others in the platoon had ventured over to help. One of them dispatched the officer with two swift blows of his bayonet. Flannigan helped Tam to his feet. 'Well done, lads,' he said admiringly. 'That was good work.'

'Aye, it was,' agreed McRoberts, who had stopped shaking. 'I think that was three-two to me, Tam?'

'I wasn't keeping the score, Jim,' replied a grateful Tam.

By midday, the division had its next objective to aim for – the so-called 'brown line', with the Point du Jour farmhouse at its centre. This section of the battlefield was heavily protected by thickets of barbed wire, which the artillery had failed to destroy. Cutters were sent forward to clear a path and Tam's platoon once again proved their worth by providing covering fire. Their task completed, they crawled through the gaps in the wire and regrouped, waiting for their next instructions. Also in this section were a number of heavily fortified German block houses, which had to be cleared before they could advance safely. Tam's platoon was assigned to what looked like a perfectly innocent house, complete with fascia brickwork, mock windows and doors, and even a chimney. The clever camouflage concealed a deep bunker. Inside, an FK 16 field gun and two machine guns had the potential to wreak havoc on any passing troops in their line of fire. Tam, McRoberts, and Flannigan were to provide support for another platoon who had the unenviable task of storming the blockhouse. The sergeant had jokingly asked if Tam wanted to sit this action out, dazed as he still was from his previous ordeal. He declined, however, wishing to be with his comrades for the next attack. They had procured a Lewis gun and started to set it up where they would get a good line of fire at the blockhouse. The plan was for a volley of smoke grenades to obscure the view from the blockhouse, so the attackers could reach it before being spotted. Tam's group was to concentrate fire on the slits in the blockhouse, to deter the Germans from firing out. It was a highly risky strategy.

A German high-explosive shell suddenly burst within yards of Tam's position. He was blown about ten feet backwards and was severely winded. Tam could see Jim Flannigan and the Lewis gun pirouette madly, high in the sky. All hell broke loose as the others tried to rush the blockhouse, only to be mowed down by machine gun fire. Tam's ears were ringing loudly as he shook uncontrollably, crawling towards Flannigan, whose limp body lay half covered by a pile of earth. He knew there was no hope for him, so turned to see if there was any sign of McRoberts. The acrid smell of smoke and cordite filled Tam's nostrils; his tongue tasted of blood. Soldiers were running backwards and forwards across his path in the chaos caused by the German artillery. He bellowed at the top of his voice, 'Jim, where the fuck are you? It's Tam, are you all right, man?'

His frantic calls only attracted German fire in his direction. He collapsed onto the muddy ground, holding grimly on to the rim of his steel helmet with both hands as bullets whizzed and cracked over his head. When the onslaught lulled for a moment, he looked up through the clouds of smoke to see, close by, a body with a large pair of boots pointing towards him. Recognising them as McRoberts', he struggled over to see what condition his friend was in. He recoiled with horror at the sight he found. McRoberts' headless torso lay motionless in the mud. A huge piece of shrapnel had ripped his head off. Tam vomited several times and began crying, just as another shell went off close by, completely deafening him and showering him in mud. He struggled to his feet and started running, but another burst of machine gun fire traced across his path, so he changed direction. He fell in and climbed out of a shell hole, clambering over the rotten corpses, whose stench made him dry retch. He discarded his rifle and steel helmet as he continued to race across the battlefield, stumbling over body parts and ducking whenever a shell burst. In his head all he could hear was the Harry Lauder song: *keep right on to the end of the road*. He repeated the line again and again and again in his head, in time with his heavy breathing. *Keep right on*, he told himself, *keep right on*. In this confused state he ran over three miles to reach the outskirts of Saint-Laurent-Blangy, a ruined village in the thick of the fighting. Allied troops were still pouring through to advance on the German lines, but no one seemed to pay Tam any attention.

He lay against the wall of a half-destroyed house and fell asleep. It was dark when he awoke with a thumping headache and, realising, he was parched and hungry, decide to search for food and water. He entered the remains of the house, which had two external walls missing. There was a hearth on one of the standing walls, but it was cold, and the only signs of food were empty tins of potatoes and green wine bottles. Tam was about to leave when he tripped on the catch of a trapdoor. Summing up his remaining energy, he pulled it open, and descended rickety wooden stairs into a cellar. The echo of his footsteps resonated off the damp walls. He peered into the half-light, inhaling a musty smell sweetened by a faint whiff of lavender. In the far corner a white apparition, holding a flickering candle, stared at him.

'This must be heaven,' Tam said to himself.

SIXTEEN
VIMY RIDGE

ndrew stood to attention beside Sergeant Dewar, Anders Halvoren, and the rest of his company in a large ploughed field behind the front line. For weeks they had been training hard on new battle tactics and formations. Now they were about to receive a pep talk from the High Command. No less than Lt-Col J.M. Ross, DSO, Commanding Officer of the 29th Battalion, took to a makeshift platform to address his troops. A tall, thin Englishman, who had served with distinction, he commanded the stage, his booming voice exhorting his troops to victory. He strutted back and forth across the platform, making eye contact with as many men as he could.

'Only yesterday men, I was in a confab with Lieutenant General Sir Julian Byng, our Corp Commander. There is a big push coming, boys, and all four Canadian divisions will play a major part. We are to storm and take Vimy Ridge, and I will not hide from you the enormity of the task in front of you. The French failed in 1915 and the British in 1916, but I have faith, in each and every one of you, that we will take it from the Hun this year. Battalion commanders will instruct you in your specific objectives nearer the time. May God protect you and bring you safely to victory.'

His troops applauded with enthusiasm. Anders, however, was not so impressed.

'Yes, he'll not need God's protection back at his cushy HQ.'

'I don't know about that,' replied Andrew. 'He speaks very well, and strangely for the first time I feel more Canadian than Scottish. I'm sure we'll show up well.'

Vimy Ridge, overlooking Arras, was indeed a formidable obstacle and its capture was key to the success of the battle. To protect their position on the ridge, the Germans had built one of the most impressive fortresses on the entire Western Front. Four Canadian divisions, consisting of 15,000 men, were to storm a seven-thousand-yard line. Andrew's Second Division had the job of taking Hill 135, so called because of its height above sea level. It was immediately north of the village of Thélus. Unlike their British counterparts, the Colonial officers were comfortable about sharing the details of an attack with the other ranks. Only the date and time were kept confidential. The enormous build-up of artillery, however, with one heavy gun for every twenty yards of front, was a clear indication that the attack was imminent. The roar of eight tank engines lumbering into position at the front was a further sign that they would be in action soon. Zero hour arrived at 9 a.m. on Monday 9 April. By 4 a.m. that morning Andrew's battalion was in place and given final orders about their objectives for the day. It was an ambitious plan with a very tight deadline. Success depended on the creeping artillery barrages which would pound the German positions just ahead of their own infantry. By dawn, Andrew could see the outline of Vimy Ridge on the horizon. The bluish-grey crest, with Hill 135 and Hill 145 at either end, looked peaceful enough through the sleety drizzle. It reminded Andrew of the foothills back in Galloway. The noise and flash of artillery fire told him that this would not be an Easter Monday stroll.

Sergeant Dewar spoke up. 'We're going over, boys. It's 750 yards to their first line. Get over there in one piece, hold the line, and wait for further orders. And remember: shoot first, talk later.'

'My pleasure, Sarge,' muttered Anders.

The driving sleet was more of a problem than enemy resistance in their first dash across no man's land. Andrew lifted his head briefly from the stinging hail to see German distress rockets shooting into the air, vainly signalling for support. The artillery barrage had succeeded in ripping their trenches apart.

'Maybe this will be a stroll in the park after all,' thought Andrew, almost disappointed, sloping his rifle to the side and sliding down into what was left of a German dugout.

The 'black line' had been reached with the minimum of casualties. Thirty minutes later the picture was much the same as they advanced to the 'red line'. One or two of the tanks were stranded in no man's land, caught in deep shell holes, diesel fumes belching from their overworked engines. A steady line of German prisoners, hands on head, were streaming back in the opposite direction. The Canadians rested at the red line for over two hours. Andrew's section had not seen much action so far, but his heart beat quickly from nervous energy, sapping his strength, and he was glad to collapse into the trench and rest up. He had no chance of sleeping, however, as the din of the battle was unbearably loud. The start of a further creeping barrage was the signal to move forward again. All Andrew and his comrades could see through stinging eyes was a wall of smoke about fifty yards in front of them, as the barrage hit with impressive accuracy.

'Don't go too fast, lads, or our own shells will hit us,' he cautioned. They dived for cover as a German machine gun fired wildly and blindly in their direction. They crawled forward into a sunken path to survey their position. Ahead of them the barbed wire appeared intact, but they could see cutters moving forward to clear a route, which they duly followed when the barrage lifted.

'By Christ, we made it,' shouted Anders, punching his fist in the air. 'This must be the top of the ridge.'

'You're right, Anders,' smiled Andrew. 'Got to take my hat off to the artillery boys; they have fairly done their job today.'

'Sure did,' Anders agreed, 'sure did.'

'Not quite over yet, though – we have one more line to take on the lee side of the ridge. They are dug in there with machine gun nests and heavy gun emplacements. We've to clear them out before the calvary arrive,' instructed Sergeant Dewar.

The sleety weather gave way to bright sunshine for a couple of hours. The view from the top of Hill 135 was impressive. The plain at the foot of the ridge was completely devoid of trees; not even stumps had survived, given the ferocity of previous bombardments. They could make out the village of Vimy nestling below the ridge, and several others in the far distance.

'Do you think we have finally got them on the run? I fancy a glass or two of fine French wine in that village in the distance,' said Anders.

'One step at a time, boy. If we don't winkle them out of those positions down the slope, they'll have the perfect position for a counter-attack.'

The Prussian and Bavarian regiments holding the lower slope had no intention of giving up their positions easily. Their emplacements had been largely unaffected by the British bombardment. The German field guns were positioned to fire shrapnel shells at close range and were ably supported by machine gun crews on their flanks.

'Ok, boys – one last big effort today. Down the ridge to the brown line and we'll stop there. I'll get you all a beer in Vimy,' said Sergeant Dewar, trying to stir up some enthusiasm from his exhausted men.

'Fuck's sake, Sarge. Are we after the Hun or chasing a bloody rainbow?' asked an exasperated Anders.

'At least we will be charging downhill for a change.'

'Too right, lad, we need to get in about them pronto, or it could be slaughter.'

The veins in his neck straining, Sergeant Dewar roared above the blast of the artillery: 'Fix bayonets. Get ready to charge. Get into their emplacements and wipe them out.'

Andrew squeezed his fists so tight it hurt. Gritting his teeth, he grabbed his rifle and led his section over the top.

'Move, move, move,' he screamed.

The German gunners were already firing shrapnel shells at point-blank range. Soldiers were falling everywhere, horribly maimed by the red-hot metal splinters. Andrew tried to blot out the screams and moans to focus on a 77 mm gun crew frantically trying to reload. He tore towards them, signalling for the others to follow. Short of breath, his heart pumping so hard it felt like it would burst out of his chest at any moment, he closed in on the crew. Shouting guttural obscenities in their direction, he could see them place a new shell in the chamber. On he drove. The chamber of the gun clicked closed. The gunner speedily took aim. Andrew grimaced and raised an arm instinctively to protect himself from the shell. A rifle shot cracked past his left ear to score a direct hit on the gunner, who crumpled to the ground. Andrew turned around abruptly to see a smiling Anders coolly rising to his feet. He had knelt to get a good aim at the German. Before any other German could fire the gun, Andrew's section was in amongst them with their bayonets. He fired at point-blank range into one and followed up with a bayonet thrust. The dead weight of the soldier fell forward on his rifle. He struggled to keep him up and eventually had to let the body and his rifle fall to the ground. Unarmed, he heard a familiar warning shout and turned to see a German lunging at him. He neatly side-stepped his attacker, whose momentum carried him past, allowing Andrew to grab the barrel of his gun with both hands and wrestle it from the German's grasp. The soldier stumbled to the ground and rolled over, raising his hands in surrender. Andrew skewered him straight in the chest repeatedly. With each thrust, warm blood splashed on his face.

'He's finished, Andrew, for fuck's sake. Leave him. We've captured the gun too,' Anders shouted at him. With his aching arms finally by his side but the adrenaline still coursing through his veins, Andrew stared blankly, looking for more Germans to kill.

'It's over, we've done it,' repeated Anders, offering his corporal a water bottle. Andrew raised the bottle to his parched lips and took a deep draft. Wearily taking off his helmet, he sat down on the edge of the gun emplacement, totally exhausted.

It proved to be a highly successful day for the Canadian 2nd Division. When news reached headquarters that every objective had been achieved and Vimy Ridge was secure, General 'Bungo' Byng decided to press home their advantage. A brigade of the Canadian Light Calvary was called up, to push into the open ground beyond the ridge. Andrew's regiment were to provide cover and mop up any German resistance which might be left.

'Remember that village where I said I would buy you all a beer? Well, you might get there quicker than you think, my lads,' said Sergeant Dewar as he roused his men from their brief rest.

'All right Sarge, what's the bloody catch now?' asked Anders, rubbing his bloodshot eyes.

'A cavalry unit will be here soon and we're to follow them down off the ridge, mopping up any Huns that are left,' replied Dewar.

'Bloody hell, the glory hunters are coming. Hope they don't expect us to mop up after their precious horses,' scoffed Anders. 'That's why they call us infantry the shit shovellers. Just hope they don't get those nice uniforms or gleaming sabres dirty.'

Andrew, barely able to raise a smile, lifted his eyes to heaven and sighed. 'Here we go again.'

A few moments later, the sound of horses neighing as they struggled up the soft ground on the ridge caught the attention of his section.

'Fuck, they're not exactly what you would call Charge of the Light Brigade material, now are they?' mocked Anders.

The khaki-clad troopers, wearing flat claps, sat astride thin, emaciated horses. They had survived the winter on half-rations of oats as a result of grain shortages caused by the German U-boat campaign, An outbreak of mange meant the horses had been clipped and were as cold as the soldiers without their greatcoats. The horses trotted past them in single file, their steamy breath emitting white puffs into the crisp late afternoon sunshine. Andrew's section trooped behind them as they made their way gingerly down the ridge. A sporadic burst of gunfire greeted them near the first village. The cavalry galloped on, clip-clopping over the cobbled road. Sergeant Dewar ordered his men to march at the double so they would not fall too far behind. Andrew's tired limbs ached for the first few hundred yards. He coughed the cold air out of his lungs. By the time he reached the village, badly out of breath, the token German resistance had been dealt with. A small group of bedraggled prisoners had been rounded up, waiting to be escorted back behind the lines.

'Next time, do you think you plodders could keep up? Not that we needed you lot anyway,' bragged a cavalry officer.

They approached the next village, a few miles further down the road. Dusk was descending and the temperature plummeting. Andrew watched the steam rise from the rumps of the horses. On the left-hand side of the road stood an isolated farmhouse and barn. The exuberant cavalry were focused on the village ahead of them as they trotted past. A vicious burst of machine gun fire scythed down men and horses in a matter of seconds. Horses reared, fell, or bolted. A few cavalry tried to return fire, using their fallen animals as cover. The familiar stench of blood filled Andrew's nostrils. He winced at the scene of butchery and felt ready to burst into tears of helplessness as Sergeant Dewar, acting swiftly, ordered his section to flank the farmhouse. With Anders, they worked their way around the building, using a tall beech hedge for cover until they were directly behind the farmhouse. Andrew had to stifle a laugh at the absurd sight which greeted them. Viewed from the front, the farmhouse had appeared intact. However, it was no more than a façade, as it was clear from the rear that more than half the building was destroyed. Clothing and paper billowed around from a large open wardrobe on the ground floor. Perched between it and a brass-framed bed, devoid of its mattress, was their target. Two German soldiers were manning a machine gun, intent on picking off the few cavalry who had survived the first deadly burst of gunfire. Andrew and Dewar flanked Anders as they slithered on their stomachs to within range of the enemy. They decided that Anders would snipe at the machine gun crew and the two NCOs would provide covering fire at any other Germans who showed up. Anders gave a thumbs up, signalling that he was in range and, taking a long calm breath, let off a shot which caught the machine gunner clean between his shoulders, sending small fragments of his uniform bursting into the air. As his colleague turned instinctively to help, he took Anders' second shot in the chest, and letting out a loud groan, collapsed on top of his friend.

Andrew whooped with delight. 'Yes, Anders my lad, that was some shooting!'

He turned to congratulate his mate at the very moment a German sniper's bullet caught Anders square between the eyes. The shot created a neat hole in his smooth forehead. Blood slowly began to seep down the curve of his nose, between his wide-open, pale blue eyes. Andrew embraced him tightly, wrapping his arms around Anders' warm but limp body. He sobbed on his dead friend's shoulder. Time stood still for a few minutes. Andrew was oblivious to the danger and turmoil around him.

'No, Anders, no, not now. You and I were meant to survive this war together,' he softly whispered in his ear.

Dewar had to prise Andrew away. 'We need to get out of here before we're hit. I'll get a mortar crew to blast at the farmhouse.'

They each grabbed a leg of their dead companion and dragged Anders back behind the beech hedge again.

'Stretcher-bearers will find him soon enough and take him back to be buried,' reassured Dewar. Andrew slumped to his knees, still weeping. He stared at his blood-soaked hands, and in that moment, Corporal Andrew McDowall of the 29th Vancouver Battalion, 2nd Canadian Division, became young Andrew McDowall, running home to his mother's house with a basket of wild fruit, his hands covered in red berry juice.

*

Andrew was not the only one with blood on his hands. Kathleen had remarked to Mary that she was up to her elbows in it, frantically trying to cope with the wounded from both sides, at the casualty clearing camp. They were well used to the rushes at Royaumont, but there everything was done with order, discipline, and precision. Now, so close to the front line, the approach was distinctly more haphazard. It wasn't that the field hospital was badly organised, but rather that the sheer volume of casualties stretched staff and resources to breaking point. A sharp blast of a bugle sent everyone scurrying to 'fall in' for the next batch of wounded, fresh from the front. Sister and the senior surgeon on duty made a quick decision about who would be treated first, irrespective of the side on which they had fought. They used the Medical Corps triage system to identify the slightly injured, those requiring further hospital treatment, and finally the group beyond help. The soldiers lay on long lines of stretchers. Kathleen and Mary worked their way down the rows as quickly as they could, searching for a pulse in the worst cases and handing out cigarettes to the most desperate. At Royaumont Kathleen had rarely witnessed shell-shocked casualties, as they were treated at a specialist hospital. Here near the front she found it a disconcerting experience. She attempted to console a young English soldier who was violently shivering and shaking. When he tried to reply to her all he could manage was an indecipherable stammer. She pleaded with him to calm down, almost crying herself, his vacant eyes staring straight through her. At night he lay strapped to a bed, screaming and shouting until eventually the reluctant sister gave him an injection of scarce morphia. Kathleen guiltily admitted to herself that she had never been so relieved to see a patient leave when the young man was taken away in a special asylum ambulance. She vaguely remembered her father telling her of an uncle who had to be taken to the asylum in Dumfries. She was never allowed to visit him, and he was never mentioned again by the family. She thought now she understood why.

In the emergency surgery tent, broken limbs, shrapnel wounds, and gas victims were dealt with. Most days Kathleen found herself in the amputation tent. She held limbs steady as the surgeon sawed through sinew and bone, blood splashing in all directions. She became almost immune to the pained cries and groans of the soldiers, rarely having time to comfort them before they had to attend to the next casualty. The operations continued incessantly for almost a week, the nurses working eighteen hours at a time, to the point of complete exhaustion.

'Kathleen, didn't you hear the bugle call? There is another batch of wounded on the way,' said Mary, shaking her friend's arm.

Kathleen stirred from a deep sleep, nursing a fuzzy head.

'Oh, I've just had the most wonderful dream!' she croaked between dry lips. 'It was before the war. I was singing in the local hall back home. My parents were there, all my four brothers, Andrew and Thomas too, I think. Everyone was on their feet, applauding me to the rafters. It was wonderful, Mary, and I was wearing my finest frock.'

'That's all well and good, Kathleen, but splash your face with water and let's go.'

She flopped out of her camp bed and straightened the uniform she had slept in the previous night. Deciding she was presentable enough in the circumstances, she ran towards Mary, who was already making her way to the edge of the camp with the other nurses to meet the incoming ambulances.

'Gas cases today, Nurses,' warned Sister. 'This will be far from pleasant, but we must do our best for these poor creatures.'

Together Kathleen and Mary helped a blue-faced casualty from the ambulance and gingerly walked him towards a tent. With each painful step, he struggled for breath. They tried to reassure and encourage him with comforting words. He could only rasp in reply. They propped him up on a stretcher with a sandbag for a pillow, and returned to help the next victim. There were more than thirty gas patients, all suffering from acute bronchitis brought on by exposure to phosgene gas. The severity of the cases depended on how quickly, or not, the soldiers had managed to put their gas masks on.

'This is awful, Mary, and no way to fight a war,' said an indignant Kathleen. She watched in horror as a young soldier, too far gone to be helped, coughed up green froth from his lungs, his eyes fixed in terror straight at her.

'There is nothing we can do for him now,' said Mary, who closed the soldier's eyelids and washed the froth from around his mouth with a handkerchief.

Those who could be saved were given fumes of ammonia and oxygen.

'These lads will need plenty of bed rest before they are fit for the front again,' advised Sister.

'That is the only thing I'm jealous about,' quipped Mary. 'I would love to be in bed for a month.'

'I'd settle for a good eight hours at the moment,' replied Kathleen.

At the end of their long and traumatic shift, the two nurses wearily trudged towards their tent.

A blinding flash of light and a whooshing roar took them completely by surprise. They felt wind rush through their hair. To their left they saw flames rising from a hospital tent and heard cries and screams from the occupants. A stray German shell had made a direct hit. They ran towards the tent instinctively, hoping to help in any way they could. Half of it was engulfed in flames, and patients scrambled to get out the other end. Fire buckets were brought up to douse the flames but were too late to contain the blaze. In the flickering light of the fire, Sister was attempting a roll call. At least seven patients were unaccounted for. In the mayhem a shell-shocked patient was screaming at the top of his voice. He marched purposefully towards Kathleen and Mary, shouting obscenities at them.

'Oh Lord, we will have to calm this poor man down, Mary. I'm not sure what to do for the best.'

As Kathleen raised her hands in an appeasing manner the soldier lunged at her, spun her round, and grabbed her fiercely around the neck with one arm. She choked and struggled to free herself. With his other arm, he produced a bread knife from his jacket and held it against her face.

'Get him off, get him off!' screamed Kathleen.

'Don't move or I will kill you, you German bitch,' roared the soldier.

By now several other nurses and two auxiliaries were at the scene but were unsure what to do next.

Mary had gathered her composure and tried to reason with the disturbed man.

'You have my friend, Kathleen. We are Scottish nurses, not Germans. We mean you no harm, young man; we are here to help you. Please let her go.'

'Shut up,' he replied. 'Shut up. You are lying.'

Mary responded quickly. 'But we are speaking English to you, so we can't be German, can we?'

That seemed to strike a chord with him, and momentarily he paused and lowered the knife from Kathleen's throat. Remembering a women's lecture she had attended on how to deal with overzealous policemen,

Kathleen simultaneously fired her heel back into his shin and stuck a sharp elbow into his ribcage. As he recoiled in pain and dropped the knife, the onlooking nurses swamped on top of him to restrain him.

Kathleen and Mary stood staring at each other and then burst into a fit of nervous laughter.

'You should get a Victoria Cross for that, Kathleen,' joked Mary.

'More likely to be struck off,' she replied.

'I think we need a hot cup of disgusting tea now.'

As they drank the, for once welcoming, beverage, they complimented each other on how brave they had been in the circumstances.

'But you know what, Mary? After the week and day we had today, I wouldn't have cared if he had done for me.'

SEVENTEEN
TRIAL

T am blinked and took a deep breath. The apparition remained motionless. The only movement came from the candle in her hand, which cast an animated shadow on the cellar walls. Tam straightened himself up, drew his hand through his unkempt hair, and tried to make sense of his surroundings. On the floor in the corner lay a bundle of bedding and clothes. He thought he detected something moving there, but thought that it may have been the flickering candle playing tricks with his eyes. He focused on the figure standing directly opposite him. He could see she was a youngish woman, around twenty-five to thirty years old. She wore a full-length white nightgown with a blue woollen shawl draped over her slim shoulders. She had medium-length straight black hair.

Tam took a few slow steps towards her. She turned her face, cowering against the wall, but held out an outstretched arm, wielding a butcher's knife. Tam stopped in his tracks, raising his hands submissively. He attempted to make himself understood.

'No, no, *mademoiselle*, I mean you no harm, eh…*je suis écossais*. Put the knife down, please, everything will be fine.' He smiled weakly.

She stared intently at him. '*Allemande. Allemande*?' she accused.

'No, no, I'm not the Boche; my name is Tam,' he replied.

Realising she did not understand, he tried again.

'I'm called Thomas, you know, Tommy.'

The slightest of smiles flickered across her face.

'Ah! *Anglais*,' she said, relaxing a little. She lowered her arm, motioning to him to sit down on a wooden stool by her side. He was struck by her beautiful green eyes as she sat down next to him on an upturned crate. He also noticed that she had been crying heavily; lines of tear tracks ran down her cheeks. She pointed to herself, saying, '*Je suis Lisette*.'

They spoke to each other in broken English and French for nearly an hour, although Tam could understand very little of what she said. From a canvas bag she produced a photograph of a dashing young French soldier in full dress uniform.

'*Mon mari*.' She pointed and then shrugged her shoulders, which Tam took to mean she didn't know where he was, or what might have happened to her husband. She began to cry again and, for some reason he could not explain to himself, Tam began to cry too. The pair sat sobbing for the best part of half an hour, when Tam was startled to hear a high-pitched wail rise above his own spluttering. Lisette jumped to her feet, dusted herself down, and from the pile of bedding lifted her crying infant son. She shushed and consoled the child before putting him to her breast. Tam looked on in bemusement before turning his head until the child finished suckling.

'*Bonne nuit, petit Pierre,*' she said, returning the sleepy and content child to his bed of blankets.

She lay down beside the child and indicated to Tam that he too should get some rest.

Tam had a long and deep sleep. When he awoke, he was surprised to find himself lying next to Lisette and Pierre, given he had fallen asleep at the opposite end of the cellar to them. He was grateful for her body heat, though, and guessed they must have huddled together for warmth as the early spring temperature plummeted overnight. The intense, gnawing feeling in his stomach reminded him how hungry he was. He had shared the few dry biscuits in his pocket with Lisette the previous day. He stood up and surveyed the cellar in the dim daylight. Other than the makeshift chairs and bedding, there was precious little else in the room, bar a metal coffee pot. There was no obvious sign of food. An hour later Lisette stirred to feed her son again.

When she finished, she used signs to let Tam know she would go out to look for food. Once she was satisfied that he understood, she handed a dumbstruck Tam a gurgling Pierre to look after while she was gone. Tam held the child at arm's length for a while, which Pierre found amusing, judging by his smiles and laughter. Tam instinctively laughed back at him but was less amused when the child burped milk over his uniform.

'Oh shit,' he said loudly, causing the infant to cry.

'Damn – what do I do now?' he asked himself.

He started to pace up and down the cellar with the child tucked into his chest. As that seemed to make little difference, he sang a Scottish lullaby:

'Ally bally, ally bally bee,

Sittin' on yer mammy's knee.

Waitin' for a wee bawbee,

Tae buy mair Coulter's candy.

Poor wee Pierre's lookin' awfy thin

A bag o' bones covered ower wi' skin

Soon he'll be gettin' a wee double chin,

Fae sookin' Coulter's candy.'

Lisette had stopped at the top of the cellar stairs to listen, and she smiled broadly at Tam's efforts to pacify her boy.

'*Très bien, très bien*,' she said approvingly, as she lay the spoils of her scavenging on the ground. She had found a stale loaf of bread, a tin of prunes, and best of all a packet of coffee from the rubble of what had once been a local shop. Tam looked on hungrily, licking his lips. She took Pierre from him, saying, '*Merci*, Tommy,' and laid him down to sleep. She gathered the food together and skipped up the stairs. '*Allez*, Tommy, *allez*.'

He emerged into the bright sunlight, blinking his eyes. Lisette pointed to the empty hearth in the corner of the ruined house. It didn't take him long to understand she wanted him to collect firewood. He returned in a short while with two wooden crates, which he smashed with the heel of his boot. When the fire lit, Lisette put the pot of coffee on to boil. They munched on the stale bread and warmed their hands by the fire as they waited on the coffee to brew. Tam used a knife to stab open the tin of prunes and they scoffed them greedily. The strong bitter coffee was the perfect complement to the sickly-sweet tinned fruit.

The village, or more exactly what was left of it, was almost deserted now. The Allies had pushed the front a mile or so to the north. A few older folks shuffled along the ruined streets, searching for whatever scraps of food they could find. There was a stench of decay in the air coming from the damaged sewers. A swarm of rats scurried from one side of the street to the other. In the distance, the continuous rumble of thunder indicated the ongoing artillery bombardment. By the time they had drained the last drops of coffee from their chipped china cups, the noise had become louder and nearer. A shell flashed and burst about five hundred yards along the road, showering splinters in every direction. They quickly made for the shelter of the cellar again. Lisette lifted a bawling Pierre to her chest, and the three cowered together in the far corner. Tam was shaking uncontrollably again. A near hit rattled the floor above them and released a thick cloud of dust into the cellar.

'*Mon Dieu!*' coughed Lisette. She quickly wiped the dust which had settled on her baby's face and clothes. She looked up at Tam, and he at her. He burst into fits of laughter. He thought she looked so comical, covered as she was in dust from head to foot. It took him a second or two to realise he must look the same. Lisette's giggles were a clear indication that indeed he did. At least he had stopped shaking. They did their best to clear the dust from each other. Tam enjoyed the feel of her hands as she gently brushed his shoulders, back, chest, arms, and legs. They sat together quietly until the bombardment was over. The time passed quickly enough as they continued their clumsy communication with each other. He gathered her parents had owned the local bakery, but fled as the Germans approached the village. Lisette had decided to stay to look after the shop and take her chances, hoping the enemy would show humanity towards her and her infant child. When the Allied counter-attack shelled the area, she took refuge in the cellar where Tam had discovered her.

By late afternoon it was Tam's turn to leave the cellar to search for food. He headed along the main street, stumbling over bits of fallen masonry. He passed a couple of corpses lying by the road, one a civilian and the other in a German uniform. A larger, whitewashed house, which was still in reasonable condition, caught his eye. He turned the brass handle on the door and it opened easily. It became clear that the Germans must have used it as a temporary headquarters. A German flag was pinned to the far wall and the large dining room table had been moved to make a desk for the commander. Military papers littered the floor, but Tam didn't pay them any mind. The adjoining kitchen was completely devoid of food, much to his disappointment, but he did help himself to a couple of copper pots which he thought Lisette might find useful. At the far end of the long kitchen there was a pantry door. *Oh well. Nothing ventured...* Tam thought to himself.

He tried opening the door, but it was locked fast. He put his shoulder to the door several times, optimistically thinking it had begun to weaken. Three sharp kicks to the lock had more success. With his fourth kick, the pantry door burst open noisily. It was still surprisingly well stocked.

'Oh yes, oh yes, oh yes,' he shouted to himself. 'Dinner is served.'

'This is the best dream I have ever had,' he said, as he grabbed two tins of sausages, a large bag of rice and two bottles of fine red wine.

'Just wait until Lisette sees what I've found. She will be so pleased, and it'll help her feed the bairn.'

He carefully closed the pantry door, intending to come back for more pilfering in the coming days. Lisette was indeed pleased, clapping her hands as she exclaimed, '*Très bien*, Tommy, *très bien!*' She gave him a peck on the cheek, causing Tam to blush from head to foot. He hastily went upstairs to cook the food on the open fire, stirring all the ingredients together in an old copper pan, impatiently waiting for the food to heat through. When he finally thought it ready, he pulled his sleeve down over his hand and lifted the pan from the fire. He triumphantly marched down the stairs holding the feast aloft, at one point tripping on a step, causing Lisette to let out a screech of mock horror. He set the pan between them and they used their hands to scoop the food into their mouths. Tam fetched one of the bottles of wine and pushed the cork down into the neck of the bottle with his knife, spilling some on his hand, and licked it.

'Aye, no bad at all,' he said, taking a large swig from the bottle, before wiping the top and presenting the bottle to Lisette. She took a sip and returned the bottle to Tam. When the meal and wine were finished, Lisette fed Pierre, and then settled him for the evening.

Tam was feeling quite merry, so decided it would be an excellent idea to open the second bottle of wine. 'I think it's time for a wee song, lassie. But don't worry; I'll be quiet and no' waken the bairn.' Before Lisette had a chance to understand what he meant, Tam had cleared his throat and given a hushed but passable rendition of his regimental marching song, 'Blue Bonnets O'er the Border'.

Taking another slug from the bottle, he encouraged Lisette. 'It's your turn now.'

Shaking her head at first, but not wanting to disappoint Tam, she sang 'Joli Tambour' while marching around the cellar, much to Tam's delight. The second wine bottle was almost finished when Tam remembered he had also helped himself to a fat cigar, which he had come across in a desk drawer. He unwrapped it carefully from its greaseproof paper-cover, and climbed upstairs to light it on the embers of the fire. It was dark outside, apart from the odd Very light, which lit up in the distance. He puffed on the cigar, inhaling a satisfying lungful of smoke.

'What a great day it's been, just grand,' he thought to himself. 'Lisette is such a lovely girl, even if she is married. Who knows, maybe her man is dead? I think she thinks he is,' he reasoned with himself. His wine-fuelled amorous thoughts got the better of him, and he decided he would chance his arm with Lisette. He need not have bothered.

By the time he had finished the cigar, she was fast asleep. Tam drained the last of the wine and lay down beside her. He smiled ruefully to himself, thinking: *Somebody up there doesn't like me. I missed my stop to see Anne when I was on a promise, the lass in the brothel was so sad I felt sorry for her, and now Lisette is sound asleep. I'll likely die a virgin.* He leaned over and gave Lisette a peck on the cheek. Within five minutes, he too was asleep.

He awoke the following morning with a pounding hangover and a racing heartbeat, shaking in panic.

'Oh Christ, what the fuck am I doing here?' he asked himself, springing to his feet. 'I should be back with the lads; I better get moving.' To add to his confusion there was no sign of Lisette or her child. 'This is far from clever,' he said to himself. He pulled on his army tunic and boots and rushed towards the cellar stairs. He could hear muffled voices, so stopped to make out what was being said and by whom. He could detect Lisette's voice and at least one male voice, possibly two. He thought they were speaking in English, but with German accents. Alarmed at the thought that Lisette might be captured by the Germans, he decided to brave it and burst open the cellar door, kitchen knife in hand. Lisette and a South African Military policeman turned around in astonishment. Before Tam could do anything else, a second policeman, who had been searching through the ruins, drew his truncheon and whacked Tam over the head from behind.

When he came round, Tam was lying on the ground with his hands handcuffed behind his back.

'On your feet, boy, you useless bit of shit,' a voice growled at him.

For a second Tam thought he was back at Étaples, on the training ground with the sadistic sergeant. Groggily he looked around him. The two tall military policemen were standing opposite him, arms crossed. Lisette was sitting next to them, cradling Pierre close to her chest.

'What's your name, boy?'

'Thomas Murdoch, sir.'

'And your regiment?'

'Kings Own, sir.'

'So, Thomas Murdoch of the King's Own, can you tell me why you are shirking back here with this French whore, when you should be up the line?'

'She is no whore, sir. Leave her out of it.'

One policeman stepped forward and belted Tam across the stomach with his truncheon.

He fell to the ground in agony.

'We give the orders here, sonny, and we can do whatever the fuck we like. Explain yourself.'

Tam breathlessly rose to his feet again. 'I don't know exactly, sir. I was in a battle… must have got lost. Ended up here. I was only looking after them until I got back. I was heading back today, until you arrived…'

'Not bloody likely, boy. If I had a shilling for every time I'd heard that tale, I wouldn't need my army pension.'

'You're coming with us.'

And at that, the two MPs grabbed Tam by the arms and frogmarched him to a waiting truck further down the road, leaving a despairing Lisette behind. Tam could hear Pierre wailing as he was bundled into the lorry. A short journey took them back to a local British Army headquarters, but in that time, Tam learned the South Africans had taken over that section of the front, and the MPs were on patrol looking for looters.

'Just my bloody luck,' thought Tam.

The South Africans swiftly handed him over to a sergeant major and two guards from his own regiment. The officer looked at Tam with a mixture of disgust and pity.

'Bad enough you were picked up by another regiment, but did it have to be those smug Colonial bastards? This won't end well for you, son.'

'It's no' starting very well either,' Tam replied.

'Oh right, you're a joker as well as a shirker. I've got just the place for you to laugh your head off.'

They were back at brigade headquarters, about a mile behind the front line. Mainly the army had commandeered civilian buildings, but there was also a number of purpose-built army constructions, mostly Nissan huts. Tam was escorted to a small wooden hut known as 'the cage.'

He had his handcuffs removed and was unceremoniously dumped inside. The door was banged shut and the bar slammed into place, imprisoning Tam in a stuffy, dark, confined space. Hours went by and no one came near. He could sense it was evening, but still there was no contact with the outside world. Tam had been alone, tired, and hungry before, roaming the Galloway hills in search of lost sheep. But this was so, so much worse. He was desolate.

Finally, the following morning, the door was unbolted and a soldier pushed in a tin plate with a slice of bread on it and a mug of lukewarm tea. He made no attempt to speak. Tam consumed his breakfast without enthusiasm or enjoyment. An hour later, the door opened again and in stepped a tall, thin bespectacled officer. Tam rose to his feet.

'At ease, soldier. I am Dr Alec Jones. It is my duty to decide if you are fit for trial or not. Do you understand, Private?'

'Yes, sir. Well, not sure, sir. What trial?'

'You do know that you are facing serious charges, don't you, Private Murdoch?'

'I know I am in a lot of trouble, sir, aye.'

'Well that's one way to put it, I suppose.'

The doctor cast a medical eye over Tam, who was in a highly dishevelled state. His crumpled uniform was filthy and lousy, his tousled sandy hair was in very bad need of a cut, and his stubbly chin required a shave. Tam had developed a stoop which made him look shorter. In the doctor's opinion, he looked every inch a soldier who had let himself go.

'Stick out your tongue, soldier,' ordered the doctor, examining his mouth. Apart from very bad breath and a broken tooth, he appeared in fair health. The rest of his physical examination confirmed that was the case. The trickier part of the doctor's assessment was to decide on Tam's mental health. He had noticed that Tam had shaken mildly during his visit, but that was not entirely unusual and could be a sign a soldier was merely 'windy' rather than something more serious. He asked Tam what he could remember about the last few days and how he had come to be arrested by the MPs. Tam didn't really give a plausible or coherent answer, but the doctor concluded that he was alert and fit enough to stand trial. He informed Tam of his conclusion, then took his leave.

Later the same day, the door to the cage was opened again, and Tam blinked towards the sunshine to see the figure of Captain Denis Wilson enter.

'Christ, I'm popular today,' Tam muttered to himself.

The captain spoke formally. 'Private Thomas Murdoch, of the 6th Battalion King's Own Scottish Borderers, it is my duty to inform you that a Field General court martial has been arranged for noon tomorrow. You have been charged with desertion on active duty. You will, of course, enter a plea of not guilty. I am prepared to be your defending officer, if you so wish.'

Tam took his time to consider what he had been told by the captain.

'I don't think I've been too well, sir. I don't remember too much. I know a lot of the lads were killed and that spooked me. What will they do to me, sir?'

Captain Wilson cleared his throat. 'These charges carry the maximum sentence, but I'm sure we will get it commuted to imprisonment. You had a very good record up until now, Murdoch.'

Tam was finding it difficult to take in all the captain's information. The first thing that crossed his mind was why had he not stayed at home on the Major's estate when he had the chance? He also remembered his radical cousin from Glasgow advising him to never trust a judge or lawyer. They weren't the 'workers' friends', or something like that.

Wilson could see that Tam was losing concentration.

'I need to know now if you want me to be your defending officer. The court calls me the 'Prisoner's Friend.' I don't have much time left to prepare your case.'

The captain's comments did not chime right with Tam.

'If it's all right with you, sir, I think I'll defend myself. After all, is that no what us soldiers are supposed to be good at?'

'As you wish, Murdoch,' replied Wilson, turning in disappointment and locking the door behind him.

The following day, before noon, Tam's guards arrived to escort him to the courtroom. They brusquely ordered him to his feet, instructing him to remove his belt.

'Don't bother with your hat; you're not allowed that either.'

Tam cut a pathetic figure in his tawdry uniform, head bowed, flanked by two tall, upright soldiers in immaculate uniforms, rifles at their side. He was quick-marched into the courtroom and ordered to halt at attention. The courtroom was a requisitioned office of a small French stationery business. At one end sat three officers behind a long writing desk. An officer-lawyer from the Judge Advocates branch was seated to their left, with a volume of the *Manual of Military Law* open on his table. Few officers, prosecuting or defending, were well-versed in legal procedure, so his role was to advise his fellow officers on the fine details of military law.

Tam recognised the officer in the middle as a major, from the crown insignia on his uniform. He informed Tam that he was the President of the Court Martial, then turned to a lieutenant on his right and asked him to read out the charges against Tam.

'I notice you have declined the offer of a defending officer, so when I ask you how you plead against these charges, you should say, "Not Guilty". Do you understand?'

Slightly bewildered, Tam did as he was told. He was following standard procedure for a soldier charged with a serious offence.

Tam was then asked to give the case for his defence. He stuttered through the next five minutes, trying to explain the impact of witnessing the terrible death of his friends, the frightful noise of the battle, and how it had shattered his nerves. He also admitted to memory loss and blackouts in the days between the battle and his arrest. The Major was not impressed by his story. Wearily, he asked Tam, 'Do you know, that of the last *twelve* discipline cases I have had the misfortune to deal with, every single one claimed to be shell-shocked when they deserted their post? And further, each and every one of them was a lying maligner! Why should I believe you, Private Murdoch?'

'Because I'm telling the truth, sir.'

The officer turned his attention to Tam's army record, poring over the details.

'I see you served at Gallipoli and were wounded; cited for bravery too. Was it a serious wound?'

'No, sir, not really,' replied Tam, naively.

'But you were invalided home, were you not?' persisted the puzzled Major.

'Aye, but that was the army's mistake, sir,' replied Tam.

At that point the lieutenant interjected. 'Hmm. I served at Gallipoli too, and it was chaotic at times, not to put too fine a point on it. However, some wounded men took advantage and wangled their way home. It wouldn't surprise me if Murdoch was one of them.'

The Major nodded and said, 'Thank you, Lieutenant Marshall,' before addressing Tam again.

'You were relieved from Army service for a time, I see. Had you had enough?'

'Maybe at the time, sir,' admitted Tam, 'but I did volunteer to come back later.'

The lieutenant, who Tam had sensed had taken an instant dislike to him, interrupted again.

'I believe there was a police charge against him back home for assaulting a police constable. He was mixed up with those damned Bolsheviks. Would it be too much to suggest he joined up again to avoid prison?'

Tam shook his head vigorously, but the comments had sowed a seed of doubt in the other officers' minds. Finally, the major brought proceedings to a temporary halt.

'I think we have heard all we need to hear for now. Escorts, take the prisoner outside while we deliberate on the case. Private Murdoch, you will be recalled to hear our verdict in due course. Dismissed!'

The trio of officers discussed Tam's case in his absence.

'An unusual case indeed,' began the Major. 'We have no witnesses from the time of his desertion, as they were all killed or wounded.'

'I'm not in the least convinced it was shell shock. I could accept he might retreat when his unit was wiped out, but it was days later when he was found miles from the front,' argued the lieutenant.

'Besides, the Military Police report said they had found wine bottles and cigar stubs where they arrested him, so probably guilty of looting, too.'

'My take on him,' commented the captain, 'is this: here is a soldier who served in the Territorials. He knew what he was getting into. Lucky escape at Gallipoli, then enjoyed the good life at home. Who knows why he returned? Probably in trouble back home. First time under fire again, he gets 'windy' and bolts. Meets the *mademoiselle* and decides he prefers her to the front line.'

'I think that just about sums it up, Captain, thank you,' agreed the major. 'So, gentlemen, have we decided Private Murdoch is guilty as charged of desertion while on active duty?'

They nodded in accordance.

'If I could make a point now, Major?' asked the officer-lawyer. 'In fact, if I may read from a recent War Office instruction,' he said, putting on a pair of horn-rimmed spectacles. 'Desertion during active service is one of the most serious crimes a soldier can commit, a fact which does not appear to be everywhere sufficiently appreciated by the officers, who as presidents and members of courts martial have to deal with this offence. Sentences in not a few cases have been exceedingly lenient.'

'That is a pretty clear message,' conceded the Major, 'and I think we all know what it means for this present case. Captain, can you fetch the prisoner for sentencing?'

Tam was brought before the court martial again and ordered to stand to attention once more.

The Major began:

'Private Thomas Murdoch, of the King's Own Scottish Borderers, you have been found guilty of the capital offence of desertion while on active duty. Private Murdoch, you may now make a statement of mitigation of punishment to the court.'

Tam's head was spinning from lack of sleep. He had not yet processed the verdict of the court. This much was clear from the bewildered look he gave the major.

'What have you to say for yourself, soldier? You are facing the death penalty for your crime. Why should we give you a lesser sentence?'

Tam stood in silence, his head bowed.

'Nothing at all to say, soldier?' prompted the lieutenant.

'I'm no coward, sir. I volunteered twice…was wounded…I can't explain what I did.'

His pathetic defence did nothing to encourage compassion from the officers.

'It is the decision of this court, subject to confirmation of sentence, that you will be executed by firing squad, two days hence at 06:00 hours.'

Tam, shaking, was led away by his escort, back to the cage. He collapsed to the ground, sobbing. The confirmation process began with Tam's commanding officer, Captain Wilson, writing his views on his record, discipline, and qualities as a soldier. He endeavoured to write a sympathetic report on Tam and recommended that his sentence be commuted to imprisonment. This, along with the court martial proceedings, was passed up the line to the Brigade commander, Brigadier General Stubbs, who was unimpressed with Tam's case and concerned about general discipline in his command. He concluded that the death sentence should be carried out. Finally, the commander in chief, Sir Douglas Haig, holding the power of Royal Warrant, confirmed the death sentence.

Captain Wilson had the unpleasant task of informing Tam of the army's decision.

Tam had assumed he would be shot anyway, so was nonplussed by the captain's news. Since his arrest by the military police he had descended into a fatalistic mood. He was more concerned about the information his family would receive about his death.

'Will my mother be told I was shot for desertion? I don't think I could bear that. Can't have her thinking I was a coward,' he asked, hesitantly. Wilson was quick to reassure him that he would personally write a letter to his mother stating simply that he was shot on duty, and how brave and popular a soldier he was with his comrades. With tears streaming from his eyes, Tam thanked the captain profusely.

'I will see to it that you get a bath, haircut, and shave today, Murdoch, and I'll find you a clean uniform if I can. The padre will visit you later.'

Tam saluted his officer. 'Sir. Thank you, sir.' Then, chancing his arm, he added, 'And if there is any rum going, that would be a great help, sir.'

Sighing at Tam, Wilson finished. 'I'll see what I can do, Private.'

The captain was as good as his word. That afternoon Tam enjoyed a lukewarm wash in a tin bath. A corporal barber cut his hair to a close crop and shaved him with a blunt open razor, leaving Tam's fledging moustache. He was then given a clean battle tunic and a regimental kilt of blue and green Leslie hunting tartan to wear.

Well, I'll be damned; I'll be the smartest soldier to be shot in the whole fucking British Army, he thought ruefully to himself.

The padre, an affable, short older man with a mop of grey hair, was Tam's last visitor to the cage. He carried a black leather-bound Bible in one hand and an army water bottle in the other.

He introduced himself as Chaplain Grey.

'Grey by name and grey by nature,' he joked, attempting to lighten the seriousness of his visit.

Tam replied with a formal 'Good evening, sir.'

'We both know that your time on this earth is drawing to a close, so I would like to pray with you for God's forgiveness and mercy, my boy. A better world awaits you after this one. You can confess anything you like to me now. It will be good for your soul and you will go in peace.'

Tam knew the padre was being sincere, so let him finish his spiel.

'I don't mean to be insubordinate, sir, but I have never believed all the heaven and hell stuff. Even over these last few days, when I've had plenty of time to think to myself, I'm still not having it. Don't get me wrong, I've seen plenty of lads get comfort from reading their Bible, or fingering their rosary beads, but it doesn't mean anything to me. But

I would be pleased if you would stay with me for a while, just so long as we don't talk religion, that's all.'

The padre smiled at him. 'Thank you for being honest with me, Thomas. The good Lord did say to visit the prisoner, so that's what I'm doing. I don't think I could face what you are tomorrow without my faith in God. You are a brave young man, in your own way.'

'I don't really have a choice about tomorrow now, do I, sir?'

'I concede that is true. However, we can chat for a while, Thomas, if it's what you want.'

'Thank you, sir, but just call me Tam. Only my mother calls me Thomas.'

'Very well, Tam, but you must call me Henry.'

Tam laughed loudly.

'I didn't realise my name was so amusing,' said the perplexed padre.

'Oh sorry, sir. It's just that I could never imagine the stiff shirts I had as ministers back home ever saying that to me.'

Grey smiled again, relieved he was not the centre of fun. 'Well, this war has changed a lot of things, Tam.'

They spent the next two hours chatting about their lives. Tam discovered Grey had served as a minister in a small village in the south of England, but volunteered to serve as soon as war broke out. He was torn between either staying at home with his young wife and two small daughters or serving his God, king, and country. Tam said that he thought the padre had made a brave decision and remarked that he would have liked to have become a father someday himself. Lisette had said he was good at looking after her child.

Grey, too, had been at Gallipoli for a time, and they both agreed it was a disaster from start to finish. In turn, the chaplain was interested in Tam's experiences with the conscientious objectors and was very impressed with his decision to return to the front so his disabled comrade could get his job.

'Now, you say you are not a believer, Tam, but that was a very Christian thing you did for your friend.'

'It was nothing, really. But does that mean I get to go to Heaven, if there is one?' joked Tam.

'In my experience non-Christians are capable of very Christian acts, and sadly the opposite is also very true,' suggested the padre. 'Do you regret coming back to the army when you could have seen out the war safely at home?'

'No, not really. No point in thinking about that now, is there? But tell you what I do regret, and I don't want to shock you, but I never got a chance to, you know, do it with a girl. Came close a few times, mind you. I've thought about that a lot recently and it makes me fucking sad,' he replied, clenching his fists tightly.

The padre took no offence whatsoever, but seeing Tam was becoming agitated, decided it would be best to bring their conversation to an end. A man in Tam's predicament needed to be alone with himself and his thoughts.

'Will you join me in saying the Lord's Prayer before I leave, Tam?' he asked.

'I don't suppose it could do any harm now, Henry, could it?' Tam smiled, and just for a second an impish gleam returned to his vacant eyes. They bowed their heads and recited the prayer quietly.

As the chaplain rose to leave, he hesitated. 'Oh, I almost forgot.' He handed Tam the water bottle. 'Captain Wilson asked me to give this to you.'

'Thank you, sir. That was good of him.'

As soon as Grey left, Tam eagerly unscrewed the cap, and held the bottle to his nose. The rich, sweet smell of dark rum confirmed Tam's hopes. He took a mighty swig and held the bottle high saying, 'Cheers to you, Captain Wilson, an officer, a gentleman, and a man of his word.'

After several more mouthfuls, Tam entertained himself by singing a few of his favourite marching songs. Tiring badly, he was halfway through 'Keep the Home Fires Burning' when he fell into a deep sleep. Captain Wilson had asked an army doctor to put a couple of doses of morphia into Tam's last drink.

EIGHTEEN
AFTERMATH

ndrew wakened in a panic. He was in total darkness. His eyes were burning as if they were on fire and his eyelids felt as if they had been cemented closed. He lifted his hands to his face, only to discover they were both heavily bandaged. The strong smell of disinfectant suggested he may well be in a hospital, but the air in his lungs felt fresh and outdoorsy. He heard footsteps approach his bed, then was startled by a strangely familiar voice saying, 'Everything will be fine, Andrew. I'm here to take the very best care of you. Please be still.' He felt the sensation of lukewarm water gently press against his eyes and drops of the cooling liquid trickled down his cheeks.

'I'll do that one more time, and then I want you to open your eyes if you can. It will be very painful, I warn you.'

Andrew attempted to do what he was told. His left eye opened slightly, but it felt as though shards of glass on the inside of his eyelid were scraping his eyeball. His fingertips within the bandages curled inwards as he tried to brace himself against the pain. For a split second he could see the blurry image of a red-haired nurse.

'Don't worry, Andrew. I'll be back in an hour to try again. Just try to rest for now,' she said.

In his semi-conscious state, a sudden wave of relief shot through Andrew's body.

'Oh, thank God, thank God,' he thought. 'I'm dreaming of Kathleen; all those awful things were just a horrible nightmare. What a relief.' Despite the acute pain, his mind was at rest, allowing him to drift off to sleep.

Half-awake again, he could feel the dabbing of water on his inflamed eyes once more. A second attempt to open his eyes was just as excruciatingly painful, although this time both eyelids lifted briefly. Seeing Kathleen's blurry silhouette brought home to Andrew the sickening realisation that he had not been dreaming after all. So, the last few days had indeed been a nightmare, but one of brutal reality. He pieced together the awful events in a haphazard way. He remembered being at a grave and smelling the whiff of horseradish, the telltale sign of a mustard gas attack. Then nothing more, until his presence in the field hospital where, for some inexplicable reason, Kathleen Marr was nursing him. His mind drifted back further in time as he agonised over the death of his friend Anders, and the rage and fury he had felt holding the dead body in his arms. Then the furious scramble which followed to avoid the deadly German sniper, who claimed another victim by shooting Sergeant Dewar in the back. He recalled making it back to the newly dug

Canadian front-line trenches, exhausted and emotionally drained. He reported the events to his company captain, who confirmed the death of Sergeant Dewar from other reports. The deaths of a dear, close friend and a sergeant he respected and trusted, in the space of a few hours, was hard to bear. He had barely had time to take it all in when he was taken aback by his captain's decision to immediately promote him to the rank of sergeant, and put him in charge of a makeshift platoon made up of the survivors from different units. He only knew a few of his new unit and found it difficult to process the names of individual soldiers who were unfamiliar to him. He wasn't even sure if there was an experienced corporal in the unit he could rely on.

There was no time to consider his promotion, as he was immediately ordered to round up a dozen men for firing squad duty. He was given scant information, other than the fact that the deserter was from a Scottish regiment close by. He remembered thinking, 'I've lost two good men and friends today, and some weak cowardly bastard has scarpered and deserted his comrades, so he's going to get what's coming to him.' He could feel a rage building within him, and even now, lying invalided in his hospital bed, he sensed the veins in his forehead begin to bulge.

His train of thought was interrupted by the sound of a new voice; a lilting Highland voice, if he was not mistaken.

'It's my turn to bathe your eyes, Andrew. It should get easier for you every time we do it. I am Nurse Mary McLeod; Kathleen has told me all about you.' Then, to try and cheer him up, she added, 'Kathleen talks about you a lot and she often wondered what became of you. Isn't it remarkable that you have ended up here together? Maybe it's fate, do you think? She said you were handsome, but you're not looking too bonny at the moment, are you? Never mind, we'll have you as right as rain in no time. The doctor will be doing his rounds soon, so you just rest until then.'

Andrew tried to reply but a fearful pain shooting through his mouth, like chewing on barbed wire, stopped him dead.

'Oh God,' he thought to himself. 'Is there any part of my body which isn't in agony? This must be God's way of punishing me for what has happened.'

A short while later the medic on duty, Dr Alexander, gave him a medical explanation for his extremely painful condition.

'You have been exposed to dichlorodiethyl sulphide, briefly, but long enough to cause severe blistering to your hands, face, and even tongue. You also have extreme conjunctivitis in your eyes, but with continued treatment this will clear completely. Your blistered tongue will also heal in time, but it will be far too painful to eat now, so I have arranged for the nurses to feed you by nasal gastric tube. With luck, that will only be necessary for a few days. Let's see how that goes,' he ended positively, before moving to his next patient.

The best that Andrew could manage was a weak nod to indicate he had understood the doctor's comments. 'So, I'm not permanently blind, that's something at least,' he thought. And the pains in the rest of his body now made sense.

'But I need be able to speak soon, or else how I can explain to Kathleen the dreadful thing that's happened?' His mind was back at Arras, the new sergeant in charge of his firing squad. A captain from the KOSBs spoke to him briefly. He was from the division raised in Dumfries, but there was no time for pleasantries or reminiscences. He led the men into the chalk tunnel and lined them up. They were issued with pre-loaded rifles, some with live ammunition, others with blanks. Andrew ordered his unit to line up opposite the wooden stake where the prisoner was being tied. He was already blindfolded; of average height, Andrew thought, shaven-headed and wearing a stubbly fair moustache. Someone had thought it appropriate to dress him in the regimental kilt. Just at that moment, one of his own men fainted and had to be led away. Something in Andrew snapped.

'For fuck's sake,' he bawled at the private, 'do I have to do everything myself?' He grabbed the soldier's rifle and took his place at the end of the line.

*

'It's time to feed you now, Andrew. I'm sorry,' said Kathleen apologetically as she approached his bed, holding a porcelain funnel and a length of rubber tubing. Mary was close behind, carrying a mug of beef tea. The nurses were thankful that Andrew could not see how nervous they were, as this was the first time they had carried out this procedure. Kathleen had read many accounts of how women campaigning for the vote had been brutally force-fed while on hunger strike in prison. She remembered being outraged, and telling her unsympathetic father that it was nothing more than a form of torture. She had never imagined that one day she would have to do something very similar to a patient. At least she hoped Andrew would cooperate, but the thought of causing anyone hurt, albeit for their own good, was not something Kathleen found easy. She lubricated the rubber hose with warm water, explaining to Andrew that she would need to insert it through his nostril, as his mouth was still so badly blistered. Andrew braced himself for the discomfort to come. As the tube inched its way down his nose and into his oesophagus, he felt the need to simultaneously sneeze, cough, and vomit. He almost passed out with the pain. He felt the strangest sensation in his stomach, as if it was on fire, followed by the sickly feeling of an over-full belly. Mary had very gingerly poured a pint of warm beef tea down the funnel. He retched several times when the tube was removed, but managed to keep down most of the nutritious liquid. This torturous procedure continued for a week, at which point the doctor decided Andrew's mouth had healed sufficiently for him to be fed with a spoon. The feel of the cool metal utensil on his tongue was the first pleasant sensation he had had since the gas attack. After another few days of mashed potatoes and milk, he was well enough to be on his feet to continue with the next part of his treatment.

Every morning a long truck rumbled into the field hospital, steam billowing from a capped chimney pot on its roof. This was a specially adapted lorry, complete with a hot water boiler and fold-down shower heads for use by the mustard gas patients. Soap and hot water were the most effective remedy available to treat the effects of the gas on human skin. The gas casualties trooped into the back of the truck in groups of six, stripped naked, and stood under the hot shower for five minutes. Initially, the water stung, but each day it became a little easier to bear. An orderly issued clean bedgowns to each man as he finished. Eventually, Andrew's bandages on his hands and arms were removed to allow the red-raw skin to heal. Talking became more of a discomfort than a trial, but he was advised to say only a few words at a time until he fully recovered. His conjunctivitis was also improving, although his eyes remained bloodshot and his sight blurry. Despite his physical improvement, Andrew did not feel any better within himself. He was plagued with thoughts of what had occurred before the gas attack and, more crucially, how he would ever be able to tell Kathleen what had happened.

He recalled his anger at the firing squad and in particular the soldier who had fainted. Lifting the fallen man's rifle, he stared down the barrel at the pathetic prisoner, feeling absolutely no pity for the man, and fired in unison with the rest of the squad. He tried very hard to recollect the exact moment he pulled the trigger. He was desperately attempting to remember if the shot felt like a live round or a blank. The extent of the recoil was usually the telltale sign, but at the actual moment he could not have cared less. Now, he convinced himself it must have been a blank, as the alternative was just too horrifying to consider. Frustratingly, chances to talk at any length to Kathleen were few and far between. All the nurses were incredibly busy, dealing with the constant flow of freshly wounded soldiers and patched-up discharges. He was into his third week at the hospital when he was told he would be fit to return to the front in another week or so. This news prompted a sense of urgency in him to confide in Kathleen. A part of him thought it might be better not to say anything and simply head back to the front, but he knew he could not live with himself if he were to do that. He was at least reassured that Kathleen had made a very good friend in Mary, whose cheery disposition and little jokes and quips brightened up the monotony of hospital routine. Two days before he was due to be released, and with the hospital relatively quiet, Kathleen arrived at his bedside with a mug of tea and some time on her hands.

'At last we have time for a proper talk, Andrew. You'll have noticed how awful this stuff is,' she said as she handed him a mug of hospital brew, 'but it's all we have, I'm afraid. And no china cups or scones either.' She smiled.

Andrew realised at once she was alluding to their last, rather more civil, cup of tea together, in the sitting room of her family house back in Creetown, before the war started. To both, it now seemed like a lifetime away. He sat up to take a good look at her. She appeared worn out, he thought, although her long red hair was still striking, and she had not lost the sparkle in her green eyes.

'I remember that last meeting well, Kathleen. I was so nervous about how you would react, but as usual you took everything in your usual calm way,' he said, before continuing. 'I expect you will go back to Creetown when the war is over?'

Kathleen replied that she probably would, although she wasn't entirely sure. She thought of telling Andrew that she had a new ambition to become a professional singer, but chose not to from fear he might think her silly. Instead, she answered:

'When your hands heal properly, you can get back to playing the fiddle again. I miss our singsongs together.'

'Yes, me too,' he replied, 'although I have not had much chance to practice recently, of course.'

He fondly remembered their times together, playing at local halls and listening to her wonderful voice. In his heart of hearts, however, he knew he had made the correct decision to emigrate to Canada.

'How are all your family, by the way?' he asked next. 'Do you hear from them at all?'

She then gave him the sad news about the death of her elder brother.

Genuinely saddened to hear this, and noticing how emotional Kathleen was becoming, Andrew now dreaded the topic of Tam coming up, as he did not want to upset her further. Fortunately for him, Kathleen asked him something entirely different.

'You know you will be released from here in a day or two, Andrew. How do you feel about going back to the front again? It always grieves me to see you young lads, who we have helped to recover from awful wounds, going back into that hell again.'

Andrew looked at her closely. 'To be honest, I would much rather stay here with you and Mary, and even the awful tea. But it's my duty, isn't it? I'll go back to the front like everyone else and just get on with it. At least we seem to be making some progress at last, and my lads will need me.'

Kathleen held his hand gently. 'Every year I pray that this will be the last year of the war, so I hope this one actually is. And what will you do, Andrew, after this wretched war is over? Will you go back to Canada?'

'I most certainly will, Kathleen. It's a wonderful country, if you can put up with the cold winters. There are so many opportunities out there for me, with new people arriving all the time. Vancouver is such an exciting place; I think you would like it, Kathleen. I was beginning to settle in nicely when the war broke out. I felt I had to join up, though, as there was great support for the war in Canada. If only we had known.'

'I know. None of us could have guessed what was in front of us when we volunteered,' agreed Kathleen. 'But I can sense your enthusiasm for your new country, Andrew. You really must return, then. Have you made many friends over there yet?'

'Yes, a few,' he replied, 'and I expect I'll keep in touch with the lads from my regiment when the war is finally over.'

Kathleen agreed again. 'I have made such a good friend in Mary; we keep each other going, you know. I'm sure we will be friends for life now.' She then took the conversation in the direction he was dreading.

'I saw Thomas back in 1915, just before I left for France. He had been wounded at Gallipoli and was back home recovering. He was the same old Thomas, cheery and joking all the time. He promised he would write to me. But you know what he's like, so I've not heard anything since.'

Andrew remembered that Kathleen was one of the few to refer to Tam by his full name. Her obvious affection for him was painful to witness.

'I don't expect you have heard anything about him either, have you, Andrew?'

The image of the executed soldier's identity tag flashed through his mind, bringing him out in a cold sweat. *Private Thomas Wallace Murdoch, Kings Own Scottish Borderers, Church of Scotland.*

Andrew took a gulp of tea, giving him a few seconds to compose himself, as his mind worked frantically to compose an answer. A distant droning sound distracted both of them at that very moment. Andrew had a puzzled look on his face. 'That doesn't sound like any artillery I have ever heard, and I don't think it's a tank, either.'

The sound was increasing to a loud throb, over which they struggled to hear each other.

'Could it be an aeroplane?' shouted Kathleen.

'Yes, I expect that's exactly what it is. Let's hope it's one of ours,' responded Andrew.

Unfortunately, it was a flight of three Gotha G.IV twin-engine bombers of the Imperial German Air Service. The first aircraft dropped a bomb, which hit a marquee tent full of wounded soldiers. Kathleen and Andrew saw a flash of light through the canvas and heard a loud crumpling noise. A few seconds later Mary flew into the tent and shouted at Kathleen: 'We're needed outside, quickly, hurry after me!' Kathleen did as she was told and ran out of the tent. The scene outside was one of mayhem. Flames were licking from the top of the stricken tent, lighting up the night sky, men trapped inside were screaming for help, and nurses and auxiliaries were frantically beating back the flames to rescue them.

Andrew was slower to make it outside, as he was still weak from so much bed rest. He surveyed the scene unfolding before him and realised that water was badly needed to douse the flames. In an instant he thought of the shower truck, parked close by. He rounded up a group of walking wounded, and using his new-found authority as a sergeant, ordered them to line up at the lorry. They drained the water boiler into buckets and formed a chain along to the burning tent, throwing bucket after bucket on the flames which they finally brought under control, saving around half of the marquee and, far more importantly, the patients trapped inside. Andrew and his makeshift fire brigade joined with Kathleen, Mary, and the other nurses to help the survivors to safety at the edge of the camp. For the first time in a while, he felt like he was doing something positive and helpful.

Meanwhile, the aircraft had made their first pass over the field hospital and nearby army base, but then banked and turned to make a second bombing run. On the ground, they could hear the dreaded noise of the heavy engines grow louder and louder. Everyone scattered for cover. Andrew fell to the ground and shouted to Kathleen and Mary to do the same. This time a stray bomb hit the nurses' compound, which consisted of a row of smaller tents. One took a direct hit and was blown sky-high into smithereens of canvas. The adjoining tents were set ablaze instantly. Kathleen was first on the scene to pull a badly burned nurse from a flaming tent. In the process her forearms were also burned, but with the adrenaline pumping through her veins, she hardly noticed. The others joined in to assist the stricken nurse to safety. She was weeping loudly, but also trying desperately to tell them something. Kathleen was first to realise she meant someone else must be still in the burning tent. Despite being told to remain where she was for her own safety, Kathleen ran towards the flames again, just as the last of the three aircraft was passing overhead to release its remaining bombs. The shock wave from the high explosive knocked her off her feet and sent her crashing onto the hard ground. She lay spreadeagled and still, face down on the ground. The others had instinctively ducked for cover, but as soon as the bomb had exploded, Andrew leapt to his feet and ran towards her, shouting, 'Kathleen, are you all right?'

He crouched down beside her and softly turned her over on her back. Her face and body were completely unmarked. Relieved, he tapped the side of her face gently and repeated, 'Kathleen, are you all right?' He turned towards Mary, who had arrived on the scene, saying, 'I think she's unconscious, Mary, knocked out by the bomb. I've seen it happen to soldiers a lot. Can you help, please?'

Without saying a word, Mary was already bent over Kathleen, listening and looking for any sign of breathing. She lifted her limp wrist searching for a pulse. Next, she put her hand on Kathleen's neck and whispered to herself,

'Come on, Kathleen my girl, don't do this to me. Please, God.' The next few minutes felt like hours. There were still nurses running here and there, helping other casualties. Everywhere there was frantic noise and movement, and in the midst of it all Kathleen lay silent, still and lifeless. With tears streaming down her face, Mary looked up at Andrew. She did not have to say anything to him. The look in her eyes was enough for Andrew to know. He bowed his head in his hands, shaking it backwards and forwards. 'In the name of all that is holy, will there be no end to this? Why the fuck did they have to bomb a hospital? And of all people, Kathleen …' At which point he fell to his knees, crying. Mary had composed herself again and put a hand on his shoulder, 'Come on, Andrew, let's get her body to a safe place away from the flames.'

'Of course, Mary, of course,' he replied, jolting himself into action. The need to do something, anything, overrode his emotions. He found a stretcher easily enough and, with the help of an auxiliary, carefully lifted Kathleen's body onto it. Mary, also working automatically, placed a hospital blanket over the body of her dear friend. They slowly walked away from the flames to a field on the edge of the camp. They sat together, holding hands but barely able to speak, so stunned were they by the suddenness of the evening's events.

By sunrise, all the flames were extinguished. The hospital now resembled a battlefield, and Sister was able to do a head count. She had made arrangements for the transfer of the wounded to other hospitals in the area. Sixteen patients had been killed and a further thirty were wounded. Two nurses, including Kathleen, were dead, and another four were wounded. Andrew and Mary had sat all night in the cold, damp field. consoling each other. A thoughtful auxiliary had brought them blankets and mugs of sweet, hot tea. Mary grimaced at the first sip and, quick as a flash, using humour to cope with her grief, turned to Andrew, saying, 'At least Kathleen will be spared drinking this horrid stuff.'

He sprayed out the mouthful he was about to drink, laughing and releasing his emotions. 'Only you could have thought of that, Mary.'

'Well, she did always see the funny side of things, Andrew. I hope you don't mind, but while you were dozing earlier, I took the liberty of looking in her uniform pockets before she was taken away. Look what I found.'

She handed Andrew two strong manila envelopes.

'Go on,' she said. 'Open them. I'm sure Kathleen would have wanted you to.'

Andrew nodded, cutting open the first sealed envelope. It contained a beautifully handwritten letter, in what he could tell was not Kathleen's handwriting.

'Oh, what is it, Andrew?' Mary asked impatiently.

He scanned the letter briefly. 'Well, it looks like a letter of introduction to a music hall in London, if I'm not mistaken. How very strange.'

'Oh, it's not strange at all, Andrew. One of the posh nurses at Royamount worked there before the war. She heard Kathleen sing and encouraged her to think about a career on the stage. It certainly appealed to Kathleen, poor thing,' explained Mary.

'Well I never,' Andrew responded.

He opened the second, unsealed, envelope. It contained a white silk handkerchief, which he unfolded carefully. Nestled in the middle of the material was a shiny silver cap badge of the King's Own Scottish Borderers. Soldiers called them sweetheart badges.

Giving a loud sigh, Andrew said, 'Oh, I think I know who gave her this.'

NINETEEN
REMEMBERING

A ndrew gripped tightly onto the armrests of the BOAC Boeing 377 Stratocruiser as it made its approach to land at Prestwick Airport. In the late evening sunshine, he could see the small island of Ailsa Craig from his seat window, and then the ploughed fields of the Ayrshire coast as the aircraft descended rapidly. He gave a sigh of relief as it completed a bumpy landing, waiting for the four large propeller engines to come to a halt before he and the other passengers could disembark.

'We're home, Andrew!' said a delighted John Halliday.

'And still in one piece,' replied a rueful Andrew.

The idea for this trip of a lifetime had been Halliday's from the beginning.

Andrew had survived the last year of the war; mainly on desk duty, because the mustard gas had affected his eyesight. He worked for the Canadian 'Khaki University', his teaching background making him the ideal choice to deliver education courses to his fellow soldiers. An office job made it easier for him to keep in touch with nurse Mary McLeod, who also continued to serve until the end of the war. They corresponded regularly by letter, frequently sharing their memories of Kathleen. Her writing style was as witty as her personality. To his slight surprise, at the start of 1919, as he waited impatiently back in England to be returned with his unit to Canada, he found himself writing a proposal of marriage to Mary. To his even greater surprise she had accepted, making some comment about how winters in Vancouver could not be any worse than in Inverness. They set up home in the Canadian city and had a very comfortable life together. Andrew became headteacher at a local elementary school, and Mary a sister in the nearby hospital. Mary was disappointed not to have had any children, but she knew from the start of their relationship that Andrew was not a particularly physical person. She loved him dearly and consoled herself with the comforts of her home, a large group of mainly Scots immigrant friends, and a lifestyle that would not have been possible back home.

A few years after the end of the war, Andrew had attended a meeting of the Vancouver branch of the Great War Veterans Association, a campaigning group for veterans' rights and welfare. As he sat drinking tea in the meeting hall, he heard a familiar inquisitive voice, which he was able to place immediately.

'It can't possibly be. Can it?' he thought to himself.

Turning round, he saw a slightly thinner, but larger than life, Private John Halliday.

'Good evening, Corporal McDowall. How are you?' said a beaming Halliday, somewhat formally.

'Well, I'll be damned; it really is you, Halliday. How the hell did you get here?' asked a puzzled Andrew.

'By tram, of course. I don't live far from here,' responded an equally puzzled Halliday.

Andrew laughed out loud. 'That's not what I meant, you clown. We all thought you were dead or had cleared off, that night you disappeared. What did happen to you then, John?'

'I'm still embarrassed about it now, Corporal. The Germans surprised me and knocked me out. Don't remember much after that until I was in a German dugout being questioned by an officer. Only gave them my name, rank, and number. Took a few beatings before they got fed up with me and sent me to a prison camp. By God, that last winter was hard. We were all starving. Put it this way, if I never see another turnip in my life again, then I'll die a happy man.'

His story made sense to Andrew and explained Halliday's thinner frame.

'Just one thing, Halliday. Will you stop calling me Corporal? Even though I was a sergeant by the end of the war, please just call me Andrew.'

'OK, Sarge.'

Andrew couldn't quite tell if Halliday's response was in jest or not.

*

The two veterans met regularly after that, at association meetings and on Remembrance Day parades. Halliday married a local Vancouver girl and they had three boys. He was obviously a very proud father and took delight in informing Andrew of their progress. In 1927, as the tenth anniversary of the Battles of Arras and Vimy Ridge approached, some of the veterans organised a trip to France to honour their fallen comrades.

'Do you think you would ever go back to the site of the battles?' Halliday asked Andrew. 'I would certainly like to do so someday,' he continued.

'Well, you should be safe enough from German soldiers capturing you this time, John,' Andrew joked, then added, 'I've never really given it much thought, to be honest.' Andrew had never been able to tell anyone, including Mary, what had happened to Tam. Nightmares about that fateful morning would torture him throughout his life.

By the thirtieth anniversary, in 1947, it felt too soon after the end of the Second World War to consider a trip to France. The two veterans had watched, aghast, as a new generation of Canadian soldiers went off to fight and die in Europe. Halliday was mightily relieved that his sons were too young to be conscripted. The years slipped by, and as the fortieth anniversary approached, Andrew realised it would coincide with his retirement from teaching. His army and teacher's pensions combined would see himself and Mary live comfortably for the rest of their lives. The journey itself would be a lot quicker than it would have been previously, thanks to the development of transatlantic passenger flights. Halliday had finally convinced him to go one evening, as they sat after a veterans' meeting browsing through old photographs of their regiment.

Andrew produced the Brownie photograph he had taken at the Étaples army base camp in France. They stared at the twelve grinning faces, recognising themselves and naming most of the others, including Andrew's friend, Anders. Halliday said, in his inimitable style: 'Andrew, you and I have worn well, but we're none of us getting any younger. You're sixty-five this year and I'm sixty-three. If we don't go soon, we will probably never do it.'

Mary encouraged him to go too, but declined the offer to journey with them, as she still had several years to work at the hospital. Besides, she argued, who would look after their collie dog, Sammie? It was their third dog of their life together and Andrew had insisted every time on a collie, which was always called Sammie. Mary liked nothing better, when she came off a shift, than to take Sammie for a long walk in Stanley Park, to clear her head before going home to sleep. It was one such morning when she thought to herself that if Andrew and John were going all that distance to France, then they should stop in Scotland first. She discussed it with Andrew that evening ,and he agreed with his wife that it was a very good idea.

So here they were at Prestwick Airport, travel bags collected, organising a hire car to take them to Galloway. Halliday grinned broadly at the shiny blue Morris Minor awaiting them.

'Eh, Andrew, what exactly is that contraption, and how far do we have to drive it? It's so small.'

'You're back in Scotland, John; everything is smaller here. But for God's sake don't say anything like that to the locals. They will be far from pleased. I'm going to drive first, down to Creetown. But remember, when it's your turn, they drive on the left side here, John.'

'Right you are, Sarge. I'll remember,' joked Halliday.

'Just you admire the scenery and don't put me off my driving,' retorted Andrew.

The interior of the car was far more spacious than either man had anticipated. Andrew glanced at himself in the rear-view mirror. His hair and moustache were speckled with grey and his build was stockier than when he had left Scotland all those years ago. He thought locals would still recognise him, even though he now wore dark-rimmed spectacles. Halliday was impressed by the scenery along the Ayrshire coast as they headed south towards Girvan. Andrew explained to him that the large island of Arran, whose outline dominated the horizon to the west, was described as 'Scotland in miniature.' From Girvan, they took the road inland through the Galloway forest. The well-handling Morris Minor was more than a match for the twists and turns of the narrow country road, despite Halliday describing the noise of the exhaust as being like a herd of moose's farts. As they passed the small village of Bargrennan, Andrew mentioned that, time permitting, they would return in a few days to visit the nearby and beautiful Loch Trool. By the time they reached Creetown it was dark. They had booked into the Ellangowan Hotel, and in the gloom it appeared to Andrew to look no different from when he had last seen it before the First World War. The bald hotel manager also looked familiar, and almost simultaneously they recognised each other.

'Well, you're a sight for sore eyes, Andrew McDowall,' beamed his old friend Davy Kennedy.

'I was hoping you might still be here,' replied Andrew. 'Almost like old times.'

'Aye, almost,' said Kennedy. 'You probably heard by now that Tam Murdoch never made it through the Great War?'

'Yes, I did,' replied Andrew, thinking to himself: *If only you knew the half of it, Davy.*

'Anyway, come away in, it's getting cold out here. I'll get your bags to your rooms, then we'll have a dram or two before dinner,' offered Kennedy.

Turning to Halliday, Andrew remarked, 'Now that's what you call good old-fashioned Scottish hospitality. Let's get inside quickly.'

As they sat in the lounge, sipping on their generous measures of whisky, Andrew recalled the last time he had had a drink in the bar with Davy, on the evening of his mother's funeral. He properly introduced John Halliday to Davy Kennedy. Halliday then explained that his family left their home village of Kelty in Fife when he was very young, so he had very little memory of the old country. Davy promised to show him the local sights the following day. The dining room was full of wildfowlers, enjoying the last weekend of the goose-shooting season. Steaming plates of mince and potatoes were ferried from the kitchen to the hungry guests. There was a pleasant hum of conversation in the room.

'Oh man, that's the first time I've had a plate of mince and tatties in a long time,' said a satisfied Andrew, wiping his moustache with a linen napkin.

'You'll have a nightcap before bed, lads?' suggested Kennedy.

'Don't mind if we do,' replied the visitors in unison.

Although wearied by their travels, they sat up till the wee hours of the morning, catching up on old times. Using the interrogation skills he had honed as a head teacher interviewing school pupils, Andrew gleaned a lot of information from Davy Kennedy about the locals. Tam's brother William had moved to Glasgow for work, but his younger brother, Alexander, or Sandy, still lived in the area, working for the Forestry Commission. Of Kathleen's surviving three brothers, only one had returned to the area, taking over from his father as the manager of the local bank.

The following morning, a full Scottish breakfast helped to clear his hangover, and Andrew announced he would try to find Sandy Murdoch for a chat. John Halliday was only too delighted to agree, as he had already decided to join Davy Kennedy for a day of shooting wildfowl on the nearby Cree estuary. Although invited, Andrew explained that he had never lifted a gun since the war ended and did not intend to now, using his deteriorating eyesight as an excuse. He said his goodbyes for the day and headed north to the village of Glentrool, where Sandy Murdoch worked. Andrew parked the Morris Minor at the small wooden Forestry Commission office and went in to enquire if Sandy was in the area.

'He's most likely around here somewhere, probably skiving off for a smoke,' replied a half-interested receptionist. 'If you don't mind hanging around here for a bit, they will all be in shortly to refill their flasks from the tea urn. Would you like a cup yourself? Sorry, I didn't catch your name.'

Andrew introduced himself, but politely declined her offer, preferring a stroll in the crisp spring sunshine. In the near distance, he saw a team of Clydesdale horses with a sled full of timber logs, heading towards him. The horse driver had a familiar look about him in terms of his height and awkward gait. He would be in his early fifties, but the resemblance to Tam was astonishing – it could only be his brother Sandy. He tethered the horses, pulled a twenty packet of full-strength Capstan from his dungaree pocket, and lit one. Without breaking stride, he inhaled deeply. As he exhaled, he greeted Andrew:

'How are you doing, stranger? It's no' a bad day now, is it? Did you smell Annie's tea on the brew? Better come in quick before the others arrive, or there will be none left.'

Andrew smiled at Sandy and agreed to join him.

Once inside, he explained to Sandy the purpose of his visit.

'My name's Andrew Murdoch. I don't suppose you will remember me, Sandy, as you were too young. I was a friend of your late brother, Tam; we both served in the war, although I was in a Canadian regiment by then. I'm on a short holiday in Scotland and thought I would look up his family. Hope you don't mind?'

Sandy sat quietly and motionless for a while, making Andrew feel nervous. Then suddenly, pointing at Andrew, he blurted out, 'Aye, ah mind of you now. You were the schoolteacher. Tam thought the world of you. Always telling me and my brother how clever you were. Tam could barely read and write, you know.'

'Yes, I did, actually. He was very embarrassed about it and I offered to help, but he joked that he didn't fancy going back to school at his age,' replied Andrew.

'Aye, that would be Tam all right. Always joking and never taking life too seriously. My ma was surprised when he went back voluntarily; broke her heart, actually. But tell you what, his pal, John Glendinning, who got his job with the old Major, was always grateful to Tam. After he found out Tam had been killed, he would always stand me and my brother a pint in the pub. He would say to the barman, "A pint for the brother of the bravest man I ever knew." Always made me feel very proud, that.'

'And so it should.' Andrew added, 'I had no idea he was home and then volunteered to go back. Sounds like Tam, right enough.'

Sandy composed himself and lit another cigarette, offering one to Andrew, before continuing.

'And here's another strange thing I remember. When we got the news of Tam's death, the old Major took it really badly. Maybe he felt guilty he had let Tam go back to the front. You would honestly have thought it was his own son who had died, the way he carried on.'

Andrew was intrigued. 'So how did your mother take the news, then?' he asked nervously.

'Oh, really badly, as you'd expect, but she was very proud at the same time, you know. The neighbours were a great help to her, and of course we weren't the only family in the village to lose a son or brother. The worst was our neighbour, Mrs Grant. Can you believe it was Armistice Day? The church bells were ringing, we got home early from school, which was great, everybody out in the street just chatting and glad it was all over. Then the telegraph boy arrives on his bike and stops next door. He hands Mrs Grant a telegram to tell her that her only son, Kenneth, had been killed two weeks previously. Now that was bad, the worst fucking timing ever. Hit the whole village; nobody felt like celebrating much after that.'

'That must have been really tough,' said Andrew, sympathetically. Then he asked the question which had been troubling him. 'Did the family get much information about what happened to your brother?'

'No, not really, just that he was killed while on duty. We knew from the newspapers that his regiment were fighting at the battle of Arras at the time of his death, so we guessed it must have been there he died. We aw knew he was daft, but Tam was a brave lad, too. We imagined him leading a charge over the top.'

'I think you're right,' said a relieved Andrew, who had let go the tight grip he had on the edge of the table. And Tam's brother had raised an issue which had troubled Andrew all his life whenever he recalled the traumatic events of Easter 1917. Tam was a very brave lad, so what could he possibly have done to face a firing squad? The captain at the time had said he was a deserter, but Andrew found that so hard to believe. Maybe it was a tragic case of mistaken identity. One thing was for sure; he would never know now. Sandy Murdoch interrupted his line of thought with another question.

'There were a lot of Canadian troops there too, weren't there? Papers here were full of it. How brave they were, and all the usual.'

'Yes, I was there too, Sandy. It was a hell of a time,' admitted Andrew.

'Well, fancy that, you two great friends, then miles apart when you went to Canada, only to end up fighting at the same place in France. That's quite a coincidence.'

'It certainly was,' agreed Andrew and, before he could add anything, Sandy was on his feet.

'Right, Andrew, nice to meet you after all those years, but they trees won't chop themselves down. The foreman will be after my blood if I don't get back to work. If you're in the Barholm Arms before you go back, I'll let you buy me a pint.'

And with that he was off.

Andrew sat for a minute, gathering his thoughts. He imagined Tam would have been so like his brother, had he survived the war. He was very relieved that the family did not know the circumstances of Tam's death and although he had thought about telling Sandy, he was glad he had not done so. There would have been no point in sullying Tam's reputation now. He finished his mug of tea, thanked Annie, and headed back out into the spring sunshine. He thought it would be the perfect afternoon to continue along the road to Loch Trool, but then remembered he had promised to take John Halliday there. Instead he headed south again, back to Creetown. That evening, over a fine meal of steak pie and chips, Halliday was exuberant about his day of wildfowling. He had bagged three fine geese and his host had complimented him on his shooting skills.

'And the best things were the weather and the scenery. The Cree estuary is a lovely spot and the view of the hills was great, even if they are a bit…'

'Don't you dare say small,' interrupted Andrew, laughing.

The following morning the two veterans took the pleasant drive to Loch Trool. The long, thin loch was nestled into a valley in the Galloway hills, its sparkling waters reflecting the peaks of the local mountains. It was a rigorous five-mile walk around the loch, but both men agreed that after all the eating and drinking of the previous few days, the exercise would do them no harm at all. From the top of the loch the road took a stiff climb up past the Buchan Burn. They had to stop once or twice to catch their breath.

'We're definitely not as young as we used to be,' panted Halliday.

'I'd say amen to that, John,' agreed Andrew.

At the top of the brae, Andrew spotted something new, or at least something that had not been there the last time he walked the route in his youth. A large, inscribed granite boulder sat on a prominent crag. They scrambled up to read it. The stone, called 'Bruce's Stone', commemorated King Robert the Bruce's victory over an English force in 1307.

Andrew, reverting back to his schoolteacher's role, gave John a potted history of the Wars of Independence. Halliday listened attentively, before concluding, 'You know what, Andrew? Throughout time we've always found something to fight about and have wars over. Christ, our war was meant to be "the war to end all wars", and we know how that turned out.'

'That's pretty profound for you, John, but I agree. And you know what an awful lot of good men are still going to die in the future, for one cause or another.'

'Right: enough of the philosophy. I'm parched. Is there a pub around here?'

A day later, they began the long journey to France. An overnight sleeper train took them from Dumfries to London, then another train to Dover and the ferry to Calais. Finally, another train journey to Lens and the small hotel they had booked in advance. They were both so exhausted by their trip that they quickly thanked the owner and headed straight to bed.

'This is rather better than the breakfasts we were used to back in the day, eh Andrew?' said an appreciative Halliday as he tucked into his third croissant and jam, washed down by strong black French coffee.

'No question about that, John, no question about that at all. Drink up and I'll use my best French to find out how we get to the Vimy Ridge memorial.' They were wearing their best Sunday suits and Halliday was wearing his British War Medal and Victory Medal on his chest. Andrew engaged the affable hotel owner, Pierre, in conversation as best he could. A look of admiration spread across the Frenchman's face when he realised who they were.

'Ah, *les anciens combattants canadiens!*' he exclaimed, shaking Andrew's hand vigorously. Then he shouted towards the kitchen: '*Allez*, Camille, a*llez!*'

A pretty, dark-haired girl of around twenty appeared. The conversation between father and daughter was too quick for Andrew to follow, but resulted in the girl driving them the short distance to the Canadian Vimy Ridge Memorial. Camille parked the green Citroen 2CV close to the adjoining Moroccan war memorial and explained to the veterans it was only a short walk from there to the Canadian site. She was studying English at university, so gave them very clear instructions and promised she would wait for them to return. The path to the memorial was flanked by large Canadian and French flags, fluttering in the light breeze. The memorial itself completely dominated the surrounding landscape. Andrew and John Halliday stood in awe for a moment, looking up at the two thirty-metre high limestone pylons designed by Canadian sculptor Walter Seymour Allward. They were drawn to one carved figure at a corner of the memorial, a weeping woman known as Mother Canada. They stood close by, heads bowed in silence. Andrew was first to speak.

'John, I've just realised we are standing on top of Hill 145. Look, you can still see the remains of the trenches down there, and shell holes too. By God, it takes me back.'

'Makes you proud to be Canadian, Andrew, doesn't it?' added Halliday, who was wiping his eye with a white linen handkerchief.

They walked around to the outside wall of the memorial, where the names of over 11,000 Canadian soldiers with unknown graves were inscribed.

'I wonder how long it took them to do that?' asked Halliday.

'Well, however long, it was worth every minute,' said Andrew emphatically. 'I'm going to take a closer look.'

Andrew found the name of Sergeant Dewar, but nothing for his good friend Anders Halvorsen.

'That must mean he has his own grave somewhere, Andrew. I wonder if we could find it?' suggested Halliday.

'Don't think we will have time for that, sadly,' replied Andrew.

The two men stood silent again for a few minutes, deep in their own thoughts.

'Had enough, Sergeant?' said Halliday, with a weak smile.

Andrew nodded and they walked back to the car. On their return to the hotel, Camille asked them to wait in the car for a moment while she rushed inside. After a minute or two she returned to usher the puzzled pair inside again. A French Tricolore and the Canadian maple leaf flag had been draped on the far wall of the small dining room. The owner, Pierre, had rounded up a few of the locals, including two veterans. An accordion player, perched in the corner, played lustily as the others gave a warm round of applause. Pierre produced a fine bottle of Armagnac, which he cheerfully shared with the gathering. Andrew and John were gobsmacked by the warmth of their reception. They shook hands heartily with their fellow veterans and did their best to exchange tales of the war, despite the language difficulties, which counted for less as more brandy was consumed. Their unexpected evening ended with a singsong of the old wartime favourites. Someone even managed to find Andrew a fiddle, and although his playing had slowed a little, he thoroughly enjoyed accompanying the accordionist. He gave a solo rendition of Tam's regimental tune, 'Blue Bonnets O'er the Border'. 'That's an old Scottish song,' he explained, at which point Camille rose to her feet and exclaimed, '*Monsieurs*, I know an old Scottish song which my grandmother taught me. Would you care to hear it?' Without waiting for an answer, the young girl cleared her throat and began:

'Ally bally, ally bally bee,

Sittin'on yer mammy's knee.

Waitin'for a wee bawbee,

Tae buy mair Coulter's candy...'

Andrew beamed a broad smile, wiping a tear from his eye. When Camille had finished singing he beckoned to her to join himself and Halliday.

'This evening has been such a wonderful surprise,' he enthused, 'but your song was the cherry on the cake. Was your granny Scottish, by any chance?'

'No, not at all, *monsieur* Andrew. She was born and bred in this village. When I was a child, she would tell me her story before she sang me the lullaby. Would you like to hear it?'

'Of course,' replied an intrigued Andrew.

'It was during *la première Guerre mondiale*. Our village was so badly damaged by the Germans. My grandmother was hiding in a cellar with my father, who was only an infant. She was terrified they would be killed. A kind British – how would you say – Tommy? found them and protected them. He went out to find food for them and kept them company. She thought he was very funny and quite handsome, and she knew that he liked her too, but at that time she did not know if my grandfather was alive or dead. She told me he was a fine Scottish gentleman and that he taught her the lullaby to soothe my father to sleep. Later, soldiers came and arrested him, and sadly Grandma Lisette never found out what happened to him.'

Andrew took a deep draught of red wine as he contemplated Camille's story. It couldn't possibly be, could it? he thought to himself. The coincidence was just too far-fetched to be plausible. Yet he would never know unless he asked her the obvious question.

'I don't suppose your grandmother told you the name of the kind soldier, did she?'

Camille's eyes lit up. 'But of course, because they joked about it. He wasn't any old Tommy; he was her Tam.'

Andrew reached over to Camille, giving her a warm hug as he planted a kiss on her forehead.

'What's that all about?' asked a perplexed John Halliday.

'Too much French hospitality and wine, I think, John,' replied Andrew, 'I'm going to call it a night.'

Apologising to Camille, Pierre, and the other guests, he made his way unsteadily to the bedroom and slept soundly.

'I'd like to visit one more memorial, John, if that's all right with you?' asked a bleary-eyed Andrew the following morning. 'It's not too far, and Camille has kindly offered to drive us again.'

'That's fine by me, Andrew,' he replied, tearing apart his second croissant of the morning to dip in his coffee.

On the short journey along the Arras to Douai road, Camille explained that the local countryside was still a dangerous place to roam, as there were still so many unexploded munitions. Every year some unfortunate farmer was killed or maimed while ploughing his fields. She pulled up at the site of the 9th Scottish Division memorial. It was not on the grand scale of the Canadian memorial, but was still impressive in its own way. The centrepiece was a thirty-foot-high cairn made of imported Scottish granite. Ringing the cairn were twenty-six smaller granite boulders, bearing the names of the units that had served in the division. Andrew singled out a particularly jagged boulder inscribed with '6th Battalion King's Own Scottish Borderers', the last unit Tam had served with. Meanwhile, John Halliday walked up to the main cairn, the better to read its inscription. He read it aloud to Andrew. 'Remember with honour the 9th Scottish Division, who on the fields of France and Flanders, 1915 to 1918, served well.'

Andrew contemplated the typically Scottish, modest words.

'Who served well,' he thought, taking a long deep breath. He remembered his fallen comrades, he remembered Kathleen Marr, and he remembered Tam Murdoch.

He asked himself: 'Who served well?'

FURTHER READING

Max Arthur, *Forgotten Voices of the Great War*, Ted Smart

Cathryn Corns and John Hughes Wilson, *Blindfold and Alone*, Weidenfeld & Nicolson

Eileen Crofton, *Angels of Mercy: A Women's Hospital on the Western Front 1914–1918*, Birlinn

Robert Duncan, *Objectors and Resisters: Opposition to Conscription and War in Scotland 1914–18*, Common Print

Peter Hart, *Gallipoli*, Profile Books

Lyn MacDonald, *The Roses of No Man's Land*, Penguin

Jonathan Nicholls, *Cheerful Sacrifice: The Battle of Arras 1917*, Pen and Sword Books

Julian Putkowski and Julian Sykes, *Shot at Dawn*, Pen and Sword Books

Paul Reed, *Walking Arras*, Pen and Sword Books

Gavin Royon (ed), *A Prayer for Gallipoli: The Great War Diaries of Kenneth Best*, Simon & Schuster

This book is printed on paper from sustainable sources managed under the Forest Stewardship Council (FSC) scheme.

It has been printed in the UK to reduce transportation miles and their impact upon the environment.

For every new title that Matador publishes, we plant a tree to offset CO_2, partnering with the More Trees scheme.

For more about how Matador offsets its environmental impact, see www.troubador.co.uk/about/